Pictures of You

A Novel
By Juliette Caron

Juliette Caron

First paperback edition: May 2014

ISBN-13:978-1499380774

ISBN-10:1499380771

Caron, Juliette.
Pictures of You / by Juliette Caron

Summary: In a moment, September Jones's life is changed forever. After her best friend, Abby, is killed in a hit-and-run accident, September struggles to face each day. She turns to junk food, bad TV and journaling to cope. When September meets handsome, mysterious Adrien, who's given himself two weeks to write the perfect suicide note, and nice guy Chris, her new coworker who has some troubles of his own, she realizes she's not the only one dealing with personal demons. *Pictures of You* reminds us of our human capacity for resilience, forgiveness and hope.

Ages 12& up

Cover photo credit: Depositphotos

For Anne, who was my Abby.

For Jeff and Mom who helped me get through losing her—and a whole bunch of other stuff.

For Grandma Pat who lost her best friend in a tragic car accident.

And for all those musicians who changed my life by having the courage to share their amazing talent.

Prologue

Abby,

Your last words didn't surprise me. You said, "September, I'm sorry to say it, but rock 'n roll is dead." That's exactly something you'd say and although the phrase may be trite, to me you couldn't have been more brilliant. And I said, "Yeah, this crap makes you lose your faith in humanity." And then we burst into laughter. I loved it when I made you laugh.

Our cheeks hurt from laughing all the way from Los Angeles to New York. High on sticky, carefree early summer air, we were in the anything-became-as-funny-as-hell state of mind. We'd taken a road trip across the country—a trip we'd promised to go on together since we were thirteen. With stiff backs, numb butts and stomachs sick on junk food, we were more than happy to get back home to familiar beds.

We were just thirty minutes away from home. Thirty minutes away from safety.

I didn't see the man in that ugly van. I only saw a flash of brown racing diagonally across the freeway, over into our lane. I wondered if my frail, mortal experience would be coming to a halt as I let off the gas and swerved, trying to miss him. People say your life flashes before your eyes at times like these, but that wasn't the case for me. Only one thing shot through my mind: I have to get out of this.

I remember the impact and the sound of crushing metal. I'll never forget that sound.

My yellow Volkswagen Beetle didn't stand a chance. The little car flew into the cloudless summer sky like hang-gliding Big Bird and turned over and over. Crushed ginger ale cans, empty Fritos bags and apple cores flew around like white flecks in an agitated snow globe. They say we flipped five times. I screamed and screamed. You were silent. Your frail arms cradled your head in an attempt to protect yourself. Your green chiffon scarf slid off your neck and out the window, slipping away like mortality. We landed upside-down. Funny how the car was broken—totaled—but the radio still played that song. To this day I don't know the name of that nauseating song.

Upside-down, we hung like sloths from our seats, our belts keeping our bodies suspended. Your long, flaming orange hair fell down, the tips sopping up blood from the ground. I noticed the sprinkling of freckles across your nose and cheeks. They stood out like the moon among stars against your salt white skin. There was blood. Lots and lots of blood. That salty, metallic scent, mixed with your jasmine perfume, overwhelmed me. Blood dripped, like a leaky faucet, to the roof of the car. Like tears, it drizzled from the gash at the top of your head and out of the corner of your perfect mouth.

I remember people calling. So many voices. "Hey! Are you okay?" "Hang in there, I just called 911." Also, "Ughhh. I can't look. I think they're dead." I looked down at my body. Was I dead? No, I saw the rise and fall of my chest. I felt strangely fine.

I turned to you. "Abby," I whispered. Your eyes met mine. You smiled weakly, your face was strangely serene. You moaned, too weak to say anything. You reached for me, but your hand, shaped like an eagle's claw, moved only a few inches and fell. You wore the silver charm bracelet I'd given you on your birthday six years earlier, do you remember? I gave you a charm to add to it every year. I saw your last breath. I watched your bright indigo eyes—those eyes that saw no bad in the world—close.

Those eyes I'd never see again.

1

I laughed out loud when they brought in the cherry wood casket. Who were they kidding? Abby wasn't in there. She was alive, breathing, probably singing in some bar in Manhattan wooing men with her dark, smoky alto. She played the guitar like nobody's business, too. She *couldn't* be in there. Life was not life without my Abby. I mean if she was truly dead, I'd have no other choice than to throw myself in front of a semi. And what was the deal with the red roses everywhere? Abby was a daisy girl. This was a weird dream. Nothing more. Right?

Her two younger brothers, Luke and Mitchell, plus an uncle and three cousins, sat the shiny, oblong box down on the special stand thingy. Luke, in hysterics, his face tomato red, fled the room. Poor Luke. The congregation turned simultaneously, creating a pretty wave, similar to something I'd seen a crowd do at a Mets game. Mitchell had a funny smile on his face, almost a confused smirk, as he sat down beside his parents.

Suddenly I noticed all the noise around me. It was awfully loud for a funeral. Further proof I was going to wake up at any moment. The noise: dreary organ music, thunderous sobs coming from some old lady sitting in front of me and a toddler throwing a tantrum. "I want the cookie. Give me the cookie!"

Between the creepy ancient-looking stained glass windows, the overwhelming smell of perfume, mothballs and perspiration and people packed in as tightly as canned beans, my claustrophobia kicked in big time. Maybe I would leave the room wailing. Maybe I should join Luke outside. Tempting, but no. What kind of BFF would I be?

Abby was apparently dead and me, well…according to the doctors I was lucky. I'd left a mangled car with only a bruise the size of a grapefruit on my leg, a seatbelt-shaped cut on my shoulder and a headache.

I hardly paid attention to the songs and prayers and the monotonous speech given by a heavyset pastor or reverend-type guy. (Abby and her family were devout Christians.)

Instead, I looked around the room, amazed at the strange variety of people sitting around me. Abby had the most unusual friends, not unlike exotic fruit in the produce department. I saw hair that made up every color of the rainbow, guys in funky ties and jackets, girls wearing rock band tees with too-casual-for-church skirts and more piercings than I could count. My gaze rested on Mary, who sat several feet to my left, Abby's *other* best friend ("My second-to-best-friend, only after you, September," Abby had sworn once). I'm ashamed to admit this, but I pretty much hated Mary because of it. This month she stained her hair an eggplant color and added another tattoo to her growing-like-dandelions collection. I knew this because she sported a white, rectangular bandage on the back of her neck, like one Abby had when she opted to have the word "Freedom" forever etched in her right forearm on her eighteenth birthday.

Then there was Abby's band mates sitting directly behind me: Marcus, the eternally frowning bassist. Guitarist Keaton, who was one funny chin short of being a supermodel. Keaton and Abby had dated off and on over the years. They were on when she died. The final member was Tyrone, a scrawny punk with pimpled earth-colored skin.

Even Abby's parents were "alternative." Her dad, Jed, sported longish hair and combat boots. Her mom, Hannah, wore heavy Egyptian-style eyeliner and a cute little nose ring. I watched the backs of their heads, wondering how they were dealing with all of this.

I took one last glance around the room and then I saw him. Probably the hottest guy I'd ever laid eyes on. I mean, I've seen my fair share of good-looking guys, but this guy was gorgeous. Who was he? And more importantly, how was I going to meet him? Why didn't Abby ever mention she had a friend/schoolmate/cousin who was so—

To my surprise, my ex-boyfriend John and my older sister April slid into the empty spot next to me. I don't know what shocked me more: my sister coming or my ex, or their coming together. Or did they come separately and just so happen to arrive at the same time?

April had always hated Abby. She thought my best friend was weird and irresponsible and had her head in the clouds and April wasn't afraid to voice her opinion about it. On several occasions. April and Abby were as alike as cheesecake and Brussels sprouts. Abby was warm, affectionate, spontaneous, free-spirited, whereas April was more uptight, demanding, goal-oriented. A perfectionist. Even the way April dressed here at the funeral made her stand out like a Disney princess in a gothy vampire movie. Hair precisely pinned back, pink cardigan and matching skirt neatly pressed. Only Michelangelo could apply makeup with such precision.

John's presence baffled me. What was he doing here, of all places? Unlike my sister, John didn't hate Abby, but he didn't exactly like her, either. Plus, he dumped me a month ago, after nine near-perfect months together. I really loved him. I would've married the guy. Well, not immediately, but maybe after we both did a little more growing up. I never thought I'd see him again. Yet beside me he sat, looking especially handsome in a sharp suit, with his sleek, gorgeous hair neatly combed (which he inherited from his Native American mother).

"Hey," John mouthed, smiling warmly, showing off his perfectly straight, glow-in-the-dark teeth. He squeezed my hand. His hand was soft and warm and comforting. A part of me wanted to hang on to it—I needed John right now, more than ever. But I quickly pulled my hand away and crossed my arms over my chest.

"Hi, John. What are *you* doing here?" I whispered.

"What do you mean? I liked Abby, too," he said. I wasn't buying it. John and Abby weren't close at all. In fact, he'd always resented Abby and Keaton's tagging along, which wasn't a regular thing. He preferred one-on-one time with me—all the time. Anyone who diverted my attention made him jealous and insecure.

I leaned forward and waved at April. She smiled, but it seemed forced. Plus, she was drumming her professionally manicured nails on the edge of the bench like she was nervous or bored, while John had the weirdest look on his face. What was that? Guilt? Amusement?

Something was up, I was sure of it.

Aunt Louisa spoke next. Her boxy dress had slipped from her shoulder, exposing much of her lacy bra, which, unfortunately for the rest of us, she never caught during the length of the talk. Her words blended together like pancake batter as I practiced my origami skills on the cheap, poorly Xeroxed program. I wrinkled my nose at the picture they chose of Abby for the cover. She had always hated that photo. She wore a phony grin and had just gotten a bad haircut. It didn't do her justice—why couldn't they've chosen a better one?

Jed, Abby's father, spoke last. I tried to pay attention, but his ocean-deep voice broke up like an out-of-range cell phone. "Abby was a special girl—er—woman." A soft chuckle. "Well, she'll always be *my* little girl, even now that she is no longer with us. Everyone who knew her…" I shoved the program into my purse and played with the silver butterfly ring on my pinky finger. "…an extremely lovable girl. Sweet as maple syrup." I moved on to ironing the wrinkles out of my skirt. Was that a Cheerio stuck to my blouse? I looked over to see if John had noticed, but he was looking straight ahead. The suspicious expression he wore a moment earlier was replaced by genuine sadness. Weird. "Everyone here knows she was an incredibly talented musician. In fact, an indie record label had expressed interest in signing her band just a week before her…" he coughed into a fist a couple of times, "passing…She had so much promise…"

When Jed finished his eulogy, I looked behind me to steal one more glance at that gorgeous boy, but he was gone. Oh well. He was probably one of those guys with zero personality.

The funeral ended with Abby's aunts and her mother, Hannah, singing *Be Still My Soul.* Hannah was the only one with a nice voice, but it came out funny when the sob-a-thon started. Aunt Louisa's voice was passable. The third lady—I forgot her name—should've been shot.

For the length of the song I urged myself to cry. This was a funeral, after all. Isn't that what people were supposed to do at funerals?

I thought of the blood in the car, I thought of the body— Abby's perfect little body—in the box, stiff and lifeless. Nothing. I forced myself to think of never seeing her again, but I didn't believe it. I *couldn't* believe it. My very survival was dependent on my best friend's existence. I needed her more than I needed anyone.

I half expected her to show up now and plop down next to me, laughing her adorable, throaty laugh, poking fun at Aunt Number Two's horrible singing, the overkill of the rose displays, this whole silly charade. I moved on to thoughts of tortured puppies, starving children in third world countries, freezer burned ice cream, World War III. Nada. My usual easily spilled tears pulled a no-show. My traitorous eye ducts refused to cooperate. What kind of a best friend was I? Couldn't I shed a single tear at her funeral? Even Mary leaked like a bad roof. I couldn't let the second-to-best friend show me up. But she did.

2

"What are you doing here?" I said, blocking the door to my apartment. It was John, of all people. Aaaand the plot thickens. First the funeral and now this. What was John up to? And why couldn't he have called first? I was all too aware of my uncombed hair, my purple fuzzy alligator-print pajamas. It was after noon and I had yet to shower and brush my teeth.

"September, you look awful," he said, his face twisted in concern.

"Gee, thanks." I tossed him a dirty look. Actually, he was probably right. All I'd done lately was listen to The Cure and play online Scrabble with other hermits until the wee hours of the morning. Whenever I'd manage to get some shuteye, it would be an uneasy sleep. I kept having unsettling dreams about cute puppies turning into vicious demons with razor sharp teeth. They'd come after me and eat me alive, one body part at a time. True story.

John looked sheepish. "I just…"

"Just what?" We both stood awkwardly for a moment. Tiger, my orange popsicle-colored cat, came over to greet John and proceeded to rub his body all over John's legs. John shooed him away before brushing the hair from his jeans. "I've always hated that cat."

"So I've heard." I rolled my eyes while he wasn't looking.

What an idiot. But the truth was, I missed him, idiot or not. "John...I..."

"September," he said, like me at a loss for words. And then he flung his arms around me, taking me by surprise. A moment later, I let my guard down and returned the embrace. I felt the even pulse of his heart against my chest as I inhaled his indescribable John smell. It was safe, familiar. He stepped back just enough to kiss me, long and passionately, like they do in the movies, like he once did when we were fresh and new.

I was out of breath when he pulled away. "What's going on? I thought you wanted to—I thought we broke up."

"I'm so, so, *so* sorry about Abby," he said, tearing up. Great. Even my ex was crying over her—and I couldn't—and he didn't even like her that much. What kind of a friend was I?

I bit my lip. "I'm sorry, too."

He took my hand. "I miss you, Tember. I really miss you."

What was he saying? Did he want to get back together? It'd been two days since the funeral and I'd already forgotten how handsome he was. He wore my favorite t-shirt of his, the blue one that complimented his light russet skin. His amazing hair fell over his almost-black eyes. His familiar, comforting, warm eyes.

"Life is so short. So uncertain. I'm just glad you're okay. I'd never be able to forgive myself if anything ever happened to you."

What was I supposed to say to that? I'm glad I'm okay, too? Because, John, actually I'm not okay. You dumped me and Abby's gone. I have no one left. But instead I said, "Thanks."

"I really miss you. I'm so sorry I..." He kissed me again. His lips were warmer than the thick summer air around us.

"But I thought you didn't love me anymore," I said, managing to pull away from his kiss. Of course a part of me didn't want to. A part of me wanted to stay in his arms forever—screw the consequences.

"September." He seemed stunned, hurt even. "I will *always* love you," he said, reminding me of a cheesy song. "Always, always."

I laughed. I do that sometimes—laugh at the most inappropriate times. At funerals, for instance. One of the many things John didn't like about me.

What was he doing here? What did he want from me? Did he want me back? Did *I* want *him* back? "I love you, too. But I thought—"

"But I can't be with you. Just because we *love* each other, doesn't make us *right* for each other." And then he stroked my hair in a condescending way.

Ouch. What he meant was: I wasn't right for him. Because if it was up to me, we'd still be together. Okay, it wasn't the perfect relationship, but are there any that are? I took a step back, crossed my arms over my chest. "Then what are you doing here?"

"I just wanted to check up on my girl." He gently pried apart my folded arms, took my hands into his and kissed each palm.

Wow, even after nine months together, he could still be confusing as hell. I yanked my hands away. "I'm not your girl anymore, remember? You dumped me, John. You can't *dump* your cake and eat it too."

"You're right. I guess I'm not being fair."

"You guess? You have no idea how big of a jerk you're being right now. Especially right after my friend's…" I didn't want to say it. The word "funeral" was like battery acid on my tongue.

"You're right, I'm sorry. I'm being a total jerk. I shouldn't have kissed you. I shouldn't play with your heart like that."

Play with my heart? There he was being condescending again, like he was the only one with any power in this relationship. Er, ex-relationship. I sighed, shook my head. "Forget about it."

Okay, despite the fact that John could sometimes be a selfish creep, a part of me still wanted to exploit his moment of weakness and beg him to come back to me. I was lonely, plus John and I had history. I've had a massive crush on the boy since seventh grade.

I can still remember, quite vividly, the first time I saw him. It was after school in late November, the day before Thanksgiving break. The weather was perfect; it was an Indian summer. Abby and I rolled up the legs of our pants to feel the warmth of the sun on our skin. We sat on a patch of grass, attempting to memorize a world map for Geography homework.

John kept distracting us. It was hard to concentrate on homework when there was a cute new kid only a few yards away playing soccer with a bunch of other boys. I loved watching the way his gorgeous hair swung back and forth as he ran, the way he grinned this big old cocky grin whenever he scored a goal. His legs weren't bad looking, either. It was love-at-first-sight.

It only took him five years to notice me. He asked me out when we bumped into each other at the city library. I was a senior and he was a freshman in college. We went to a lame romantic comedy and then walked around Times Square. He bought me a pretzel and a strawberry ice cream cone and kissed me in front of Planet Hollywood.

We had some good times together. And some bad. John was never exactly my dream guy, but he was close enough. And I missed him. I really missed him. But I knew if I let him back into my heart, he'd be careless with it all over again.

"Thanks for checking up on me, I guess. But…" I opened the door.

He got the hint. "Okay, but call me if you need anything." He touched my hair again, flashed his flawless white teeth. I would miss that cocky smile of his.

"Will do," I said, wondering if this was the last time I'd see him. I nudged him out the door, feeling confused, hurt, angry—and sort of relieved.

***

Eleven days after the accident I decided I needed more socks.

I threw my head outside my apartment window, amazed by the mild spring-like weather. Happy white clouds decorated a bright blue sky. A gentle breeze tamed the usual smoldering New York heat. It was a perfect day for shopping.

I called work, informing my boss Janice I was finally over the flu but now coming down with something else. A terrible, terrible cough. I plugged my nose and made a creative hacking noise to make it more convincing.

I wasn't going to tell Janice about my Scrabble addiction.

I took a shower and got dressed for the first time in nearly two weeks.

It took going to seven different stores before I found the right socks. I bought thirty-eight pairs. Short socks, tall socks, knee-length socks. Polka-dotted, striped, argyle. Socks with little gray kittens, socks with electric guitars.

Some people max out a credit card or drink themselves into a stupor when they find themselves all alone. Apparently, I buy socks.

After the hardcore sock shopping, I ordered some fries and a milkshake at McDonalds. Sitting all alone in a sticky booth, I felt self-conscious. Well, more than usual. I'd never done this before: ate at a fine dining establishment on my own. So I distracted myself, pulling my thirty-eight pairs of socks out of their bags and displaying them neatly on the table. Already I was having some buyer's remorse. I'd have to take at least half of them back, particularly the kitten ones. When people started giving me funny looks, I put them away. That was just what I needed: people to think I was some eccentric sock-collecting recluse. Crazy cat lady, move over.

So I people watched, hoping to find someone with a more pathetic life than my own. I spotted a frazzled pregnant woman who looked like she hadn't had a good night's sleep in five years. She made several failed attempts to quiet down her three little kids, who fought viciously over Happy Meal toys. I saw two awkward teenagers, both lamppost skinny and wearing braces, sharing a large order of fries and playing footsie under the table. And then I noticed an elderly man struggling to remove the paper wrap from his burger with hands that shook like a washing machine on spin cycle. It must've been two minutes before he got to take his first bite.

Okay, he won.

After lunch I realized I needed new bath towels and a clock for the kitchen. So I spent the rest of the afternoon in local department stores looking for the perfect cherry red towel set.

At home I flung Abby's door open, anxious to show her my new finds, but her room was empty.

***

"This one's perfect," John said, peering into the window of a Volkswagen Beetle. "Low mileage, like-new interior."

He looked annoyingly handsome in his muscle-hugging white shirt and new jeans. I had a strange urge to reach out and touch his chest, but, wisely, I resisted. It would take some time for reality to seep in—John was no longer mine. Randomly touching his chest would be totally inappropriate.

"But this one's silver. I don't want a silver one. I had a yellow one. I want exactly what I had before," I said, fingering the paint. "Plus, look at that. It has a nasty stain in the back seat."

When I'd called John earlier and asked him to help me replace my old car (my insurance check finally came in the mail), my goal was to get the same car. Same year, same color, same everything. I even planned to accessorize it the same way: zebra print steering wheel cover, colorful beads to hang from the rearview mirror and the same band stickers to slap on the back bumper. Maybe if it looked exactly the same as my old one, it would be easier to forget what happened. Plus, some of my best memories were made in that car. My parents surprising me with it as a belated sixteenth birthday present. The first time Abby and I heard her band's song on the radio. John's and my second kiss. The road trip with Abby.

"September, come on. You can't be too picky," he said, looking at the time on his phone. We were on our fifth used car lot and were both getting tired and hungry. The places before offered free popcorn, but there was only so much popcorn a person could take.

"I know I'm being impossible, but I feel cheated. That car was my baby."

An older man wearing a newsboy hat circled a blue Toyota several yards away. He tested the tires with his cane. No one else was around.

"I'm sorry." John squeezed my shoulder. "Did they catch the man who hit you?"

"No and they never will." I drew a frowny face into the dirty windshield.

"Why do you say that?"

"The day after the accident a police detective came over to ask me a few questions. I wasn't any help. When he asked for a detailed description, all I could give him was: male, Caucasian, driving an old brown van. That was it. Really narrows it down, doesn't it? I hate myself when I think of how I forgot to look for the make and model or even the license plate number. I should've studied the guy's face. He could be sixteen or sixty. Brown eyes, green, hazel, or purple for all I know. Abby's dead and this bastard and his stupid van are still out there."

"You can't be too hard on yourself. No one thinks to look at the license plate when their life flashes before their eyes."

Maybe he was right. I was being too hard on myself. "I'll never forgive him, John. What kind of a scumbag leaves two girls for dead, in a mangled car on the side of the road? And the worst part is he will never have to pay for what he did."

"Well maybe it's a good thing they'll never find him, because if I ever meet the guy, I'm going to kill him with my bare hands." He gave me a quick side hug. "I'm so sorry you're going through this."

"Thanks," I said, willing myself to cry. No luck.

John opened the driver's door and slid in. "It's got lower mileage, Tember. Ten thousand less than your old one. You can't get a nicer car with that money."

"Wait, how did you know what my mileage was?"

He laughed. "I'm a guy. We notice these things."

"Okay, I'll think about it, at least," I said, to shut him up.

"Are you interested in the Beetle?" a middle-aged woman with an Australian accent asked as she approached us. "Would you like to take it for a spin?"

"Yes, we would," John said, fiddling around with the buttons.

"Okay, let me know if you have any questions," she said, handing me the key.

"Will you drive?" I asked John, suddenly feeling woozy. Maybe this wasn't such a great idea.

"Why? We're car shopping for you."

I shoved my hands in my pockets. "I just. I'm…"

He shook his head and climbed over to the passenger seat. He popped open the glove box and inspected the contents.

I felt sicker by the second as I stood and gazed at the empty driver's seat. "Think happy thoughts," I whispered. "Happy thoughts."

John growled. "Just get in and drive the damn car."

Reluctantly, I slid behind the wheel and started the engine. The car exuded a strange smell I wasn't used to: cigarettes plus that gross cleaner stuff car dealerships use to mask somebody else's stench.

"Ready?" he said, smiling apologetically for snapping at me. I loved that about him—he could never stay angry for long. Abby thought of John's mood swings as a manic, but I'd argued it was more of a talent to snap back.

"I don't know." As soon as I put the car into reverse, my lungs seemed to shrink into the size of an apple and my heart began pulverizing my rib cage.

"Are you okay, Tember?" John studied my face. His revealed a mix of concern and impatience. "You're shaking like a—"

"I-I don't know."

"Deep breaths. Take deep breaths." He rested a reassuring hand on my knee.

As we pulled out onto the road, the cars around us disappeared and were replaced by images of the brown van flying across the freeway. And then I felt the impact, heard the sound of twisting metal.

"This can't be real. This can't be—"

"September? What's going on? You're going to get us killed."

There was screaming. Lots of screaming. Was that me?

Abby was there beside me as I saw the car flipping through

the air. Her green scarf escaped through the window. I saw the blood and Abby's clawed hand. I smelled that metallic, salty smell, her jasmine perfume. I saw her serene face again.

"Abby. Abby. Abby."

"September!"

I moaned. "Abby. Abby. Abby."

"Pull over!"

Strong, warm hands pried mine from the wheel.

And then I snapped back and saw John sitting next to me, panic written all over his face. "John, I can't-I can't!" I crossed my arms over my face. "I can't-I can't-I can't."

"Come on, September. You can do this." John helped me steer as we dodged several honking cars and a man mouthing a string of profanities. "Let up on the gas. Shhhh. Calm down, Tember. Let up on the gas. I'll help you pull over."

I was ready to throw up by the time he managed to direct me to the side of the road. I pushed the door open and my breakfast poured right out, onto the newly paved road.

"What *was* that? Are you okay?" John looked almost as freaked out as I was.

"I don't know. I'm so sorry. I just—I saw it all over again. I saw that hideous van. I saw her killed all over again. Oh, John, I can't do this."

He held me as I trembled. I buried my face in his chest. "We'll take the car back. You're not ready."

"I'm not ready," I said, the words echoing over and over in my mind.

3

"It's been two weeks and I haven't shed a single tear," I said, ringing the bottom of my t-shirt, growling in frustration.

"Everyone deals with grief in different ways, September. I think you're still in shock. That's perfectly normal," my shrink Dr. Griffin said, who insisted I call her by her first name, Rose. Although with her giant poof of frizzy graying hair she looked more like a poodle than an elegant flower. Her jacket and makeup were as outdated as her office furniture. The pastel overstuffed chair I sat on reminded me of one my parents bought when they were newlyweds. And speaking of my parents, they were the ones who insisted I go to therapy, the ones who coughed up the dough for these costly visits. I protested at first, telling them I was fine, but they insisted. Anything to get me back to "normal", whatever that was.

Mom had dropped by twice over the past couple of weeks with a casserole or a basket of fancy cookies and breads. Each time she'd stay for only a few minutes. We weren't very close and Mom didn't do messy emotional stuff well.

"She was only eighteen. Barely eighteen. People shouldn't die that young," I said, toeing the ugly carpet.

"This is good. Let it out," Rose said, nodding in encouragement.

"Every day—sometimes two or three times a day even—I go

into her room to complain about something or to show her my latest photos, or to borrow a CD. But I have to face it all over again: she's not there."

"And how does that make you feel?" Rose leaned back in her chair, pen on notepad, scribbling down notes.

I didn't know how I felt. I guess I felt a lot of things. And nothing at all.

Numb.

I looked around the office, studied a photo of a group of people in matching white tops and dark denim, framed on the desk. Rose's family, I presumed. I counted the heads. Fourteen people. Three with Rose's frizzy hair. Eight grandchildren?

I saw books, probably hundreds of books. *Why Men Hate Women.* (Nice.) *I'm OK, You're OK.* (Oh good, everyone's okay!) *Ten Days to Self-Esteem.* (More like ten years.)

Behind Rose, I saw two or three dozen troll dolls neatly lined atop her filing cabinet. The creepy bug-eyed dolls with unruly hair (not much unlike Rose's mop, actually) seemed to be staring down at me. Judging me. Taunting me. *Your best friend's dead and you can't cry. You're dead inside. Dead inside...*Abby had collected troll dolls herself when she was about eleven. She'd find them at yard sales and on eBay. She had at least a hundred. Sometimes she'd use her entire month's allowance on the ugly little beasts. I wondered if she still had them around and the idea of starting my own collection was strangely tempting all of a sudden.

The tapping of Rose's press-on nails against her Formica desk brought me back to her question: *How does that make you feel?* How *did* I feel?

"I just don't believe she's dead."

***

On eBay they had 1,466 troll dolls listed. I found myself bidding on seven of them, including two with bright tangerine hair which reminded me of Abby.

Because I was already on the computer, I spent two hours on another online shopping site, I'm embarrassed to admit. I ordered three books I'd been meaning to read, two boxes of gourmet Belgian white chocolate peanut butter cups and an at-home microdermabrasion kit, which promised to clear up my acne and shrink my pores. The damage? $139. But I didn't feel too guilty, I simply "borrowed" from my backpacking Europe fund. Although Abby and I had finally scraped together enough money to take our coast-to-coast road trip, I had been secretly setting aside money for three years for part two: Europe. I was going to surprise her with tickets on her nineteenth birthday.

After the online shopping spree, I took a long, hot shower and used Abby's expensive almond honey shampoo. I was sure she wouldn't mind. By the time I got out, the bathroom was so humid I had to wipe the mirror with a tissue to see myself. I studied my face, my tired mud-brown eyes. I hardly recognized the girl staring back. Not because I looked awful—the junk food and sleepless nights were taking a toll—but because of the strange, haunted look in my eyes.

And because now that Abby was gone, I didn't know who I was anymore.

We'd been besties for so long and we were so much alike, I sometimes didn't know where I ended and she began. I guess you could say we were like conjoined twins, only we were always together by choice. She was the only one who really knew me. The real me. She knew all my crap, my darkest secrets, all my hopes and dreams, my fears, my quirks. I hadn't been close to anyone in my family for years (April and I were good friends when we were little) and not even John understood me the way

Abby did.

In the mirror I watched a single drop of shower water begin to slide down my dewy face, mimicking a tear. I yanked my chin upward in an attempt to immobilize the drop and rushed into my bedroom to grab my Nikon DSLR. I turned it on, put it on the black and white setting, increased the ISO rating and took a few shots of my face. The white curtain in the bathroom window softened the late morning sun, resulting in perfect ambient lighting.

For a small moment I got lost in the magic of creativity. I felt the familiar rush, the rush I got whenever I was in the process of making something beautiful, something unique. One of a kind. My very own. Beauty could be found anywhere, sometimes where and when you least expected it.

I put my camera back into the bag and watched the droplet leap from my jaw onto my bathroom robe. I took a shaky breath.

Was this the closest to crying I was going to get?

After the impromptu photo shoot, I finished dressing myself. I towel dried my hair with one hand and rummaged through drawers looking for the hair dryer with the other.

My phone rang, making me jump.

"Er, hello?"

"September? Hey it's Becky. How's it going?"

"Oh. Hey, Becky. Long time. I'm…good. I'm good. How are you?"

Becky was a casual friend from high school. So casual, this phone call caught me by surprise. We'd shared two photography classes together—and one science. Human Anatomy, I think it was. We were never very close, but she did go to a few lame parties with Abby and me. Actually, that was how it was with all of my friends, Abby aside, of course. None of them knew the real me. Abby was always enough for me. I never felt I needed to make room in my heart for anyone else—until John came along.

"September, you're not going to believe this," Becky said in a breathy voice, "I'm moving to India."

"Wow, no way," I said, trying to match her enthusiasm, while tearing the house apart in search of my elusive blow dryer. "That's so—"

I tripped over poor Tiger, yelping when my bare knees and my right palm hit the unforgiving hardwood floor.

"Are you okay?"

"Yeah, just super uncoordinated."

Becky proceeded to blab for fifteen minutes about some crazy photojournalism internship she'd taken. She was leaving in a week.

I fell back into my Tiger-hair-coated couch to nurse my throbbing knees. Finally, she said, "Enough about me. What's new with you?"

"Oh, same-old, same-old."

"Still taking amazing photos?"

"I try."

"How's Abby?"

Oh. I guess she hadn't heard the news. I'd assumed everyone knew by now. I took a deep breath and said, "She's great." I didn't feel like talking about…the thing. It was hard enough in therapy, but in real, everyday life, it was easier just to *not* think about stuff, let alone say it out loud. "She'll be thrilled to hear about your exotic adventures," I said, opening the freezer to grab a bag of peas to use as an ice pack.

And there it was—the hair dryer—wedged between frozen lasagna and a pint of mint chocolate chip ice cream.

***

At Barnes and Noble the smell of coffee and fresh pastries made my stomach rumble as I browsed the blank notebook section. I have to admit I spend a very uncool amount of time at bookstores, mostly this one.

Abby loved joining me. She'd grab a pile of *Q* and *Guitar* and other music books and magazines while I'd snag *Digital Photographer* and *American Photo* and a few biographies. Armed with ample reading material, we'd squeeze into the same overstuffed chair and read for hours, often losing track of time.

Today I was here for a very specific purpose. Rose, my shrink, had given me a "homework assignment": to buy a journal in which to record my thoughts and feelings. It was apparently a good way to sort them out on the days I needed someone to talk to (because, unfortunately, they did not make a pocket-sized Rose to take everywhere I went).

She said I could also write the things I wished I'd said to Abby, that most people had regrets like that. Maybe use it as a gratitude journal to help me deal with the intense grief I'd be experiencing.

Would be experiencing. I guess I was still in denial.

My hand rested on a butterfly journal. Abby loved butterflies. But then I spotted a diary with Van Gogh's *Starry Night*, my favorite painting of all time and I chose that one.

On the L train I sat by a man with B.O. wearing an Armani suit. Although he seemed like a nice guy, I had to breathe shallowly to avoid inhaling the stench too deeply.

I opened the diary and held a ball point pen over the first line. What should I write? B.O. man sat and watched me write nothing. I looked around me and saw an African lady and her son staring, too, along with an older woman who looked like she'd blow away if someone sneezed in her general direction.

Finally, I wrote:

Abby,

Um, hi. It's me. You know, your best friend? The one you abandoned? I don't know what to say. I'm so confused about everything. I can't believe you're really dead.

Where are you??? Come back. Now.

I snapped the diary shut before nosy B.O. man could read it.

Any sensible kid would be working towards a practical, play-it-safe career. Legal Secretary. Web Developer. Registered Nurse. As for me, I was an aspiring artist. A photographer to be specific. It was my passion. I loved it more than anything. More than family, more than food and sometimes even more than cute boys. Black and white portraits were my specialty. People intrigued me. Captivated me. I currently had work displayed at two local galleries. Actually, one was my aunt's friend's gallery and the other was a coffee shop just off NYU campus. But art didn't pay the rent. Not yet, anyway. So on the side, or rather front and center, I worked at Anderson Art and Frame, which was walking distance from my apartment—can't beat that.

One day I got tired of playing online Scrabble and—coincidentally—finally recovered from my terrible, terrible cough and made it back to work. My boss, Janice, bless her heart, accepted me back with open arms. Okay, maybe not quite with open arms. But thankfully, she didn't fire me.

"I'm going to be in the back stocking paint," Janice said, watching me suspiciously through thick glasses which made her eyes look small and squinty, reminding me of little bugs. Her short, feathered hair and her grandma-style shoes with built-in arch supports added years to her look. Today she wore tight white pants that showcased her spongy cellulite thighs.

"Okay," I said, straightening the Monet, Klimt and Warhol postcards displayed next to the register, trying to look helpful and busy.

The truth: I was pretty much useless today. I may as well have had Alzheimer's. More than once I had to call Janice over to fix a mess I'd made ringing up a customer. If I kept this up I'd be fired in no time.

I watched Janice leave before resuming my comatose state on the stool behind the register.

And then a really hot guy suddenly approached me. He set a Moleskine notebook, plus two of the nicest pens the store offered on the counter. He had disheveled chestnut hair and was maybe a year or two older than me. He looked familiar, but I couldn't pin down where I'd seen him before. I didn't notice my mouth gaping open at first, much like a fish, in awe of his masterful face. He was extremely good-looking, but not in the predictable soap-star sort of way. More in the intriguing rock god way. A little flawed, but the flaws only made him more compelling. Also moody. Morose. So brooding, he put James Dean to shame. He did crack a smile when he noticed the look of wonderment frozen to my face.

With shaky hands I proceeded to ring him up. I wanted to say, "Run away with me, we'd be perfect together," but instead I said, "Did you find everything you needed?"

"Yes, thank you," he said so politely it felt like we were attending an etiquette class. ("Pardon me, would you please pass the butter?" "But of course.")

"Are you an artist?" I asked, my knees turning into pudding.

"A writer."

"I see." I wanted to add something clever but fear and intimidation paralyzed me.

Now James Dean studied *my* face. Suddenly I wished I'd gone to bed earlier last night. Maybe then I wouldn't have giant duffel bags under my eyes. I regretted not taking an extra five minutes to fine-tune my makeup, perfect my hair. I could've done better with my outfit, too. Was that a hole in my shirt?

I blushed like a total idiot as I placed his items in a paper bag. He finally fixed his gaze elsewhere, to my relief.

He fiddled with stuff around the register, picking up and examining a miniature watercolor set, poking some Life Savers, running a finger along the edge of a Picasso postcard. I stole more sneaky glances while he pawed everything around him—I couldn't help myself. He was clearly a troubled guy, with sad eyes and shapely lips curled downwards in a slight frown. His asparagus-colored shirt brought out the green in his eyes. He had lovely hands, I couldn't help but notice.

Suddenly I felt guilty. Should I be salivating over a guy like this when Abby just died? What the hell was wrong with me?

"Two hundred and ten dollars please," I said, breaking the awkward silence.

"Excuse me?" He looked at me like I had a whole salad stuck in my teeth. Or did I put my underwear *over* my clothes today? Was there a large bird nesting in my hair?

"Two hundred and ten dollars please?" I repeated timidly.

"All I'm getting is a notebook and two pens. That shouldn't be more than twenty-five bucks."

"Oh, you're right. I'm so sorry. I must've added an extra zero somewhere."

Then I remembered I'd have to call Janice over to clean up the mess. Maybe I could fix this one myself, I thought. Save a teaspoon of pride. Not a good idea. I shot my finger forward, aiming for the clear button, but missed, hitting something else entirely. I'm not sure what I pressed, but the total doubled.

Ready to commit to a nunnery where I'd never have to

interact with another cute boy again, I called Janice over. My cheeks scorched, turning a deeper shade of crimson by the second. Was it possible to suffer second degree burns due to blushing?

James Dean smiled politely—too politely—and tapped his slender fingers on the counter. Even his nails were perfectly groomed. I had to restrain my eyes from wandering over to my own, far inferior, fingertips. I didn't have to look to remember my red polish was peeling like a long abandoned home.

I heard grumbling before I saw my boss, hands on her hips, eyes rolling. "What now, September?"

I cleared my throat, three times. (Curse the mucus-producing bread-and-cheese sandwich I'd eaten at lunch!) "I overcharged him."

Janice sighed heavily as James Dean glanced at his watch. Like a mother speaking condescendingly to her pregnant, heroin addicted thirteen-year-old, she said, "September, when are you going to learn?"

Now I was ready to die.

***

"Tell me about the past week, September," Rose said, scratching the side of her nose with a leaky pen, rubbing a path of blue ink into her skin.

"I don't know. I guess I'm…I don't know…" I crossed my arms and began counting tiles in the water stained ceiling. Rose fell silent for a moment and looked over her notes. We could hear the clock ticking impatiently, bustling traffic outside, a woman sobbing from the office next door.

I let out a theatrical sigh and forced myself to focus on the frizzy-haired woman in front of me, who was wearing waaaay too much foundation. She practically looked like a clown with the stuff caked on so thick. Her orange face sharply contrasted her cauliflower-white neck. Why do old people go out in public looking like that? I'm never going to be old.

It was kind of funny, actually. Every week I had to see this goofy looking lady—someone who was a stranger to me a few weeks ago—and spill my guts out. Share things I wouldn't have shared with anyone but Abby. Although I felt vulnerable, I also kind of liked having an audience, someone to watch me wallow. Someone who was paid to care about my miserable life. It was almost like having my own reality TV show, only with an audience of one.

Another sigh. "I'm ticked, actually."

Rose seemed pleased with this. Her usual tired-looking gray eyes lit up like Las Vegas at night. "You're angry. Good. Why are you feeling angry, September?"

"They say there are five stages of grief: Denial, Anger, Bargaining, Depression and Acceptance. There must be something seriously wrong with me. It's been three weeks since Abby died and I'm only now entering stage two." I'd read all about it in Kubler-Ross's book, *On Death and Dying*. "Not to mention no tears."

"Everyone deals with grief in their own way. Some people skip phases or jump around. Your friend meant a lot to you. This isn't something you're going to get through instantly. Grieving takes time. It's not like cooking ramen noodles."

Ramen noodles? I laughed a full-throttle, gut-busting laugh.

"It's nice to see you laugh," Rose said, resting her elbows on the desk, smiling.

Between the ink on her nose, the sinister trolls hovering over us and the ramen noodle comment, I was now in hysterics. And once I start, I can't quit. Tears began cascading down my face.

It finally hit me like a falling plane: Abby was gone.

Just as quickly as my laughing episode began, I began crying. Three weeks worth of stored up tears poured out of me. Snot, too. Rose leaned across the desk, resting a hand on mine. Another hand slid a tissue box over. I grabbed fistfuls and started wiping, blowing and tossing them aside until white giant popcorn-looking balls encircled my ankles on the floor.

"Tears," Rose said, frowning sympathetically, squeezing my hand.

At the end of our fifty minute session (which ended up being two percent talking and ninety-eight percent crying), Rose scribbled something on her notepad, ripped out the page and slid it across her coffee-stained desk. "Your homework for this week."

Express your anger in constructive ways.

"Like how?" I said, standing.

"Go somewhere private and scream. Beat a pillow. Break something," she said as she opened the heavy office door. A man with wet hair, a crooked tie and plastic grocery bags covering his feet sat in the waiting area.

"Hello, Steve," I heard Rose say as I swung the glass door of the main entrance open. Hamster-sized drops of rain greeted me outside.

5

Twinkies. I love them. Too much, maybe. But you see, Twinkies and I have a love-hate relationship. So you may or may not be surprised to hear that, for the past three years, Twinkies and I hadn't been on speaking terms. While I allowed myself a *respectable* portion of dessert on special occasions—a sliver of cake at a birthday party, three bites of rich cheesecake at a wedding, two or three red vines at the end of a long day—I vowed to give up Twinkies when I reached a size fourteen my freshman year of high school. It was the only time I ever struggled with weight. It was the same year my parents separated for eight months and my next door neighbor, Adam Christensen, turned into a vegetable after bashing his head in a skateboarding accident. You see I love Twinkies, but Twinkies don't love me. I'm allergic to them. They make my thighs swell.

So there I sat on Abby's bed, armed with a box of Twinkies. Although my happy-go-lucky size four jeans screamed in protest, my longtime lust for creamy, spongy goodness forced me to succumb. I carefully opened the box and laid out all ten oblong shapes of heaven in a neat row. I squeezed, poked, prodded and lifted one to my nose to inhale the sugary vanilla scent. Prudently, I placed it back on the bed.

Looking around me, I noted the room was exactly as Abby had left it. Her neatly made bed clashed with the tornado-hit room. She'd made her bed every morning, but rarely touched the dust-collecting crap on the floor. "It gives me a sense of order. Having all my stuff laid out in clear view," she'd once explained when I questioned her.

Rumpled clothes, chunky boots and *Rolling Stone* magazines camouflaged every inch of the ancient orangey-brown carpet. Dripping candles, odd knickknacks and guitar picks covered every surface of furniture in the room. Postcards, magazine clippings and posters of rock stars dotted plum-colored walls. Her favorite poster of the '80s goth band, The Cure, hung on the ceiling directly above the pillow on her bed. She would gaze into singer Robert Smith's heavily made-up face as she drifted off each night. April said a face like that would give her nightmares, but Abby loved her men moody and weird. A younger version of Robert Smith was Abby's dream boy.

Actually, we were both huge '80s music fans, which is pretty rare for people our age. We both got a real kick out of the big, teased hair, the heavy eye makeup, the melodramatic vocals, the robotic synthesizers. We liked most of the stuff from the era, but considered New Wave the best. We loved to mimic some of the over-the-top fashion we'd see in music videos on YouTube. We'd go to '80s theme parties wearing thrashed-and-safety-pinned t-shirts exposing one shoulder, fluorescent leggings with fedoras or big obnoxious bows in our hair. We watched *Pretty in Pink* and *Ferris Bueller's Day Off* more times than I can count. We had several lines from *The Breakfast Club* memorized. Molly Ringwald was our hero. Abby would often joke we were born in the wrong era.

I ripped the Twinkie wrapper open just a tad to get a better whiff. Three years of self-control dissolved as I took my first bite. Sticky sweet love exploded in my mouth. I savored the first cake, but barely noticed my rebellious hands tearing through the plastic barrier of cake number two.

It didn't make sense, how Abby's material stuff carried on, life as usual, while her lifeless body was stuck in a box, buried deep in the earth. Shouldn't her earthly treasures disappear in a poof like she did? Even her alarm clock acted as if nothing happened, obnoxious and perky, stating the time in bright red numbers. I grabbed the gloating machine, ripped the plug out of its socket and threw it across the room. I was pleased when it hit the wall and tore one of Abby's Morrissey posters.

There. Now something was different. The room needed to know Abby was not here. That she would never be here again.

I began to nibble on cake number three. The experience brought me back to scorching summer days with Abby and I sprawled on her living room floor like cats, too hot to move. A vintage fan blew cool relief, the breeze running its fingers through our sweaty hair. Twinkie wrappers ever encircled us. Like dozens of other times, we played our favorite game, *Would You Rather...?* Would you rather go a week without makeup or a month without shaving your legs? Lose your hearing or become paraplegic? Make out with the young version of U2's Bono or have the perfect boyfriend?

When we wore that out Abby said, "What's your greatest fear?"

"I don't know. Maybe going blind. Not being able to see the beauty around me. Not being able to take another photo. Why?" I rolled onto my side to study her face. She was beautiful even at fourteen, with unlawfully clear skin, chopstick thighs and silky orange hair.

"I don't know. Just wondering." She bit her lip.

"What's yours?"

"Losing you," she said without hesitation. She was gazing at the ceiling then, playing with the charm bracelet on her arm, the one I gave her on her twelfth birthday. She did that—looked away when things got too sentimental, too gushy.

"You won't lose me," I said, but I knew it was a promise I couldn't keep. Even then I knew life was unpredictable, like the weather on a spring afternoon. There were no guarantees. "What else are you afraid of? Besides spiders and country music," I added, jokingly.

"I don't know...well actually...promise you won't tell anyone?" she asked, her eyes cutting into mine.

Surprised by her sudden intensity, I laughed. "Sure, I promise."

She hesitated before saying, "I've always been afraid of dying young. And...I've always thought that maybe—"

"What?" Again, I laughed. "Of course you won't die young. You're not allowed to. We're growing old together, remember? We're going to be each other's maid of honor and our kids are going to be best friends...You're going to be a rock star, just like you imagined. And then someday we're going to be the coolest old ladies around."

She tugged her brows together and bit her lower lip. "I guess you're right."

"You'd better not die on me," I threatened. "If you do, I'll make you eternally miserable, I swear it. I'll put spiders in your casket. Lots of spiders. And I'll play country music at your funeral. I'm not kidding."

She raised her hands, stick-'em-up style. "Okay, okay. I get it. I'm not dying young."

"That's right. And never forget it," I said before throwing a Twinkie at her face.

As I came back to the present, I was shocked to see half of the Twinkies gone. High on a sugar buzz, I took the remaining five and hid them under the bed. Maybe the cat would find them and finish them off. I stretched out on the bed, upside-down and hugged her pillow against my chest. I noted her scent of Jasmine and Suave shampoo and her natural Abby scent in her bedding. The smell filled my throat with cotton balls and caused my insides to ache. And then I felt a crushing feeling, like a brick wall fell over onto my chest.

I sobbed fiercely, the kind of sobbing that causes your whole body to tremble. And then, without fully realizing it, I kicked Abby's headboard. One swift blow punctured the flimsy wood. A strange noise escaped my throat. A sound so alien, it scared me. But seeing the hole somehow filled the void in my heart—just a little. I kicked some more and some more and laughed a bitter, angry laugh. The kicking/laughing/crying felt oddly therapeutic. Cleansing. I stopped kicking when a splinter pierced the sole of my shoe, the sharp edge poking through my sock. I only felt a tad guilty for ruining her bed frame—she told me once it had been her grandmother's—but overall I felt relieved to have damaged something.

So much for expressing anger in *constructive* ways. I rolled up into fetal position, smashing my face into the pillow.

"Why did you leave me? *Why?*" I whispered.

Despite my sugar high, grief yanked me down into a long but restless sleep.

***

In the morning I had a throbbing headache. A Twinkie hangover. Realizing I should take some aspirin and go to work, I called in sick instead. On the phone, Janice sounded, well, unconvinced. I was lucky she didn't fire me right then and there for lying. But I wasn't being totally deceitful. I felt completely trashed—physically and emotionally. Flattened by a steamroller.

I tumbled out of bed and peeled off my strangling clothes. There were seam marks in my skin where my jeans had been. I raked through Abby's drawers and pulled out a massive vintage Depeche Mode tee and a pair of plaid boxers and dressed myself. Her essence engulfed me, giving me the impression I was being hugged. My eyes got all leaky again.

As if she had psychic abilities and sensed I was coveting Abby's things, Hannah, her mom, called to say she was coming over tomorrow afternoon to collect Abby's things and would I please leave a key under the doormat for her?

Crap. The headboard.

"What are you going to do with her stuff?" I asked, an ice-cold panic washing over me. I picked up her favorite guitar, a Yamaha acoustic-electric and pressed it against my chest. She can't take the guitar. That thing was a part of Abby. Like an appendage. It still had her fingerprints all over it. It was proof she was once here.

"Keep a few things that are sentimental. Donate the rest to Goodwill," Hannah said absently. I heard Abby's brothers wrestle in the background.

I wanted to say, "How can you get rid of her stuff like that? She died like *three weeks* ago. Are you really that anxious to put her behind you? Maybe you should scratch her face out of all the family photos while you're at it. She was only your *daughter*. Shouldn't we leave things be? Leave her stuff the way it is? Maybe even consider opening an Abby museum?" But instead I said, "I'll be here. Come over whenever you'd like."

I looked around Abby's room and suddenly felt like hoarding. My inner pack-rat began scheming. *I* wanted her stuff. All of it. I'd lusted after her music collection for half of my life. Although she was a size smaller, some of her clothes were baggy and I often borrowed them. And her scrapbooks. I could not let

Hannah take those. They meant the universe to me. Untidy and swimming in graffiti, those scrapbooks sandwiched our dearest memories. Dozens of photos of us, spanning eleven years of friendship. Her crazy poems and lyrics and memorabilia flat enough to stuff under a plastic sheet protector overflowed the binders. Not to mention the hundreds of concert ticket stubs. Like me, she kept each one.

Like a winner of a thousand dollar mall shopping spree, I began grabbing fistfuls of stuff, shoving whatever I could into a Washington Apples cardboard box. First I snagged the scrapbooks, then some of my favorite clothes: her band tees, her punk-rock plaid pants with zippers, her military-style jacket with a Siouxsie and the Banshees patch sewn on the back. Next the CDs. I considered taking them all, but then realized Hannah would be suspicious. So I took the most coveted ones. The imports, the bootlegs. The rare ones: Cuddly Toys, Freur, Dali's Car, Celebrate the Nun. *The Top* album signed by Robert Smith himself.

I decided to keep her favorite guitar. I would let her family have the red and white Fender. I had no use for that one. After all, my only musical talent was appreciation. Plus, Hannah would probably notice if that was missing. Her folks splurged and bought it for her for Christmas two years ago.

I scanned her jewelry and grabbed a favorite turquoise ring and her sterling silver cat necklace. She loved cats. (Tiger was actually Abby's cat.)

I stopped cold. Would Hannah take Tiger? Definitely not. I would not allow that. As far as I was concerned Tiger was as much mine as she was Abby's. I'd helped raise the silly cat since he was a clingy kitten, pawing my every body part, looking in all the wrong places for milk. We found him abandoned in a grocery cart at a Trader Joe's parking lot three days into senior year. It was love at first sight. We knew we had to take him home.

Another thought crossed my mind. Was I stealing? Technically this stuff belonged to Abby's family now. Was I breaking some moral code? Robbing my dead best friend? Besides taking a gummy worm out of the bulk bin when I was six, I'd never stolen anything before. But she was my *best friend*. We were practically family. *More* than family. I deserved a few things for myself. I considered asking Hannah if she'd mind if I took a few things, but what if she insisted on keeping the scrapbooks for herself? I couldn't bear the thought of losing them. I treasured them more than any of my own belongings. More than my beloved camera.

I didn't get out of bed in the morning—Abby's bed—until eleven. I'd stayed up late watching a *Gilmore Girls* marathon, wiping out an entire frozen pizza and the remaining five Twinkies. I sat up, gasping in pain. My head felt like it was being twisted by two ugly sumo wrestlers.

Maybe I should kick the Twinkie habit now while I still have a chance.

I noticed my diary, which I'd absentmindedly placed on the nightstand. It looked so lonely there. Out of guilt, I picked it up and wrote:

Abby,

I miss you so much. You'll never know how much I miss you. Why did you have to leave me????

PS I've taken over your bedroom. Hope you don't mind.

I plucked up my bathrobe and headed for the bathroom to take a shower. I stood for a bit, opting to simply gawk at the shower instead. If I stared long enough, would it magically make my matted hair, my offensive garlic breath and oily skin just somehow disappear? Where was Mary Poppins when I needed her?

Instead of showering, I melted into the couch and watched

Dr. Brown's lover wake up from a year-long coma on TV. Little did she know her ruggedly handsome boyfriend with the perfect length of stubble on his chin had an evil twin brother, also romancing her.

Tiger curled up next to me, purring with contentment—as if his owner didn't die three weeks ago. I shoved fistfuls of Cheerios into my mouth (I was out of milk) and washed it down with ginger ale. Abby loved ginger ale. Our fridge was still stocked with about a month's supply.

At three Hannah came over. She was armed with eight boxes and packing tape.

"Oh, Tember," she said through wet eyes, giving me a massive hug, the stud in her nose catching my hair. She looked around the front room. "Looks like you're all settled in. I just love what you two have done with the place."

The entire apartment was slapped together with various creative finds. The purple couch had been snagged at a wealthy man's estate sale for only $80. The coffee table was simply an old door placed on two cinder blocks. A wicker chair in the corner was found dumpster-diving. Our impressive vinyl and CD collection was neatly placed in stacked antique milk crates. The leaning tower of vintage board games was another yard sale find. My photos decorated the walls. Nag Champa incense burned eternally on the side table next to a monkey lamp.

"Thanks. Um, Hannah, there's something I should warn you about." The headboard. I turned into a crazed lunatic and pulverized it.

"Tember, are you okay? You don't look too hot." She eyed me up and down and frowned. Abby's Depeche Mode tee and boxers were messy and wrinkled now. Last night's dinner stuck to the lead singer's face. It was something like three days since I'd showered. I didn't even want to imagine how I must've smelled.

"I'm…surviving." I laughed a nervous laugh. "Don't worry about me. I can't imagine how it must be for you to lose your mother *and* a child in the same year. How are you holding up?"

Hannah did look tired. Since the funeral she'd aged about ten years and for the first time ever she wasn't wearing her signature Egyptian eyeliner.

"We all miss Abs terribly. I still can't believe she's gone." Everyone in her family called her that, everyone except her grandfather who insisted she be called Abigail. "But we know she's with Jesus now."

I led her into the bedroom, dreading her reaction to the late grandma's murdered headboard. Hannah was usually a cool, laid-back mom, but I'd annihilated a family heirloom.

"Oh September. What happened here?" A heavily ringed hand covered a gaping mouth.

I was going to tell the truth, I swear, but fear clung to me like a sticky shirt on a hot summer day. "Um, er, Abby did it."

Great. Blame it on the dead person. Who was I becoming? Lying to my friend's mom, skipping showers and work, binging on pizza and sugar. I used to be so with it. What was *wrong* with me? Where was the honest, trustworthy September we knew and loved?

"Abby what?"

"Abby did it. She was having this terrible nightmare. A headboard monster was attacking her. She kicked the crap out of the poor thing." Oh, that was horrible! If I was going to tell a lie, it may as well have been a *good* one. A *headboard monster?*

"That was my mother's headboard. My great grandfather built it for her when she was eleven. That just breaks my heart."

I had to look away when Hannah teared up again.

It took two hours to box up all of her things. I helped Hannah haul the headboard to the dumpster and load her car with Abby's stuff. It nearly killed me when she drove away with it. It was almost like losing my friend all over again.

Much to my guilty relief, Hannah didn't notice the missing CDs. She didn't even ask about the scrapbooks and when I asked if I could keep Tiger, she shrugged and said, "Oh, of course."

We'd also managed to fill up an entire box of Mary's things. Abby's other best friend. Apparently, they borrowed each other's stuff as much as we did. I threw the box in the back of the closet, wondering if I'd ever get around to returning it.

Hannah let me keep Abby's posters up. After all, we adored most of the same bands. Aside from a few candy wrappers, eighty-seven cents and a moldy burrito (I found behind the hamper of all places), the room was empty.

Suddenly a surge of energy shot through me. I vacuumed Abby's floor, wiped down the dusty walls and gave the windows a Windex shine. Next I pushed and pulled and tugged my furniture into the empty room. Seeing it bare was too painful. I'd rather see my own room vacant. She had the better room anyway, with two windows and a bigger closet. We'd fought over the room when we'd first moved in but quickly resolved it with three rounds of Rock, Paper, Scissors.

I worked up a sweat by the time I pulled my dresser in the room. When the last photo was hung—one of full-grown Abby riding one of those fifty cent kiddie rides—I collapsed, exhausted. Staring at the ceiling, I realized I had to rent out my room. I couldn't afford this place otherwise. But who would even begin to compare to Abby? She was the perfect roommate. Aside from being a little messy, she never hogged the bathroom, stole my food, or borrowed my clothes without asking. When I thought about some stranger coming in and marking her territory, someone who'd listen to gross music, take over more than half of the fridge and bring creepy guys over, suddenly I craved Twinkies.

***

On my way to the grocery store to buy frozen pizza and Twinkies, I happened to see John who also lived in East Williamsburg. (He actually encouraged me and Abby to find an apartment nearby so we could spend more time together.)

Crossing paths with John wasn't the worst part. Neither was being dressed in a dirty tee, boxers, with grungy hair and no makeup. Never mind my I-haven't-showered-in-three-days stench or my unbrushed teeth.

It was *where* I saw John. He was at a jewelry store, looking at rings of all things. When he saw me watching him through the pristine glass storefront, he ducked behind the earrings like he was dodging a bullet. It was all very James Bond. I must've lost it because rather than listen to my inner voice telling me to mind my own business and avoid entering a fancy establishment in a ratty rock shirt and men's undergarments, I went in.

"Oh, September. What are you doing here?" John said, straightening up, pushing gorgeous hair out of his gorgeous face, looking anxious, guilty and perplexed all at once.

An older man standing behind the display case with a nice suit and a comb-over eyed me with disdain.

"No, the question is, what are *you* doing here?" I said, ignoring the snobby man's glare.

"I'm, um, buying earrings for my mom." He looked over to the left and rubbed his nose like he always did when he lied.

"You and I both know that your mom only wears native stuff. I saw you looking at rings. Why were you looking at rings?" I knew I was being demanding, unreasonable, obnoxious, but I'd suspected something wasn't right with us weeks before he dumped me.

John's arms fell to his sides, his face divulged defeat. "You win. You want to know what I'm doing here, September? You're going to find out soon enough."

I nodded, folded my arms. His cringe made me think maybe I didn't want to know. Maybe ignorance *was* bliss.

He sighed. Cringed again. Sighed again. Wow, this was painful for him. Whatever it was. Suddenly I was feeling sympathy pains. I'd take them back if I'd known what he was about to tell me.

He let the words tumble out. "I'm buying your sister an engagement ring."

He may as well have kicked me in the stomach.

"What? April?" I said, as if I had more than one sister. I started laughing. He's kidding, I thought. He *has* to be kidding. And anyway, they're only a year older than me. Waaaay too young for something as grown up as marriage.

He shoved his hands into his pockets. "I'm sorry, September. We're both sorry to hurt you like this."

"What?" I said, stunned. When did this happen?

He shrugs. "If I'm going to be honest…I've always had a thing for your sister."

Ouch. I couldn't believe he'd just said that. "You what?"

"When her boyfriend broke up with her, she was lonely and well…"

The more things sunk in, the more breathing became a struggle. His words were like an anvil on my chest. "You're with my *sister*? You're proposing to *April*? Abby died a few weeks ago and now you're telling me this?"

"I know the timing's rotten. April and I weren't going to tell you for a while." *April and I. April and I.* When did this *April and I* crap start? I must be a total idiot to have missed this. Oblivious.

And then I remembered the funeral. John and April showing up at the same time, sitting together. I should've known.

"Why April? She's nothing like me."

"She's pretty great...I mean, you're great, too. That came out all wrong. April's...driven. She has a ten year plan. She's going to be a lawyer. She wants to *do* something with her life."

"I'm driven, too. I'm a photographer. That's something."

"You're an artist. You work at a craft store, for heaven's sake." He said *craft store* like it was a red light district or a co-op for cannibals.

"Art supplies store," I corrected.

But he was right. John and April were more alike when it came to future aspirations. John planned on attending dental school. (I know—dental school. Could it *be* any more boring?) They both wanted a cushy suburban life with two point five children, a Labrador Retriever and a cookie-cutter home. Like me, John came from an upper-middle class upbringing, but unlike me, he wanted our parents' lives. Nice, conservative neighbors in khakis and polo shirts to invite over for barbeques. A boat, a sports car, a minivan. I wanted to take photos and see the world. Maybe I was too bohemian for him.

"When did this happen?" My heart sped up like a tape stuck on fast forward. Maybe I didn't really want to know.

Snooty Guy was leaning over a case of pendants, eyes cemented to us, chin cradled in hand, his thin lips curled up in an amused smile. What a jerk—he was enjoying this.

John looked down at something on the floor. He scratched his head. His voice cracked a little when he finally answered, "Three months before you and I broke up."

"I'm sorry, three months?" I was choking on my words. "You cheated on me—with my sister—for three whole months?"

"I know. I'm slime. I'm worse than slime, I'm..." A list of

expletives came to my mind. His face twisted up in pain. He was angry at himself. I wasn't surprised. John liked to follow all the rules, do everything the right way. Cheating on a girlfriend was out of character for him. "I feel bad. I've felt bad for months. But your sister and I...You can't help who you love, September."

"Right." You can't help who you love, huh? You poor, helpless guy. I wanted to smack him but I refrained. "Why did you kiss me then? Why did you come over after the accident and kiss me?"

"I know. It was wrong. April and I had a big fight and well, the truth is I missed you. We were together for so long."

Nine months, I thought. Only apparently three of them didn't count because you were slobbering all over my sister. Ughhh. "You can't—you can't have it both ways. You can't come running to me whenever you and April—"

"I know, I know. I don't know what I was thinking."

"You really hurt me, John. My *sister*. I can't believe it." Was I shrinking? Every minute I felt a little bit smaller.

"You'll find someone soon, Tember. You'll find yourself a nice artsy-fartsy boy and travel the world."

Now he was patronizing me. What a pig. What a stupid, freaking pig. I hated him then. As much as I hated the man who killed Abby.

I threw my hands in the air. I couldn't take it anymore. I said, "You know what? I hope you'll be happy. You and April both. Welcome to the family, John." I turned then, fearing he'd see the tears escaping my eyes.

"Tember, wait—"

I didn't care that everyone was watching—I couldn't keep my composure any longer. I fled the store like a frightened little rodent.

Blinded by my tears, I zigzagged my way to a convenience store bathroom and locked myself in a nasty smelling stall. I let myself go and sobbed like I never had before. A desperate, frantic, heaving cry. I didn't care who could hear me. I cried until my stomach muscles burned, until my head throbbed. It felt like I was in there for hours. A small handful of women came in to reapply lipstick or use a toilet and two of them asked me if I was okay. I lied and said I was. What else was I supposed to say? I quieted down until I was sure they were gone.

I blew my nose a few times and dabbed the mascara trails on my cheeks. I fished a pen and my grief diary from my purse. After studying the Van Gogh painting I scribbled a few lines:

Abby,

Where the hell are you? Why did you leave me? You promised me you'd always be there for me. I don't know who I am without you. I'm lost. So, so, so lost.

I shoved the book back into my purse and sat on the hard, cold toilet seat for a while. I reminisced. I thought of the first time I saw Abby, in second grade. She was missing her two bottom front teeth. Two yam-colored braids dangled over her bony shoulders. She wore a Tinkerbell dress, one she begged her parents to buy her for Halloween the previous year. But she wasn't a girlie-girl. She was feisty and she was messy and she was boyish. A tough girl in a fairy dress.

I was the new girl in school and Isaac, a boy with the biggest feet I'd ever seen on a kid, chased me at recess, stomping on my brand new Mary Jane shoes, using me as a target for spit bombs, calling me a baby when I began to cry. Abby saved me that day. She stopped Bigfoot dead in his tracks. She threatened to tell the whole second grade he peed his pants the first day of Kindergarten if he ever bothered me again.

I thought of the time she broke her arm roller skating. I felt so protective of her, I even cried sympathy tears, but she just sat and gritted her teeth like the tough little girl she was.

She didn't take crap from boys. When she found out her first boyfriend Brandon Westmoreland cheated on her, she swiped the ketchup and mustard bottles from the school cafeteria and painted his entire front side with the red and yellow condiments.

Abby was adventurous. Unlike me, she was never afraid to experiment with her hair or try weird seafood or rock climb or bungee jump or go on a thirty day raw vegan cleanse. I'd always envied that part of her. She was larger than life. Like a Hollywood star. Someone you couldn't imagine doing something as mundane as laundry. Of course, living with her, I saw her do all sorts of mundane things, but she did even those in a cool/quirky/cute way.

It will be forever tattooed in my brain the day she announced in front of our entire career class she wanted to be a rock star. It was the first day of eighth grade. Junior high—the time when kids caring what others think skyrockets. Mrs. Berger asked each of us to introduce ourselves and say what we wanted to be when we grew up.

I heard lots of the usual stuff: nurse, scientist, preschool teacher, vet, stay-at-home mom. But Abby, whether intentionally or not, let the truth spill like a bag of marbles. "My name's Abby Irvine and I want to be a rock star," she'd said with a kind of confidence I'll always envy. The dream of being famous one day is a delicate thing. A thing to safely tuck away and *maybe* share with a few close, trusted friends. It could be extinguished by those who meant well but didn't understand, a blanket over a timid flame.

I didn't have that same fearlessness. I would not, in a million years, announce matter-of-factly I hoped to be a hot-shot photographer one day. So I wasn't a bit surprised when a rush of giggles and snickers filled the room. Mrs. Berger said, "That's nice, dear. But maybe you should have a back-up plan. Something *practical*." Michael Garcia yelled out, "Yeah, right. Like you'd ever become a rock star. You're more likely to be hit by lightning. Loser!" Soon the entire class chanted "Lo-ser! Lo-ser! Lo-ser!" until Abby was on the verge of tears (she was tough but not bulletproof) and Mrs. Berger slammed her attendance log and yelled, "That's enough!" My turn was next. I did what any best friend would do in the situation despite being so nervous I nearly puked—I committed social suicide and said, "My name is September Jones and I want to be a fairy princess." I didn't hear the end of it until Cassandra Abraham's D-cup bra broke in co-ed PE a week later.

I gathered fistfuls of toilet paper and mopped up the tears and snot hanging from my nose. I noticed words scribbled on the wall in purple ink: *It's not like you have anything better to read.* (True.) And then with a sharpie on another wall: *I feel like this is the only mark I'll ever make in the world.* (Sad.) And then in pencil: *Do you idealize the past or see it as broken?* (I'm definitely guilty of idealizing.) Someone wrote in reply: *I'm just trying to take a dump.* (Funny.)

I pulled out my own pen and scrawled: *My best friend's dead.*

I thought a while about the idealizing the past bit. I smiled, realizing things I hated about Abby were endearing to me now. Now that she was gone. The way she'd always lose her keys and blame it on me. The way she'd shake her leg when we watched movies, rocking the whole couch. Her nervous ticks: chewing gum with her mouth open, pawing through her hair to find and chomp off split ends. Her flaky side: borrowing my clothes and forgetting to wash and return them, committing to quality time then crashing parties instead, showing up reliably late for everything.

My tear ducts dried up the same time my stomach protested in hunger. I hadn't eaten since breakfast.

It was 6:39 PM now. I toyed with the idea of buying a few groceries. At home the choices were sparse—peanut butter, mayonnaise, six saltine crackers (yes, I counted) and Abby's ginger ale, of course. But when I saw my face in the compact mirror, I wanted to scream. It was as red and blotchy as meat-lover's pizza and my eyes were nearly swollen shut. I looked like I'd gone a few rounds in a boxing ring.

I considered staying in that nasty restroom stall forever, living off the breath mints and stale animal crackers in my purse.

***

After the John incident, I didn't leave the apartment for several days, possibly even weeks. Every day I sat on the sagging couch and watched the hair on my legs grow. For the first time in my life, I went many days without bathing. When my head began to itch like mad, I envisioned all sorts of scary bugs I was sure had made a home in my hair. I finally summoned the strength to take a long, scalding shower (convinced the searing water would kill the tenants in my hair). After bathing, I was weak and drowsy and my muscles ached. Just washing my hair alone caused my arms to feel like they would fall off. I finally threw my soiled clothes into the hamper. The Depeche Mode shirt and boxers were stiff as cardboard and smelled like road kill. I traded them for Abby's vintage *Princess Bride* tee and my own sweat bottoms.

Rose, my shrink, called twice, but I couldn't bring myself to pick up. Janice from work called every day, leaving me a message. At first she was angry, but after a week I could hear concern in her tone. I wanted to pick up, tell her why I'd deserted her. But how do you explain it? "I'm sorry. I can't come to work. The boy I loved is marrying my sister and my best friend is dead." Who would believe that story? I may as well throw in that my mom broke her back and my house was robbed. I was kidnapped by aliens. Michael Jackson is back from the dead and asked me to star in his next music video.

After a week and a half she left a message, firing me and added, "You'd have to be dead to get your job back." That last part made me laugh and laugh and laugh. You see, grief does funny things to people. When I wasn't in a zombie-like stupor, I was crying and when I wasn't crying, I was laughing like a deranged woman.

I craved chow mein noodles like a blues singer craves his ex and ordered them every night. I made the cute Chinese take-out boy rich with tips. (My folks had sent me a check for a couple thousand bucks. They believe shopping could cure all ills.) My Twinkie stash dwindled. I forced myself to have no more than one a day. I cheated twice. I had only six beloved Twinkies left. Once they were gone, I wasn't buying more. I had to kick the habit—I wasn't going to let myself get fat again. (Did the nearby convenience store sell Twinkie patches?)

The TV became my new best friend. I watched all sorts of sitcoms, talk shows, fashion shows, travel logs. The nature channel became strangely soothing. I watched three documentaries on elephants and they are now my favorite animal. I saw four on sharks. Two told explicit real-life stories of perfectly nice, unsuspecting people torn to pieces by the devilish creatures. One was about a surfer girl who lost her arm. I wondered how it would feel knowing a large part of my body became a sea monster's lunch. They say you are what you eat. The shark would then be part me. Creepy. I wasn't sure I'd ever set a toe in the ocean again. I also watched a half a dozen home style shows. By now I had the equivalent of an associate's degree in home design. I couldn't wait to arrange my furniture in a harmonious Feng Shui fashion, paint my living room walls lemon yellow, add splashes of green with dozens of exotic plants.

I managed to write in my diary once during this bout of depression:

Dear Abby,
You suck for leaving me! I hate you.
(Okay, you know I don't hate you.)

***

I dreamed of Abby every night. Three times I dreamed of her, John and me looking down the mouth of the Grand Canyon. They would take each other by the hand and jump, falling, for what felt like forever, down the endless red abyss, leaving me behind, alone. Each time I woke up screaming, followed by violent sobbing. They left me. They were gone. I missed John, but mostly I was mad at him. But I ached for Abby. Sometimes I missed her so much, it hurt to breathe.

When my Twinkie stash ran out, it gave me the much needed kick in the butt to finally rejoin civilization, because I decided I wouldn't be able to quit cold-turkey. I'd have to buy more.

I took a long, tepid bath, using aromatherapy oils. I shaved my caterpillar legs. I gave my pores a deep cleanse with a Dead Sea black mud mask. The *dead* part comforted me. No sharks would be popping out of the jar. I stocked up on all sorts of fruits and veggies from every color of the rainbow. Mom would be proud. I went to see my therapist. "You're having panic attacks," Rose said after I told her about my breathing problems. She scribbled a prescription for generic-brand anxiety pills. I started doing squats and lunges to undo the binging damage—the bathroom scales smugly informed me of a six pound weight gain. I called NYU, where I'd planned to start my secondary education this fall and told them I wouldn't be able to attend until January and would that be a problem? Because I needed to sort things out. I even bought a nice bamboo plant housed in a ceramic elephant to sit in the living room windowsill.

When my last minuscule paycheck arrived in the mail, I knew it was time to go job hunting. I still had the check from my car insurance stashed away somewhere, but I knew if I cashed it, it would be gone in no time. I decided to hang onto the money until I collected the courage to drive again, which would be soon (hopefully). My electric and phone bills loomed over me like giant, hungry spiders and I was dangerously close to losing my apartment.

And then there was the roommate issue I managed to largely ignore up until now. The truth: rent was killing me. While I did live in East Williamsburg, an industrial neighborhood in Brooklyn, a place starving artists and musicians flocked to, attracted to the cheaper rent, I still struggled to scrape by and that was *with* Abby paying half the rent.

Just as I began looking for a roommate in the classifieds, there was an eerie knock on the door. It was very Edgar Allan Poe. My first thought was: It must be Hannah. She was back to claim the scrapbooks and guitar I'd stolen. I never would've guessed, not in a million years, who was on the other side of my grimy apartment door.

"Mary?" There she was: Abby's *other* best friend, my arch enemy, armed with an old suitcase, a grocery sack crammed with clothes, a sleeping bag and a pillow. Her zebra hair—alternating chunks of black and white—was tied back in a messy knot and heavy crimson lipstick colored her pretzel shaped lips.

"Hello, Abby's friend," she said, dropping the sack of clothes. She smelled faintly of hairspray, musky perfume and pot.

"Having you been smoking pot? What are you doing here?"

Tiger strutted into the room, wondering the same thing, his pale green eyes inquisitive. Tiger remembered Mary. Mary was around a lot. Usually when I was gone, at work or out with John.

"I don't do pot. My roommates did. Drugs are stupid." She squatted in her black velvet dress to greet Tiger on her level, scratch his furry neck. Tiger purred in appreciation. Mary purred back.

"Okay, okay. Good. But what do you think you're doing here? For Abby I'll let you stay for one night, okay? Just one—"

"I'm moving in."

"Excuse me?"

Mary grabbed the sack and brushed past me, sneaking in like a yucky street rodent.

"Tiger, there's an invader in our home. Attack!" I said. Tiger looked bored with the idea and curled up in a perfect circle on the recliner, ready for another nap. Maybe I needed to get a dog. A watchdog.

Mary wandered down the hall, her boots clunking against the

wood floor, peeked into Abby's old room, backtracked to my old room and dropped her stuff inside the door. "You moved things around."

"What happened to your old place?"

"Got kicked out," she said nonchalantly, plopping down on the couch.

Should I have bothered to ask *why* they kicked her out? "Um, you can't live here."

She shrugged, made bored clicking noises with her tongue. "Sure I can."

"No, you can't," I said firmly, hands on hips.

"You need rent money, don't you?" She began digging through her purse.

"Yeah, I guess."

"Okay, then." More digging. She began tossing things onto the couch. Her phone. Dark lipsticks. Tissues. A wallet covered in lace and metal studs. Scissors. Hair spray. A little *Emily the Strange* doll. How much crap did she keep in there? She was worse than Abby.

I opened my mouth to protest, but nothing came out. Rent money. I needed some pronto. I guessed it wouldn't hurt to let Mary stay for a few days. "Do you have money? I'll need some up front."

She found what she was apparently looking for. A white envelope. She ripped it open, pulled out some cash. Counted the weathered bills and handed it all over. I wasn't going to ask how she got it. "There's more where that came from. Just give me a few days."

"Fine," I said, snatching the money.

"What're you eating?" She grabbed my box of cold chow mein noodles and finished them off, making soft growling sounds. Noises of contentment.

Reluctantly, I sat beside her on the couch, keeping plenty of space between us. I flipped on the TV. The nature channel filled the screen, specifically animal's mating rituals. Mary laughed her loud obnoxious laugh when a male white rhino mounted the female.

Ten minutes into the show Mary looked over and said, "I miss her."

It surprised me. Mary and I weren't in the habit of swapping feelings. Actually, over the years we'd exchanged few words. Less than a teacup full. I sighed, shoved my hands under my thighs. "I do, too. I miss her a lot."

"It, like, literally hurts here," she said pointing to her chest.

"I know. For me, too."

"You know she ultra loved you, September. She talked about you *all* the time." She dangled the last noodle in the air and let it fall into her mouth.

"Really?" All sorts of emotions rushed through me like a waterfall, too many to name. Abby was great that way. She tossed these amazing compliments at you like candy at a parade. She recognized the good in others and was confident enough to say something. I'd kill to hear all the things she'd said about me. Knowing she spoke of me so much to her other best friend eased my longtime jealousy—just a little. Suddenly I didn't hate Mary so much.

"Really. She went on about you so much, it made me puke," she said, making a face.

What did she say? I wanted to ask, but stopped myself.

She said, "I still can't believe she's dead."

"Me too," I said. "Me too."

A couple of months after Abby died I found a job as a janitor at a stuffy office building in Manhattan. Judge if you must, but I'm not above cleaning toilets. A musician once sang, 'It's a dirty job but someone's gotta do it.' And anyway, a job is a job.

At the interview an enthusiastic man eating Red Vines said I would be cleaning two dozen restrooms each night. I couldn't help but notice the huge wet marks under his arms and yellow beads dripping from his head. I did my best not to stare and politely laughed at all his jokes. He was skeptical of my job application.

"Cashier at Anderson Art and Frame. Dishwasher at Jo's Brewery. Hotel Clerk at Comfort Inn. Flower Delivery Person at Basketful of Love…Looks like you don't keep a job long," he'd said around a mouth full of red candy. It was true. My personal record was five months. Being a free spirit and all, I got antsy if I stayed any longer. Work just seemed to suck the creativity out of me like a zealous vacuum. Ideally, one day I'll become a well-known, highly collected photographer and I'll quit working on the side all together. Despite my sketchy past, I was hired on the spot. "You'll be working with Chris. Be here tomorrow at five and he'll show you the ropes."

***

If you could overlook some acne scars, Chris, who was around my age, was a pleasant looking guy. Kind of cute, even.

He was big-boned but not fat and he kept his butterscotch hair pulled back into a ponytail. Something about his demeanor reminded me of a superhero—I'm not really sure why. He wore a blue jumpsuit that played up his wide shoulders. I couldn't help but stare at them as he mopped.

"September, huh? That's a name you don't hear every day. Artsy parents?" Chris said, dunking the mop into a yellow bucket and then wringing it out. The room smelled of urine and coffee and Pine-Sol.

"Far from it. My parents are actually pretty boring. They named me and my sister, April, after the months we were born in. I had a brother named December. He died at birth."

"I'm sorry to hear it," he said, staring at my shoes. I followed his gaze, wondering if I stepped in dog crap or something.

"They considered naming us after our grandmothers, but Fanny and Dorothy were a stretch," I added, mumbling now.

Chris unlocked a closet and tossed at me a blue jumper, like the one he wore. I slipped it on over my clothes. It smelled of chemicals but thankfully not of sweat. I'd take it home and wash it first thing. Chris and I got a real kick out of my little body drowning in endless blue fabric. Apparently, it previously belonged to a short guy who weighed nearly three hundred pounds. I'd have to wear it until the company got around to ordering me a smaller one, which could be never, Chris warned. Wearing it made me feel like a big blue Martian.

Armed with some heavy duty cleaner, Windex, a scrubby thing and a rag, Chris said, "Let's start with the sinks. It's not geometry or anything, but there's a cool trick to making them sparkle."

We talked and talked and talked while we worked and it didn't take long for me to notice Chris was the nicest guy in New York City. You hear that about people, but with him it was actually true. On weekends he worked as a volunteer at an animal shelter, one that refused to euthanize unwanted pets.

As a result, he had a handful of dogs and cats at his place at any given time, giving them a comfortable home until he could find permanent placements. Animals were his passion. He was currently attending NYU to become a vet. He recycled religiously. He opened doors for me—to all twenty-four restrooms—and said "please" and "thank you" excessively. He had a sweet, shy smile that made me melt like caramel.

"September, you have sad eyes," he said to me on the third day.

"Do I?" I stopped wiping the mirror for a moment to study them. I guess they *were* sad. I didn't realize I was that transparent. I mean, most days I tried to cement an all-is-well-with-the-world smile on my face. But apparently, my eyes were a dead giveaway. I may as well have been walking around with a fluorescent orange tag on my forehead that read: *Hi, my name is September. My best friend died* and *my boyfriend cheated on me with my sister. So yeah, you could say my life basically sucks.*

"Even when you smile, when you laugh, your eyes tell another story."

"I…well…" The words got caught in my throat.

"You don't have to say anything," he said. You could see his arm muscles flexing as he scrubbed a stubborn stain in one of the sinks.

"Okay," I said, kind of relieved, going back to work on the mirror.

"Although I'm here for you if you need someone to talk to," he added, putting down his sponge.

"Thanks." I smiled.

We worked in silence for a moment before I found myself saying, "My best friend died." It was still hard to say it aloud.

Chris set his sponge down again. "Wow. I'm sorry...Do you want to talk about it?"

***

"Did you know 3,000 people die in car accidents every day?" Mary said, clutching a cup of tea. She wore no makeup today. She looked even more sad than usual when she wasn't hiding behind the mask of heavy eyeliner and lipstick. More vulnerable.

"Mary, you're so morbid. Why would I want to know that? That's so depressing," I said, glaring at her above my worn out copy of *The Outsiders*. Curled up on the couch, we both wore our pajamas despite it being past noon. Tiger had jammed his squishy body between Mary's and my legs. Sometimes I rubbed my feet against him, feeling his warm, silky fur between my toes.

"Okay, whatever," she said, licking the rim of the cup the way I hated. There were a lot of things I hated about Mary. To name a few: the messes she'd leave in the kitchen, the way she'd always manage to lose the remote controls (now that takes talent), her weird breath (she always had weird breath), her lack of personal space, her slit-my-wrists-and-swallow-a-whole-bottle-of-Zoloft music she'd play waaaay too loud (I know, I know. Depeche Mode and The Cure aren't exactly cheery, but you should hear this stuff. Ughhhh.)

"If you want to talk about Abby, then let's talk about Abby." I laid the book down and sat up.

"We don't *have* to talk about her. It's just that we were her best friends, so it makes sense..."

"*I* was her best friend. You get honorable mention," I said, only half teasing.

"Well, you know I could always dethrone you." Her eyes shot daggers.

"She's dead." I was only starting to be more comfortable with saying those words. Each time was a little less agonizing. "How would you do that?"

"Abby trivia. Winner takes the title, or at least the loser has to shut up about being her *very best friend.*" She made it sound so juvenile. "And anyway, you don't know for sure that you were."

"Of course I know that, she said it all the—"

"She could've been lying to spare your feelings," she said, picking lint from her *Nightmare Before Christmas* pajama bottoms.

"You want a tournament, Mary? You really think you know Abby better? You're on."

She set her mug on the coffee table. "Okay. This will be fun. Her favorite food?"

"That's too easy. Grape Nuts and frozen burritos." She loved instant food. Anything that wouldn't get in the way of her music and poetry. Eating was sometimes a burden to her. "Your turn. Her favorite color?"

Mary rolled her eyes. "Duh. Plum. Her favorite band?"

"Oh, come on, you're not even making this a challenge. The Cure. Her favorite movie?"

"*Harold and Maude.* Her lifelong dream?" Mary said, sitting up straight.

"To make it big—become a rock star. And to meet Robert Smith."

"Right. You're ultra lucky you added the second part." It didn't take me long to discover that *ultra* was Mary's pet word. She shoved it in all sorts of sentences.

"Her first boyfriend?" I said.

"That's not fair. I didn't know her back then."

"See, that's why I win. I've known her *twice* as long." I knew I was being petty, but I just couldn't help it.

"Wait, I know this. Wait...Brandon Something. Brandon..."

"Brandon Westmoreland. Ha!"

"Hey, you didn't give me enough time. Um...Her blood type?" Mary looked smug.

"O Negative. You thought you had me there. Favorite flavor of ice cream?"

"Um, wait. Wait. Mint chocolate chip? No. Cookie dough."

I made a buzzing sound. "You're out. Abby didn't like ice cream."

Mary frowned. "Oh, that's right. I guess you win."

"You're right, I win. I totally win. I'm her true bestie," I said, getting up to do a victory dance.

But I regretted it when I saw Mary bite her lip, when I noticed her dark eyes water. I guess I didn't realize how much this all meant to her. It struck me for the first time: Mary could be hurting as much as I was.

I tried to smooth things over. "But I know she was crazy about you. You were definitely one of her top two most favorite people in the world."

"Yeah, yeah, yeah, I know." She seemed embarrassed now. She sponged her eyes with her index fingers.

I added, "And anyway, who doesn't like ice cream? You'd have to be a total freak."

"I know, right?" And for the first time in history, Mary and I—together—busted out in laughter.

***

A couple weeks into my new job, Chris asked me something that surprised me, something I'd given little thought to these days.

"Do you have a boyfriend?" he asked, his eyes not quite meeting mine. Today he wore his hair down for the first time. I liked how it framed his face like a soft blanket.

I dropped the toilet brush in the bowl, cleared my throat. My heart sped up just a little, I wasn't sure why. "Um..."

"I thought so." He went back to work, wiping lipstick graffiti off the tile wall within my field of vision.

I took a long, shaky breath, inhaling the usual stench of urine and chemicals. "No, actually I don't. Not anymore."

He stopped scrubbing, raised his eyebrows. "Oh."

Was that relief I saw on his face? "Abby dying was only part one of my sob story. Care to hear part two?"

"There's a part two? I'd love to hear part two." He grinned, appearing maybe too enthusiastic.

Another shaky breath. I picked up the brush and worked on a stubborn stain in the toilet. "My boyfriend—his name is John— my *ex*-boyfriend, I should clarify. He cheated on me with my sister."

"No way." His face scrunched up in compassion.

"Yes way. And they're getting married now. I found this out shortly after Abby died." I flushed the final toilet and made a face.

He held the door open as I pushed the monster truck cart out of restroom number eleven. "Ouch. Do you still love him?"

"Yeah, I guess I do. You don't just stop loving someone because they broke up with you. You can't turn it on and off like that." I snapped my fingers. "It takes time."

I studied Chris's face carefully for the first time. He had slightly slanted gray eyes and reminded me a bit of a young Ryan Gosling. He had an unusually cheery countenance, something you don't see every day, especially in the city. If we were close friends I could see myself calling him "Sunshine Boy." That would be his superpower, to bring sunshine to everyone around him in a bleak world. I know I for one anticipated our time together every evening. With him I almost forgot my life had gone to pot. I got a short break from the constant throbbing ache in my heart.

We paused outside the restroom to take quick sips of icy cold water from the drinking fountain. The office workstations around us were abandoned for the night and dimly lit by the moon and city lights. There was something almost intimate about being with Chris in the near-dark.

"I…" He hesitated, frozen in place for a moment. He picked up and studied a roll of toilet paper in his hand as if it was the most fascinating thing in the world. His uneasiness made me nervous.

Suddenly I felt fifteen again. Chris and I were awkward locker partners reaching for the dial at the same time. "Um, you go ahead." "No you go ahead," we would've said.

He cleared his throat. "So this might be fast. Or too soon after dealing with so much loss, but…"

Heart pounding. "Yes?"

"Do you want to grab dinner sometime? Or coffee," he added, avoiding eye contact again.

"You don't have a girlfriend then?" I had to be sure. I had trust issues now after John and April.

"Oh." Chris looked like a kid who'd been caught by the police stealing a Snickers bar.

"You do have a girlfriend?" *Aha,* I thought. So he's *not* the nicest guy in the world. Slimy, scummy cheater, that's who Chris is.

He raked his hair into a ponytail then let it flow around his face again. "Yes and no."

I sighed. "Well which is it?"

"Yeah, I guess I sort of do." His face was florid, his cheeks two pomegranates, his eyes sad, reminding me of a puppy.

I crossed my arms over my chest. "How do you 'sort of' have a girlfriend?"

"I don't know. It's complicated. I'm not a cheating…" he paused allowing me to fill in the blank. Thinking of John, a variety of colorful words filled my mind. "I swear. I'm not like Jake."

"John."

"Right, John. I'm not *that* guy…It's…it's complicated."

I managed to stifle my urge to groan and roll my eyes. "It always is."

Chris had a smudge of the powdery cleaner on the side of his nose and I resisted brushing it off.

***

Dear Abby,

A lot has changed since you left. John is marrying April. Can you believe that?! I mean for starters, John was supposed to be <u>mine</u>. But I'm actually kind of glad I now know his true colors. My sister can have the cheating jerk. And then there's the fact that they're only nineteen. I mean, who thinks about marriage when they just started college, like a year ago? I hope they're miserable and get a big fat divorce before their first anniversary.

I met a cute guy at work, but it's definitely going nowhere. His name's Chris. He's your type, other than the fact that he likes classic rock. I know, technically we like older stuff, too, but Chris likes the <u>really</u> old stuff, like The Beatles and Led Zeppelin.

You're not going to believe this: Mary is living with me. You heard me right. <u>Living with me.</u> Have you ever tried cheese and pickles on a peanut butter and jam sandwich? It sounds awful, I know. Mary forced one on me.

She said it was "ultra delicious." She practically had to pin me to the couch and shove it in my face. But I actually loved it. I'm not too proud to say I'm addicted to them now. I've had one every day for the past week.

I miss you...Are you ever coming back?

One scorching hot day I thought I saw Abby in the subway. I once heard grieving people see their loved ones in strangers' faces. But I truly, in a moment of lost sanity, thought it was her. She had the same unruly carrot orange hair, the same yardstick-thin frame, the same me-against-the-world get-up. She even wore a Striped Goat band tee. (The Striped Goat was Abby's band's name. They were an eyelash away from being signed by an important indie record label.) "We're going to be big time," Abby had said once, crushing me in an enthusiastic hug, tears of joy cascading down her freckled face. She was inches away from realizing her two biggest dreams: becoming a rock star and traveling the world. I said, "You are. You're going to be too cool and forget all about me." I was teasing, of course, but a small part of me feared it would be true. After all, along with losing my sight, losing my closest friend was my deepest fear.

When I saw Abby—or the girl I thought was her—I called, "Abby!" I didn't care if half of the people in the subway were staring at me, looking at me like I was a lunatic. "Abby! Oh my gosh, Abby!" I ran after her. I ran as fast as my out of shape Twinkie thighs would let me, bumping into people like a pinball as waterfall tears blinded me. Touching her shoulder, I felt my heart hammering faster than it ever has. "Abby!"

She turned, only it wasn't her, it was a girl with braces and purple eyeliner. This girl was a couple of years younger.

"Oh. I'm sorry. I thought you were someone else," I said, a sick feeling creeping up, like hundreds of poisonous spiders inside of me.

Abby was really dead. Why did it keep hitting me—like a kick in the stomach? When would it finally sink in?

"No, it's totally okay," the girl said, her mouth full of hotdog. I could see a little relish on her chin. She stopped and waited for the next train.

Abby doesn't even like hotdogs. What was I thinking? "I thought you were…You have the same hair. You're wearing her shirt."

"No way, your friend likes The Striped Goat, too?"

I laughed a humorless laugh. "My friend *was* The Striped Goat. I mean, she was the singer, the guitarist."

"Whoa, you know Abby Irvine?" Her violet-lined eyes widened.

"She was my best friend."

"Was? You mean…?"

"She passed away a few months ago." She passed away. Passed. Away. What a bizarre term. Who came up with it?

"No," was all she said, clutching the front of her shirt, her face crumbling like a stale cookie.

"Abby's gone," I said, more for my own benefit. "She's gone."

***

"I want to know who killed Abby," I said, on my tippy toes, struggling to reach a spider web, in a high corner of restroom number two, with my mop. "I want to know who crushed our plans, our dreams. We swore we'd grow old together. Did you know I'd been saving up for years to take her to Europe? It was her dream. She wanted to go to Europe more than anything. Arghhh. I can't reach this stupid spider web."

"You never found the guy?" Chris asked, gently taking the mop from me and reaching the intricate net with ease.

"Thanks," I said, tossing the mop into the yellow bucket.

"No problem." He grinned that grin that was really beginning to grow on me. It was a shame he was tied up with someone else. I could use a diversion right now. A rebound.

"Didn't I tell you it was a hit and run? They were never able to catch the guy. And the thing is I want to meet him. I want to tell him how he ruined my life. I want him to know who he killed, how special Abby was. I hate him, Chris. I hate him."

His forehead wrinkled up like a balled up rag. "It's understandable why you'd feel that way."

"I want him to be punished for what he's done."

"I'm sure he didn't mean to—"

"I know. It was an accident. But the coward didn't have to run. He should've stopped to see if we were okay. I can't help but hate him. Lately he's all I think about."

"I understand—"

"I guess I'm just angry. It's just not fair. I miss her so much."

That feeling I was all too familiar with, that despair, overpowered me. For weeks I was numb, in denial. But nothing could prepare me for the pain. Knowing she was really gone. It hit me like a double-decker bus. It knocked the breath out of me, fractured my heart into a million jagged, unmendable pieces. How long would I have to feel this pain? How long did this stupid grieving process have to take? "I miss her so much," I repeated.

"I bet you do," Chris said, looking helpless, shoving his hands into his pockets.

"Why couldn't it be me? Why couldn't I have been the one to

go? She was always the better person. Funnier, more talented. Prettier."

"I doubt she could be prettier," he said, looking away, but not fast enough. I caught the flash of red in his cheeks.

"That's nice of you to say, but she was gorgeous..." I shook my head. "Such a stupid waste. Sometimes I daydream that it was me. It should've been me. If I'd let us stop for dinner first like she wanted to, we wouldn't have crossed paths with that stupid brown van. If I'd driven a little more carefully. If I didn't insist we go on that stupid road trip. She wanted to go next year because her music career was taking off, Chris...If she'd never even met me..."

In awkward Chris fashion, he touched my arm. "September, you can't think that way. It's not your fault. I promise. *It's not your fault.*"

I didn't believe him and the crushing feeling would not let up.

***

Abby,

I hate the man who killed you. I know you're not capable of hating anyone being the churchy girl that you are—or were—but <u>I am</u>. I know what you'd say. You'd tell me to forgive him. You'd tell me it was probably unintentional, that he probably feels horrible enough as it is, blah, blah, blah. I don't care. He stole you from me. How can I let that go?

***

"I'd like to buy Pacific Avenue," Mary said, slapping down a pile of pastel cash. She sat cross-legged on the carpet with Tiger curled up against her crotch.

I took a sip of hot apple cider and swore when I burned my tongue. I sat my unicorn mug on the coffee table and scooted forward on the purple velvet couch. "You can't buy Pacific Avenue. You can't afford it. Wait—where did you get three hundred dollars, Mary? Oh, you're cheating."

"I am *not* cheating." Like a chimp, she exposed her teeth. She was strange that way. She had a whole attic full of strange noises and crazy facial expressions. Where Abby found such weird friends was a mystery to me. Probably the loony bin.

"I *know* you're cheating."

It was a wet, gray Sunday afternoon, a perfect day for staying in and playing an endless game of Monopoly. We could hear the soft patter of rain outside. A tree branch clawed at the living room window in this creepy way. It reminded me that summer was ending soon and brutal winter lurked around the corner. Life was tough enough without Abby, but I knew it would be harder to face the biting Brooklyn air and the gloomy shorter days.

The death of another year without my best friend.

Abby and I both had suffered from Seasonal Affective Disorder, SAD for short. They call it SAD for a reason—because it's actually a type of depression. The lack of sunshine sucked the life out of us. Each winter we hibernated together, armed with stacks of good movies, a three months supply of mac and cheese, hot cocoa and buttery microwave popcorn. We'd pull on layers of fuzzy socks and sweaters, turn on all the lights and practically live on the couch, reading fashion magazines and juicy novels, playing Risk or Scrabble, or watching our favorite dark comedy flicks.

"You're right, I'm cheating." Mary shrugged, unwrapped a red sucker and shoving it into her mouth. She scratched Tiger under his chin.

"If you're going to cheat, then I'm going to cheat—"

A soft tap on the door made us both jump.

"I'll get it. But I'm watching you," I said, almost touching her nose with my index finger.

I fumbled to open the door. Standing there looking all smug was one of the last people I'd expect to see on my doorstep: April. The slut who stole my boyfriend, who actually had the nerve to show up—with him—at my best friend's funeral. Her porcelain skin was, of course, flawless. Her silky walnut hair sat on her shoulders in perfect salon-styled waves. She held a fragrant casserole, covered in foil. I could smell onions and green beans. Although I was ticked, I have to admit the smell did make my stomach grumble.

"Tem-Tem," she said, giving me a half hug, lightly patting my back. I stiffened. I hated when she called me that. Her fruity perfume coated my nostrils, making me cough.

Had John failed to mention our little run in? Because if he did tell my sister I knew she was a back-stabbing traitor, she wouldn't be showing up on my doorstep like this. Not for a while at least, until things cooled off.

Not for a least a decade or two.

April and I were close once, about a million years ago.

When we were little we'd play Barbies day after day and never tire of it (although April always got to be Barbie and I had to be Ken).

When we grew out of playing with toys, we started making cinnamon rolls together and sold them to our neighbors for five bucks a plate. For a handful of summers, around the time April was beginning to develop breasts, we'd hop into our swimming suits every morning and lay out in the backyard, working on our tans. We'd sip homemade lemonade and take turns reading Sarah Dessen novels out loud to each other.

High school was the beginning of the end for April and me.

We found we no longer had anything in common and ran with different crowds.

"April," I said. It was the first time I'd seen her since the funeral. The first time since I learned she was a pathetic, cheating tramp.

April slid past me and paraded into the kitchen, plopping the casserole onto the counter.

"Sorry, September. I know I'm the last person you want to see right now."

Mary snorted. She was engrossed, contorting her whole body so she could be in on the action. This was entertaining to her. I threw Mary a warning glance before shooting daggers with my eyes at my sister.

Frowning while touching her obnoxiously perfect curls, April continued, "Look. I didn't want to come, but Mom made me. She wanted you to have this green bean casserole—you love green beans—and truthfully, she wanted me to come and apologize." The last part wasn't easy for her to say.

I crossed my arms over my chest. "I don't care to hear any insincere apologies and I especially don't want any pity. Not from you, anyway. I'd rather you just go."

"September, we really didn't mean to hurt you," she said, fondling the foil covering the casserole.

"Well you did, April. John was mine. He was mine. He wasn't a book or a doll you could just borrow. He was my boyfriend. I love—I loved him. What were you thinking?" I had to use every ounce of restraint to keep a lid on the tears.

"I know, it seems all wrong...but John and I are so *right* for each other." She placed a hand on her chest. Her blouse looked expensive, probably purchased at Nordstrom or Bloomingdale's.

I practically spat out the words. "It *seems* all wrong? Cheating with your sister's boyfriend? Stealing him away? It *seems* all wrong?"

"I'm sorry for stealing your boyfriend, I really am. But obviously you can't make him happy like I can." She couldn't hide her smirk fast enough.

It was a low blow. Mary whistled in the background. I couldn't believe I was hearing this. Who did April think she was? The happiness fairy? "You know what? I'd rather you just leave. Before I *kill* you."

"Do you think you'll ever be able to forgive us?" April's eyes were big and pleading. "September we *love* each other. John's *everything* to me."

I laughed. "John was everything to *me*, April."

"No, September. Abby was everything to you. It was always Abby."

"Get out," I said, grabbing a vase, threatening to throw it at her. "Get out of my house!"

"One last thing. Mom wanted me to remind you of their twenty-five year anniversary party." She slid a manicured hand into her designer bag and handed me a lavender envelope. "Here's the invite," she added giving me a huge pity smile—the one I hated most—before finally leaving.

I stood, quivering like a lilac tree in a storm, staring at the enclosed obligation.

"Wow. That was ultra intense," Mary said, her tongue dancing on the shrinking sucker. "I'm ready to buy Pacific Avenue."

10

In line at Tim's Coffee, one of my favorite places to sit and think, it hit me: I have two weeks. Two weeks to find a boyfriend to bring home for my parents' twenty-fifth wedding anniversary party. If I didn't, I'd have to face April and John alone.

I had to see them again. It was as unavoidable as puberty and taxes. See John draped on my sister. See April gaze at him lovingly. For the rest of my life. The boy was going to be my brother-in-law.

Puke.

I could *not* let him—or my sister—see me showing up to the party alone. I refused to let him see I wasn't quite over him. That I still loved him. If I brought a date, I'd be sending a clear message that I was unaffected and completely over him.

Not that he was deserving of my love. At all. But like I told Chris earlier, you can't just turn your feelings off. These things take time.

John was faaaar from perfect. That was clear now more than ever. Now that I knew he was capable of two-timing and falling for someone as obnoxious as my sister. But I could see why April was willing to jeopardize our relationship (well, what was left of it) to be with him.

John was not only smart and driven and, let's face it, really good-looking, he had a really sweet side. In our nine months together I learned he was very protective of those he cared for. For example, one time when my parents were out of town, he came over—at one in the morning—to kill a spider the size of a golf ball in my bedroom. And he was thoughtful. He gave me a ride to school every morning so I wouldn't have to take the bus, even though it was out of his way.

Plus, he could, on a rare occasion, be romantic. Last Valentine's Day he ditched English and stuck conversation hearts all over my locker. He also left a really sweet love note in my Psychology textbook.

So it surprised me—no, shocked the hell out of me—that John was hooking up with my sister for three whole months before he finally collected the courage to break things off with me.

Maybe it was meant to be. John and April did seem to be a better fit, I was starting to realize now. But it still hurt—my heart *and* my pride—to have my always-one-upping-me sister steal my boyfriend like that. And now I'd go to any length, any extreme, to get a guy to take me to my parents' party. Hell, I'd hire an escort if I had to.

A fake boyfriend would be even better because truthfully, I wasn't ready to open my heart up only for it to be battered by the next boy—and it's not like I needed a boy in my life to make me feel good about myself anyway.

Armed with my hot chocolate and bagel-with-everything-on-it, I looked around the café for a place to sit and scheme. The place was as packed as a UPS truck on Christmas Eve. There was not a single vacant table left. Even the couch and overstuffed chair in the corner that were usually empty were occupied by four elderly ladies, wearing silly hats.

I growled in frustration.

What made this place so popular? My theory: It had the best

bagels in the area—maybe even in all of New York. Or was it the exotic gourmet cocoa flavors like banana, butterscotch or peanut butter that drew people here like mosquitoes to a porch light? I for one loved the hip, artsy atmosphere. Odd, tree-like lamps hung over punchy red tables. Inspiring art adorned the electric blue walls. Old pennies tiled the floor. (Even the ground was cool. How many coffee shops could boast about that?)

I did a double take when I saw James Dean, the brooding guy I'd rung up months earlier at Anderson Art and Frame, sitting alone by the window, scribbling something on a napkin.

His outfit brought the Jolly Green Giant to mind. He wore a sea green shirt with clashing army green pants. Kelly green Converse completed the wacky outfit. He seemed lost in thought with his left hand forked in his hair, his eyes vacantly resting on a dark splotchy spot on the table. He looked so stuck in his head a store robbery involving hand grenades would probably not disturb him from his mental meanderings.

For a moment I stood beside him, maybe two feet away, until I gathered the courage to say, "Excuse me. Do you mind if I join you?"

"Fine," he said, shrugging indifferently, not bothering to look up from his napkin.

Plopping down in the seat opposite him, I took a moment to soak in the wonder of his amazing hands. One scribbled away with an expensive-looking pen while the other was now shielding the napkin, guarding it against snoopers such as myself. His most prominent feature was a strong and defined jaw. It was so exquisite, I was sure even Roman statues quaked in envy. Yet his sad eyes made him appear sensitive, vulnerable.

"Are you writing a poem?" I asked, tilting my body to the far right to catch a glimpse of his top secret note.

"Something like that," he said, still not looking up.

"Are you a writer?" I asked before biting into my bagel.

He said nothing. He was clearly not feeling social.

I wondered if it would be rude to get up and sit somewhere else, or if I should sit with him in awkward silence. I knew if I chose the latter, I wouldn't even enjoy my bagel—it was my favorite flavor and they'd ran out of it the last few times I was here, but I felt too weird getting up and abruptly leaving. I mean, what if I saw this guy again? That would be more uncomfortable than sitting in silence, wouldn't it? This was my favorite café, after all. I didn't want to mess up a good thing. Not when they had the best everything-on-it bagel around and they were conveniently located—only a block away from my apartment.

I didn't have any good options. I had to say something clever or important to grab his attention. Shocking would be even better. I couldn't help but smile when I said the following sentence: "Will you go to my parents' anniversary party with me?"

James Dean looked up at me (finally!) appearing surprised and amused. His eyes were beautiful. As green as baby grass. He cracked a half smile before going back to work on his poem. Looking up at me for only a second at a time, he said, "I don't usually date strangers. I don't even know your name. For all I know, you could be some sort of freak."

"What do you mean by a freak exactly?" I said, laughing because in a sense I was a freak. A freak desperate enough to ask a stranger to go out with me.

"Like a serial killer. Or one of those people who talks during movies." He paused, studying my face. "You do look familiar, though."

"Then allow me to introduce myself. Hi, my name is September Jones. You may remember me from the art supply store. I used to work there. I rang you up once." He looked at me blankly. "You were buying pens. I grossly overcharged you. By I think two hundred dollars?"

"Ahhh. I remember now." His green eyes flickered.

"I may be a little weird, but for the most part I'm harmless. To date, I've never killed a person. I'm so docile, I don't even eat meat. I even hesitate to kill bugs, although spiders are a different story. They are just so hideous, don't you think? The way they crawl and just sneak up on you. So maybe I'm shallow, killing creatures based on their looks and the way they move..." Great, I'm rambling. Shut up already.

"You forgot to address my second concern. Do you talk during movies?"

I laughed. Was he serious? "What's your name?"

He smiled and shook his head, completely ignoring my question. "Speaking of names, yours is interesting. September. I like it...But you have another flaw in your plan."

"What's that?" I asked, raising an eyebrow.

"You don't know a thing about me. What if *I'm* a serial killer?"

"Are you?"

"I could be."

I shrugged. "I guess I'm willing to take the risk. I'm pretty desperate."

Looking up from his work, he studied my face for a moment. I felt my cheeks flush under his stare. "You don't look like the desperate type. You're pretty, you seem smart and well-groomed. Maybe a little naive, but you're definitely a catch. Surely you have guys lining up for your number."

"It's a long, complicated story. I'll spare you the gory details. And it's not just a date I want from you. I have to confess..." My pulse picked up. "I need you to pretend to be, um, my boyfriend." I bit my lip, avoiding his gaze. His eyebrows peaked and his mouth twisted ever so slightly. He was clearly entertained by my candor.

"You want me to pretend to be your boyfriend?" He cradled his chin in his open palm, finally giving me his full attention.

"Will you?" What am I doing? I thought. I don't even know this guy. I must've lost my marbles.

"When is it?"

"Two weeks from tomorrow. On October second. It's just dinner at my folks' house. They live in—"

"I can't."

I dropped my half-eaten bagel. "Why not?"

He tucked a stray lock of hair behind his ear. "I have...other plans."

"Like what?"

"Is that really any of your business?" He took a poppy seed that fell from my bagel and smashed it between his finger and thumb.

"No. I guess n—"

"I'm committing suicide."

I laughed, nearly choking on my hot chocolate. We were quiet for a moment before I said, "You're kidding, right?"

"Would I joke about something like that?"

"I wouldn't know. I know nothing about you."

"I'm dead serious. Pardon the pun."

I studied his face. His expression was even, his eyes locked onto mine, unwavering. I swallowed hard, unsure how to appropriately respond. "Wow. I mean, I'm sorry to hear that...Do you want to talk about it?"

"Nope." He flicked his pen and we watched it roll across the table.

I sighed. This guy was impossible and about as approachable as a boarded up meth lab with a *Keep Out* sign. "Can I ask you something?"

"Shoot."

"Why plan a suicide? Why not kill yourself now?"

He laughed, his troubled eyes sparkling for a short moment. "I want to write the perfect suicide note."

"Is that what you're working on right now?" He nodded, flipping the napkin over before I could read any of it. "So why October second? Why not three weeks from now—or next year?"

"October second is my deadline. It gives me two weeks to write it. If I'm going to come up with the perfect suicide note, it's best I have a time frame. I don't work well otherwise. My best work surfaces when I'm under pressure."

"Can't you wait until October third to do it? I could really use your help…"

He shook his head, concealing his face behind perfect hands.

No longer worried so much about my own pathetic existence, I was becoming more concerned for him. Although I didn't know him I couldn't help but feel somewhat responsible now. Human life was valuable. Priceless. I knew that now more than ever after losing the two people I loved most. This guy probably had a family and few friends of his own who would miss him dearly.

"And speaking of help," I added, "have you, um, thought about getting any?"

He peeked out from behind the shield his hands made over his face. "It would be useless. I've tried the whole 'getting help' thing already and I just can't see life getting any better."

"Couldn't you give it a while longer? Things change. Life has its ups and downs. I know from personal experience—"

"I'm sorry, but I'm sticking to my plan. I'll go out with you tomorrow night, however, if you'd like. I, um, have nothing better to do."

Nothing better to do?

"You flatter me." I took the last of my bagel and shoved it in my mouth and chewed thoughtfully. "Hmm. I don't know. I'm sort of afraid of long term commitment."

"Very funny."

"Okay, let's go out. Where do you want to meet?" My heart was racing now. What am I doing? What am I getting myself into?

"There's this Indian place. Do you like Indian food?"

"I love Indian food." And it was the truth.

"Great." He penned an address on a new napkin. "See you tomorrow at seven?"

I stood, brushing bagel crumbs from my t-shirt. "Perfect. Wait, so what's your name?"

"Adrien. Adrien Gray."

"Nice to meet you, Adrien."

11

"I met someone," I said, pulling the massive janitor uniform over my jeans and t-shirt, snapping rubber gloves over my hands.

"You met someone?" Chris said, dropping his jaw.

I nodded, not bothering to hide my sloppy grin.

"A guy?"

"Of course a guy," I said, punching him in the arm.

"So does that mean you're finally over John?"

He unlocked the janitor's closet and stocked the cart with fresh rags and more toilet paper. I refilled the plastic squirt bottles with glass cleaner.

I bit my lip. "Not entirely. But I guess it does mean I'm ready to...I don't know. Care about someone again." My own words surprised me. Was I really ready to let someone into my heart? Probably not. But Adrien was safe. It was highly unlikely I'd have to commit long-term—even if I managed to talk him out of killing himself, he was clearly too big of a wreck to be serious boyfriend material. It could be like a fling. A quick and harmless rebound relationship. If you wanted to call a few dates a relationship.

I was also still hoping he'd agree to go to my parents' party with me. Not only would I be bringing a date, but Adrien was also some serious eye candy. Not that looks are everything, but they help when you're trying to make your ex and your sister jealous.

If Chris's girlfriend wasn't so jealous and possessive, I'd ask him to be my date, play my boyfriend for a night. She would never go for it. She was even threatened by our working together every night. I get that. With school and homework and other commitments, Chris spent more time with me in an evening than his girlfriend usually had with him in an entire week.

"September Jones met a guy." He shook his head, making his butterscotch ponytail swing back and forth.

"Why is that so shocking? It's been a while since John and I broke up."

"I'm just happy to hear you're okay now. Or that you're *going* to be okay." His face lit up reminding me of the nickname I'd mentally given him months earlier: Sunshine Boy.

"I'm going to be okay." I nodded, feeling for the first time it could be true.

"You've been through a lot. You deserve some happiness after John and Abby. What's he like? Did he ask you out?"

"Well—"

Chris knocked on the men's restroom door. "Anyone in here?" After waiting for a reply and getting none, I pushed the sticky door open, dropping a brown rubber door stop on the ground and using my foot to jam it under the door. Chris pushed the heavy cart full of cleaning supplies into the fluorescent lit room that reeked of urine and cappuccino—someone had left a half empty paper cup of the foamy stuff by one of the sinks.

"It's your night to clean the urinals," I said, heading over to the stalls with a brush and a bowl cleaner so heavy duty the regular exposure to its fumes will likely shave a year or two off my life.

He groaned. "I did the urinals Wednesday. It's yours, September."

"No, don't you remember? I found a wedding ring at the bottom of one?"

"That was Tuesday." He shook his head, but he was grinning. "Okay, let's flip."

"Tails," I said, before he could even fish a coin from his pocket.

"You're supposed to call it in the air."

"I always choose tails anyway. You know that."

"I know that," Chris said, smiling at me affectionately. He flipped the quarter and caught it in one quick, fluid movement. "Tails." I laughed mockingly as he grumbled. "Okay, but you're doing the boxes in the ladies room."

"I always do the boxes."

"I know. And I love you for that." He gave me a quick side squeeze.

Chris and I had become good friends over the past several weeks. Traditionally, janitorial work wasn't something to look forward to, but I found myself eager to get to work every day to spend time with the guy who'd become my closest friend since Abby. Of course no one would ever replace her, but it was nice to have a soft place to fall after a hard day. I looked forward to our long, philosophical chats and our gut-busting laugh sessions over unexpected surprises we'd find in restrooms. Once we found a decapitated teddy bear on the back of a toilet in the women's restroom, for example. Another time we found at least a couple of pounds of M&M's candy smashed into the tile floor of the men's room.

Today I had another pleasant surprise awaiting me—a plugged up toilet with fragrant yellow-brown water spilling over the rim. "Ughhh..."

"They left you a little present?" he said, laughing.

"Can you hand me the plunger?"

"Let me get that for you." He gently nudged me away to take over. He put on some protective goggles, which made me giggle. They came in handy, however. I learned that the hard way my second day when toilet water jumped out at me and hit me straight in the eye. Chris got a real laugh out of that. I smiled thanks as his big-boned frame slid past me, our bodies brushing as we traded places. We exchanged a couple awkward apologies.

"Now tell me about this guy of yours," he said as he pumped the plunger into the overflowing bowl. I took a step back as nasty poop water inched towards my feet. I grabbed the mop to start cleaning it up.

"He's not my guy—yet. Let's not get ahead of ourselves. I met him this morning at Tim's Coffee. He's, um, really…unusual."

"How so?" He flushed the toilet. I thanked him, placing my gloved hand on his upper arm. I loved how Chris was always watching out for me, taking over the nasty or more difficult jobs.

If he didn't already have a serious girlfriend…

I gazed at the toilet thoughtfully. "Well, he seems a bit intense. He's a writer. He's…I don't know. I'll learn more at dinner. One thing I do know: he's really cute. I mean, really cute. Hot, even."

Chris stopped wiping down a urinal to look over his shoulder and roll his eyes. "He can't be that good-looking."

"Oh but he is." I don't know why, but I liked making Chris a little jealous. I opted to leave out the suicidal part for now. I didn't want Chris to think I was a total weirdo. Or extremely desperate. Although I was probably both. "We're going out to-morrow night. At seven. I'll need to get off early. I was wondering if you'd cover for me."

"Of course. I'm just thrilled to see you living your life again."

I squirted turquoise toilet cleaner around the rim of the bowl and watched it fall in a swirling motion before hitting it with the brush. "Thanks, Chris. You're the best."

"I am. I am the best. Don't forget that when I ask you to cover for me next weekend. Megan and I are celebrating two years together."

Chris and Megan became serious their junior year of high school. They were an unlikely couple—Chris being a hippy-skater hybrid and Megan a cheerleader at the time. One day their science teacher partnered them up for a class project and the two have been inseparable since. I remembered Chris mentioning their relationship was complicated but I didn't feel comfortable asking for details.

"Two years? That's a long time. Congrats!" I flushed the toilet and stood up. "Don't worry. I've got your back."

***

Dear Abby,

I'm going out (on a date!) with this really intriguing boy tomorrow night. Well, if you want to call it a date. It's...complicated. But just because I'm dating again doesn't mean I miss you any less. You know that I'll never stop missing you. And I know that you'd want me to be happy.

So why do I feel so guilty?

The other day I saw the cutest old lady. She wore pigtails, can you believe that? An eighty-year-old with pigtails. I thought, that's something you would've done if you stuck around long enough to experience your senior years. Okay, I'm not going to lie. In a way I envy you. You won't ever have to deal with wrinkles, gray hair, bad knees and failing eyesight. Is that wrong of me to say?

***

At the beginning of our session, Rose was engrossed in a conversation on the phone. She held up a finger and mouthed an

"I'm sorry." Spaghetti sauce or something orangey-red stained the outer-rim of her tiny lips. That, in combination with her cotton poof hair, made me think of a clown.

I nodded politely and let my mind wander. Thinking about going out with Adrien made my stomach feel funny, like it did when I first danced with a boy in seventh grade. It would've been perfect had it not been to a nasty country song, the kind my grandpa listened to in his blue pick-up truck when he'd take April and me out for ice cream.

I listened to the sound of heavy rain slapping the roof above us as I weighed the lottery chance of getting Adrien to change his mind about his impending death *and* pretend to be my boyfriend. I pursed my lips. Maybe Rose could help me figure out how to handle this.

"Sorry about that. Just a little family emergency."

"No problem."

"How are things going?" Rose asked, carefully examining my face.

"I miss Abby, of course, but I feel, for the first time since the accident, almost like a normal human being again," I said, flipping through one of Rose's psychology books with a chocolate stain on the cover.

"That's great, September. Describe normal." She rested her jaw on a fist.

I sat the book down. "I'm taking photos again. I'm sleeping better at night. I'm actually happy some of the time now…I even have a date tonight."

"Really? Oh, September," she said, getting up from behind her desk to hug me. We embraced for an uncomfortable moment. Her rough orange sweater scratched my cheek. She smelled of wool and old lady perfume. "That's a breakthrough."

"I think it is." I smiled a big, goofy smile. "Rose, I miss Abby big time. I don't know if I'll ever stop missing her. I have good days and bad days. But I really think I'm going to be okay. I'm going to be okay."

Near the end of our fifty minute session I told her about Adrien and his suicide plans, but I just referred to him as an acquaintance, which he was. She didn't need to know *he* was the one I was going on a date with.

When I finished, she scratched her poodle-tail head with a pen. "I'd like to see him. I'd love to help. Please give him this." She scribbled a number on one of her business cards. I stifled a big grin when I saw a happy rainbow across the top, above her name. It was so Rose-like. She was the eternal optimist. "I'm giving him my cell number. The initial visit is free of charge. Even if he's broke, I'd be willing to work something out. Also, let me look up the suicide hotline. He'd be able to call anytime, twenty-four hours a day. If none of this works, September, I urge you to call his family."

"How? I don't know them. I don't even know where he—"

"Find out where he lives. Ask him who his parents are. They should know about this. Also, be there for him. Lend an ear. Most likely this is a cry for help. Whatever you do, don't pass judgment. You don't want to push him away," she said, compassion oozing from her. Rose was in her element. This was what she did best.

I nodded, feeling a budding hope. "I'm going to do whatever it takes."

12

Incense, curry and high energy sitar music hit all my senses at once. I sat on a bone hard bench, feeling as stiff as the brass elephant statue standing next to me. My heart fluttered as I waited for Adrien to arrive. Not only was I nervous to be going on a date with an attractive guy—my first real date since John and I were a thing—I also felt a great responsibility to be there for Adrien. To help him. It was like Mount Kilimanjaro had been heaped onto my back. A deeply troubled guy had chosen *me* to confide in. He'd revealed his plans for suicide and it was very likely I was the only one who might be able to stop him.

Pulling out a little mirror I kept in my purse, I gave myself a once-over, checking for streaked mascara and leftover lunch stuck in my teeth. My hair had survived the rainstorm, thanks to the expensive product I splurged on last week. I studied my big, brown eyes, my best feature. They were tired but hopeful. My biggest flaw was my nose, which was slightly large, but my dad once told me it meant I had personality. My full lips held their own against my other prominent features. I must confess I dressed up—a little—for the date. Rather than throw on my usual jeans and t-shirt, I wore a purple sweater and a pair of pants that hugged my curves perfectly.

While waiting, I people-watched, one of my favorite pastimes. People fascinate me. I saw a tall, skinny guy throwing his arm around his short, watermelon-shaped girlfriend. An elderly lady wearing a handkerchief-sized skirt and five inch heels, undeterred by her varicose veins. A woman with painfully outdated hair on a cell phone arguing with her lover over what time they had agreed to meet for dinner.

I caught my breath when Adrien entered the restaurant, bringing with him a rush of the moist night air. It was a chilly September, more so than usual for Brooklyn. I had to dodge meatball-sized raindrops on my way to the restaurant, which was only blocks from my apartment.

Adrien seemed preoccupied as he scanned the crowded waiting area. When he finally saw me, he flashed a seductive smile, but then just as fast, snatched it back, frowning at himself.

"Hey," he said, laughing nervously, rubbing the back of his neck.

"Hey," I said, clearing my throat, wondering who was more terrified.

"Are you hungry?" He shoved his hands into his pockets.

"Of course."

"Good. Then let's get to business."

Business? Was that what he thought this was? Why had he even agreed to go out with me? I eyed him up and down then unsuccessfully stifled a laugh.

"What's so funny?"

"You're wearing all green again. Do you always wear green?"

He opened his mouth to say something when a man with skinny arms and a basketball belly showed us to our table.

"Please," the waiter said, handing us menus. A black turban coiled around his head like a snake.

As Adrien looked over the numerous options, I took the liberty to gaze at his face, particularly his perfect jawbone I was becoming addicted to. I decided right then and there that I had to photograph him. He'd make a lovely subject with his flawless bone-structure and his brooding disposition.

"You already know what you want?" he said, catching me mid-gawk.

I nodded, feeling my cheeks redden. "I always get the vegetable coconut kurma."

"Always?"

"Every time. I love it so much I suffer withdrawals in between visits."

He raised an eyebrow. "Withdrawals?"

"Yes. I can't seem to try anything else. What if another dish just doesn't compare? Consequently, my vegetable coconut kurma withdrawals would intensify." I twisted my burgundy cloth napkin around and around in my hands.

Adrien laughed, seeming amused. "I'll tell you what. How about you order the regular and try something new? Then you won't be taking any uncomfortable risks."

"That sounds reasonable. I won't be able to finish it all, though."

"I'll help you. I can really pack it in." He tapped his stomach. I could see that. He was slender but very tall. Six-two? Six-three?

Our turbaned waiter took our order. I ordered my favorite dish along with aloo gobi. Adrien opted for the chicken tikka masala.

"This is my first *first* date in over a year," I blurted out. I regretted it immediately. I felt my cheeks flush—again.

"I find that hard to believe...but funny you say that. It's been more than three years for me," he said, running a finger down the side of his glass of water, collecting condensation on his fingertip.

Three years? I was shocked. "Really?"

"Really."

"Suddenly I feel like I'm in an AA meeting. Hi, my name is September. It's been one year since my last date."

"Hello, September," we said simultaneously. We broke into loud snickers. People sitting at neighboring tables threw us curious glances. A middle-aged woman tossed us a chastising glare.

"Three years. Wow. Why? If you don't mind my asking," I said, taking a long sip of ice water.

"It's really pathetic. Not first date material. Trust me, you don't want to know. It's been a while for you, too. What's your excuse?"

"I had a boyfriend for nine months and then we broke up a couple of months ago and, well, it's complicated."

"This is going to be a long night," he joked, sighing theatrically.

I played along. "It really is. We could leave now, before we bring each other down with our depressing tales of celibacy."

"Tempting. But I'm dying to know: Why did you agree to go out with me? Do you have a thing for guys with a death wish?"

"Just *cute* guys with a death wish."

He smiled, but he didn't look amused. He leaned forward, resting elbows on the table, his face serious. "No more kidding around. Why are you really here, September?"

I felt like a little mouse caught stealing cheese. Should I tell him the truth? A version of the truth? A flat-out lie? I opened my mouth to begin then closed it. I tried again. "You want the truth?"

"Yes, I do. And you'd better not say you're here to get me to change my decision. I've made up my mind and neither you nor anyone else can stop me." He leaned back in his chair, crossing his arms.

"Okay. Then I'll be completely honest with you. I'm here for *two* reasons. The first is obvious. I *do* want to stop you. I—"

"Then you're wasting your time." He set his jaw.

"Maybe. Maybe not," I said, losing my confidence.

"And the other reason?"

I wrung my napkin some more. "The other reason is…" I hesitated, knowing it would sound incredibly selfish. "I was still hoping I could somehow get you to go to my parents' party."

He shook his head and growled in frustration. "I already told you—"

"I know, I know. Look. Adrien…Never mind." I threw my napkin down in defeat.

The meal arrived just in time.

The next half an hour was consumed by polite small talk. I kept a forced smile on my lips, but my eyes occasionally gave away my true feelings. I was sad, frustrated. Annihilated.

I didn't want to like him. I didn't want to become emotionally invested. I wished him to be immature, stupid, uninteresting. But as the night wore on, he became increasingly fascinating.

I liked his nervous ticks, the way he raked his hand through his hair and twisted the silver ring on his left index finger. He seemed confident, but vulnerable. Cocky and sarcastic one minute, then humble and embarrassed the next. If Adrien was a book, he'd be a page turner, a mystery that kept a person up until three in the morning.

We swapped a few high school stories. He graduated two years before me. We spoke of our jobs. I told him I was an aspiring artist, a photographer, specifically. I photographed people, found them intriguing—and cleaned restrooms to pay the rent. He told me that in addition to writing, he sold used cars on the side.

Surprised, I said, "Really? A used car salesman? One of the more honorable professions of our day."

"I didn't really *want* to be one. I just needed a job and it was there." I snickered. "What?" he said, shoving a forkful of chicken tikka masala into his mouth.

"I'm picturing you in a brown polyester suit. With slicked back hair and tacky white shoes," I said, nibbling on a piece of bread.

"Very funny."

"Are you a shady salesman? Would you sell me a clunker? Overcharge me?"

"You'd have to find out for yourself. Are you looking for a car?"

"You don't seem like the used car salesman type."

He gave me a sloppy grin. "I'm not the used car salesman type. Not at all. How do you like the aloo gobi?"

"It's divine," I said, closing my eyes for a moment, savoring it.

"Good. Sometimes taking risks pays off." He winked at me.

"Sometimes it does," I said around a mouth full of cauliflower. My mouth burned just the right amount.

For a moment I forgot my nerves and allowed myself to relax and get lost in the magic. I was eating the most amazing food with the best-looking man I'd ever seen in the flesh. The intoxicating tastes, smells and sounds swept me away to another world.

"I'm usually not this bold, but I wanted to tell you from the first moment I saw you at that art store that, well, I thought you were really cute. Beautiful even," he said, clearing his throat, fidgeting with his fork.

"You're lying," I said, stunned. How could someone that handsome think I was beautiful? He was totally out of my league.

"I mean it," he whispered, touching my hand for a second. His hand was soft and warm.

I got the chills.

"Thank you." I didn't know what else to say.

I studied him thoughtfully. For a moment he looked

completely happy. Free from cares. His eyes even sparkled. Seeing this side of him made me sad. It was such a waste, watching a guy as likable as Adrien self-destruct. I wanted to say something, but I didn't want to fight again. I hated confrontation. But this was his life at stake—I had to do *something*. I opened my mouth and before I knew it, the words fell out.

"Adrien, don't get mad, but…you're a really cool guy. I don't want you to hurt yourself. I really think you should talk to someone." My hands were shaking now. He frowned, set his fork down. I pulled Rose's card from my purse and slid it across the table. "My friend is a shrink. I told her about you. She'd really like to meet you. She's willing to see you free of charge."

"I'm sorry, September, but I didn't come here for this." His expression became stony. He stood abruptly, his napkin falling to the floor. He opened his wallet and tossed a fifty onto the table.

"Adrien, wait—"

"I gotta go."

Like a bug caught in floodlight, he fled the room. I called after him, but he never looked back.

13

My body quaked like a rusty carnival ride as I washed the makeup from my face and brushed my teeth. Tears escaped my eyes as I slipped into my monkey pajamas and slid into my tightly made bed, rubbing my feet on the cotton sheets. I inhaled the laundry detergent mingled with vanilla scent of my pillow. I took comfort in it, its scent always smoothed things over, righted the wrongs in the world.

It was only nine o'clock, but I went to bed early, too spent and distracted to accomplish anything. The reruns on TV failed to put me into a stupor. I closed my eyes but slumber was nowhere near the neighborhood. I wanted to hang out with Mary; she could help me get my mind off things, but she was at work. It was funny I practically hated her at one time and now I found her presence oddly comforting. She never failed to make me laugh with her unusual sense of humor and her random, inappropriate comments. I was finally understanding what Abby had seen in her.

My thoughts kept wandering back to Adrien and the crazy way our evening ended. Adrien was going to kill himself and I couldn't stop him. Each time I tried to reach out, to help, he pushed me away. I'd known him for a couple of days and already I felt strangely drawn to him. His haunted green eyes were compelling. His laugh infectious. I wanted to know his story.

What had turned him into a tortured soul, ready to take his own life? What caused him so much grief?

As stupid as this sounded, I could see myself falling for the guy.

The suicidal part aside, Adrien seemed to be the complete package. Sweet, smart, funny and a little eccentric—just the way I like them. And he definitely wasn't lacking in the looks department. But loving him would be like taking a trip to nowhere. Juliet falling for Romeo, after reading the end of the story first. Maybe that was the appeal. No commitment required. No long-term .investment necessary. I could love him for two weeks and move on.

I sat up abruptly. It dawned on me that I didn't have Adrien's phone number, let alone his address. Did he even have a phone? I realized then that I'd never seen him with one. Had he joined any social networks online? Would I ever see him again? A lightning bolt of panic shot through me. I had to see him again. I had to stop him from hurting himself. I couldn't give up so easily. But how would I find him?

I crawled out of bed. Grabbed a glass of tap water and plopped down on the couch. I looked at the time on my phone. 9:07. Not too late to call. I searched for his name online and came up with a few options. I called all four numbers. I got two voice messages. Onc man sounded elderly, the other had a thick English accent. One guy answered with a tired hello. His voice was much lower than the Adrien I had spent the evening with. The last number was disconnected.

I scanned a number of social media sites. I found twenty-two Adrien Gray's, some with variations in spelling. None of them bore a resemblance to my Adrien. Did he delete all his accounts or was he not the social media type?

My breath quickened as something relevant surfaced in my

mind: Adrien was a used car salesman. I glanced at the time again. 10:18 PM. I'd start calling used car dealerships first thing tomorrow morning.

***

A familiar ringing noise pushed me out of a pleasant dream. My phone.

I reached for it, falling out of bed. "Hello?"

"Are you okay?" I recognized the voice immediately. It was Chris. He seemed genuinely worried.

"What do you mean? Why wouldn't I be okay?" I rubbed my aching hip.

He sounded impatient. "You never called me last night. To tell me about your date."

I let out a big, squeaky-toy yawn. "Oh. I didn't know I was supposed to."

"Of course you were supposed to. Isn't that what best friends do?"

I smiled. He'd never actually referred to me as his best friend before. The words warmed me like a wool blanket in the Alaska wilderness. But then I found myself frowning. Chris *was* becoming a best friend. Sort of. Or something like a best friend. Was I cheating on Abby? "I guess you're right."

"So how did it go? Do you like him? Are you going out again? Was he a gentleman? He didn't try anything, did he?"

"Whoa, whoa, whoa. Slow down. One question at a time." Chris was like that. Like a protective older brother.

"Do you like him?"

I sighed. How much should I tell him? Nothing, I decided. I didn't want to reveal the crazy secret. I didn't want Chris to think I was desperate after all. "It went…good. And yes, I think I like him."

I sat on the edge of my bed and played with the stress ball I kept on my nightstand.

"What do you mean by good? Will you be going out again?" Did I hear a pinch of panic in his voice? His reaction surprised me.

I fell back onto my pillow, folded it in half and stared at Abby's Morrissey poster.

What was *his* deal? I paused, once again weighing my options. Should I tell him? I felt bad for lying, but I didn't exactly feel like letting him see how pathetic I was.

Chris knew about Abby's death and how profoundly it affected me. He knew John dumped me for my sister. He knew about my semi-traumatic childhood. That I felt completely misunderstood by my own family. That I lived in the shadow of my obnoxiously perfect sister. That I was a control freak and naively idealistic. That I had grandiose dreams of becoming a hot-shot photographer.

That was enough.

He didn't need to know I was lame enough to start liking a nut job. (Not that feeling suicidal made anyone a nut job, but Adrien was unique in that he felt compelled to write the perfect suicide note before he kicked the bucket.)

"Are you going out again?" he repeated. I could hear one of his foster dogs barking in the background.

"It's possible...but he has plans for October second, so it looks like I'm going to have to show up to my parents' party alone."

"Ah, September, that's too bad. I know how hard this is for you. I really wish I could go with you. But you know Megan."

"It's okay. I understand. I know you'd be there for me in a heartbeat if you could." I did understand. Although it was disappointing—terrifying actually—to face my family *and* my ex alone, without a date. To endure April's gloating and John's worried, sympathetic looks. But I admired Chris for being so faithful to his girlfriend. It was a trait I wished John had.

I heard a soft voice in the background. It was Megan. "Who're you talking to Chris?"

"Got to go," he whispered. He hung up before I could respond.

I ate two graham crackers and a banana for breakfast as I proceeded to call every used car dealership within a thirty mile radius. Twenty minutes into my ridiculous undertaking I felt like I won the lottery. "Mike's Okay Cars, can I help you?"

"Hello, I was wondering if an Adrien Gray works there?"

"Yes, but he's on break. Would you like me to grab him?"

"No, thanks. That won't be necessary."

***

"Hello. Can I help you? Were you looking for something specific?"

I shaded my eyes against the hopeful noon sun. My heart clobbered my rib cage the instant I saw his face. Each time I saw him, he was more beautiful than the last. His sheepish smile made me weak in the knees. When I dropped my hand, a look of recognition moved across his face.

"Um, I'm looking for a car. Something affordable."

"September? What are you doing here?" He furrowed his brow.

I bit my lip and turned away, pretending to check out a primeval Ford. With water-stained seats, a crack in the windshield and nothing left of a paint job, it looked like it should've been put to rest years ago.

He smirked. "Don't tell me you're really here to buy a car."

I couldn't help but smile. If only he knew. I gave up on the whole driving thing since the accident. Well, since the panic attack while test driving that car with John. Anxiety was another fun perk that often linked arms with tragedy. I had recurring car accident nightmares, many replaying Abby's last moments. Some with other loved ones dying. These days I even struggled to remain calm as a passenger. I even sometimes wondered if it would be socially acceptable to wear protective gear while riding public transportation.

Adrien laughed, but he eyed me suspiciously. "Are you stalking me now? I should've made a banner proclaiming my death wish years ago. Didn't know it would make me so popular with the ladies."

I groaned at his dumb joke. "Tell me about this one," I said, pointing to the Ford with a shaky hand. Why did I feel more nervous around him now than ever?

"This one's a lemon. The engine's shot. I'm not selling it to you." He laughed that silly laugh I knew I could never tire of. A *heh-heh-heh*, followed by a sharp inhale that reminded me of a dying donkey. He laid a palm on the hood and watched me play out my charade. I snuck glances at him as I examined the car. He wore a white shirt with a pair of light green slacks and an emerald tie. His hair was messy as usual, his jaw especially prominent in the midday sunlight.

"You look pretty happy for someone who's so depressed," I said, peering into the side window, pretending to check the mileage.

"Looks can be deceiving. I even have my entire family fooled." He flashed me a sexy grin. Did he know he was flirting? "Although I don't exactly see them a lot. I left home when I was seventeen. I graduated early." Oh great. So he's super smart, too.

What's not to like about this guy? "We're not very close. I sort of pushed them away years ago."

"So they don't know of the turmoil you're in?"

He shrugged. He drew circles in the gravel with his shoe.

A man with splotches of oil on his balding head interrupted. "Adrien, there's a couple over there looking at the black Honda. Can you help them out when you get a minute? I have to take off."

"Sure thing, Mike."

Mike wiped his head with a dirty bandana. "I should be back in forty minutes." He turned to me. "Adrien here will take care of you."

"Yes, I'm sure he will." We watched Mike jog through the lot, zigzagging through exhausted, shoddy cars. Now I got the name. *Mike's Okay Cars*. *Mike's Good Cars* or *Mikes Great Cars* just wouldn't fit.

"Look, I'm not really here for a car," I said, feeling rushed now. I shoved my hands into the kangaroo pouch of my hoodie.

"I didn't think you were." Adrien gazed at me, his face unreadable.

"I'd better go in a minute. Let you get back to work. But...the reason I'm here. I wanted to see you again," I stammered.

"Wow, you're a strange girl. You know that? I like you September, but let's get real here...Maybe if we met a few years ago..."

I bit my lip. "Is that a no?"

"Why do you want to go out again? So you can play the hero and stop me from hurting myself? Because if you are, then I don't have time for you."

"Ideally, yes, I would like to change your mind. But I see it's useless. Going nowhere." I kicked the old Ford's back tire.

He frowned, inhaled sharply. "Good. You're right. Nowhere.

If you don't mind, that couple needs my attention."

"Yes. Right. Goodbye then, Adrien," I said, defeated. I brushed past him as I left, angry tears filling my eyes.

14

"September, wait."

I spun around to see Adrien running after me. His emerald tie swung back and forth like a happy dog's tail.

"What?" I wasn't sure whether to feel annoyed or triumphant. I guess I felt a little of both.

"Okay," he said, raising his eyebrows, shoving his hands into his pockets.

"Okay, what?"

He was slightly winded. "Okay let's go out again. But only if you promise me something."

"What?" I eyed him suspiciously.

"Promise me you won't try to stop me." He folded his arms, his eyes adhered to mine. He was serious, I saw it in his face, in his clenched jaw, the way his eyes met mine evenly. There was no stopping him.

Was it worth it? To spend a few days with a guy who'd just abandon me like John and Abby? I swallowed. Suddenly I was super thirsty. Fur coated the inside of my mouth. I needed water and pronto. Looking around me, I wondered where I might find it. I noted a fast food restaurant across the street. A guy in a hamburger suit dancing like a drunken ape waved an advertisement in the air: *Cheeseburgers 2 for $3*. To the right of that, a bagel stand. Did they have water? I was sure they would. I sighed, meeting his eyes again.

"Adrien, you can't ask that of me."

"Then I'd better get back to work." Without a second's hesitation, he turned and began walking away.

"No—wait." I bit my lip. What am I doing? Stupid, stupid girl. "Okay. I promise."

Now what? A promise was a promise, something I never took lightly.

What was I doing here anyway? Didn't I have anything better to do with my life?

Maybe I could still help him. Somehow. In some way change his mind. There was a pretty big chance I was utterly pathetic. Maybe too stubborn. Too altruistic. Abby and her Christian ways have rubbed off on me over the years. Heaven knows I didn't learn this behavior from my family. I wanted to stop Adrien from hurting himself and I was sure there could be a way to do it without him actually knowing that was what I was doing.

So maybe in a way I was planning to break the promise, but it was for the greater good.

Okay, this wasn't only about my noble side coming to the surface. The truth? I wanted Adrien, period. Even if it meant having a short fling. It was a breakthrough, I realized in wonder. I was finally getting over John. Or at least starting to.

"Good," he said, buying it. "What're you doing right now?"

"Right now? Don't you have to work?"

"Screw work."

"Won't you get fired?"

He chuckled, threw me a look that for a second made me question my own sanity. "Does it matter if I'm going to be *dead* in thirteen days?"

"Oh." It was all I could say. He had a point.

"I'd much rather spend the rest of my time playing than at a job I hate."

"Makes sense."

Once again, I hesitated. I could leave now. I didn't have to do this. I shouldn't have to feel responsible if some crazy guy wanted to off himself. I shouldn't be playing Russian Roulette with my already broken heart.

"So…What do you want to do?" he asked, his baby grass green eyes drawing me in.

I stiffened, feeling butterflies in my stomach. Would I be able to stay unattached? Could I do this? "What about the Honda couple?"

"Come on, September, they'll be fine. Loosen up. *Live a little*." He playfully punched me in the arm.

I snorted. "I could say the same to you, Mr. I'm-Killing-Myself-In-Thirteen-Days."

"Ha, ha."

I clutched my purse and said, "I have a few errands to run, then we could do something."

"If you don't mind, I'll join you on your errands."

"They're boring."

"Not with you. You're far from boring."

"Glad I amuse you."

***

"What made you change your mind?" I asked, examining bell peppers, shoving the biggest, unblemished ones into a plastic sack. The first errand to cross off my list: grocery shopping.

There was a sprinkling of people in the produce section. A young mother was making faces at her baby. An Asian man was knocking on a watermelon, testing it. He spoke a language I couldn't identify to a petite woman scrolling on her phone.

"About what?" Adrien said, pushing the cart, following me around the store like a lost duckling.

"About hanging out with me."

"I figure I may as well have some fun before…" He trailed off. He didn't need to finish his sentence.

I frowned as I tossed a bag of organic baby carrots into the cart. "What makes you so sure I'm fun? And why me? Wouldn't you rather spend your last days with family or something?"

"Nah. Like I said before I'm not so close to them anymore."

I shook my head. "That's tragic."

"Are you close to your family?" he asked, resting his elbows on the cart, gazing at me intently.

"No. Never have been. Well, not since I was little. I wish I could say I was." I grabbed two baskets of strawberries then led Adrien to the cereal aisle.

"Who would you spend your last days with?" His green eyes bore into mine. He was so close now I could smell him. He smelled of old cars, hair gel and something else. Sandalwood? Trying to be subtle, I stole another whiff of his scent. I found it strangely sexy.

"I don't know. My friend Chris maybe." A few months ago I would've said Abby. Without hesitation.

But that was then and this is now.

"Is this Chris a he or a she?" he asked, reaching a box of Cheerios for me.

"Thanks. Chris is a he. He's my closest friend. We work together."

"Ah. Chris the toilet scrubber." Adrien grinned.

I slugged him playfully. "Not funny. I clean restrooms, too, you know. It's a perfectly respectable line of work. It pays the bills. And it's not like your job is anything to brag about."

"What job? I'm unemployed. At last I'm a free man."

"Come in, September," Mrs. Watkins said through the dirty apartment door, her voice weak and worn, like a talking baby doll with dying batteries. I had to practically press my ear against the door to hear her.

I pulled out the key to unlock the door (she gave me a copy of it about two months ago) and let myself in. I was greeted by the scent of mothballs, dust and stale vintage perfume. "Hello, Mrs. Watkins. How're you today?"

"I'm good. But the question is: how are you, September?" She was sitting in her usual ancient rocker, a large print book in her lap. She threw me an absent smile while patting her cotton candy pink curls—she explained to me once that her medications turned her hair such an odd color.

Not only did her place smell like an antique store, it looked like one too, with dozens of oil paintings of still lifes above her Victorian style couch and old porcelain dolls and cast iron cars with chipped paint displayed in glass cabinets.

The creepiest part was the taxidermy collection in the corner of the living room. Yes, she did in fact have all three of her former canine friends stuffed and preserved for all to see—I only wish I was kidding.

"I'm all right. Mrs. Watkins, I hope you don't mind, but I brought a friend."

Adrien hesitantly stepped into the doorway.

"Oh. A man. A handsome man." She giggled like a schoolgirl. For some reason Mrs. Watkins referring to him as a man embarrassed me. I mean, I guess technically he was a man, although I was pretty sure he wasn't more than a year or two older than me.

"This is Adrien Gray," I said with a shaky voice. Why was I suddenly feeling so nervous? It wasn't like I was bringing him home to meet my parents.

"Hello, Adrien."

"Hello, Mrs. Watkins," he said, ducking his head down quickly.

I discreetly pointed to the collection of dead stuffed dogs and Adrien's eyes widened. I had to stifle a laugh and he bit the inside of his lips, smothering his smile.

"They were out of whole milk, Mrs. Watkins," I said, heading into the kitchen, which had soft turquoise cupboards and a checkerboard floor. I felt like I was on the set of a 1950s commercial. I half-expected a perky woman wearing red lipstick and a polka-dot party dress to come in carrying a relish tray. "I hope you don't mind, I got you two percent."

Adrien and I laid four paper bags of groceries onto the vintage Formica table.

"Two percent will do just fine. You know I'm grateful for anything. I don't know what I'd do without you, September."

I'd first noticed Mrs. Watkins a couple months ago. She'd labored to juggle three bags of groceries up three flights of stairs—the elevator was out of order for a while. I offered to carry them up to her apartment and she invited me in for iced tea, lemon bars and a condensed version of her autobiography. Two weeks after our initial visit, I'd heard she'd fallen and hurt her hip, so I offered to do her shopping for her. I did it every week since then and I have to admit it was nice to think about someone other than myself for once.

After putting away Mrs. Watkins' groceries, I cemented a polite, happy look onto my face (I didn't want to burden her with all my problems) and sat on the couch. "Anything else I can do for you?"

"Sit, Adrien. Please," the woman insisted.

He obeyed, sitting stiffly beside me, resting his hands in his lap. I felt the warmth of his body when our thighs touched.

She shook her head. "You look so much like Mr. Watkins, Adrien. With a nice crew cut, you really could be his twin."

"Oh," Adrien said, nodding politely.

We sat in uncomfortable silence for a moment, listening to the ticking of her grandfather clock and a cat fight outside.

Today Mrs. Watkins had drawn one of her eyebrows crooked, the right an inch higher than the left, making her appear quizzical. With a quaking hand, she reached for a beaded coin purse from the coffee table and placed two shiny quarters in my palm. Our hands touched momentarily, hers cold against mine. "This is for your help, dear. Treat yourself to some ice cream."

I didn't have the heart to tell her that fifty cents would not buy you ice cream anywhere these days.

"Keep them—"

She wagged a finger. "Tut-tut-tut. You're a big hearted young woman. I'm not going to take advantage of that."

"Well thank you. This means a lot." We went through this every Tuesday. She gave me fifty cents, from the bottom of her heart and I refused it, knowing she had so little to give.

Each time she chastised me. It was as predictable as the lines in a worn out play. She smiled at me, reaching over, squeezing my hand.

"Adrien, tell me about yourself. What do you do?"

He shifted in his seat. "I sell cars."

"He's also a writer," I added. I barely knew him and already I sounded like a proud mother.

"For heaven's sake. A writer. Mr. Watkins was a writer. If I didn't know any better, I'd think you were his ghost coming back to haunt me. What do you write?"

"I write fiction."

"Oh? Have you had anything published?"

"I just finished writing my first novel a few months ago. I'm not published, though. Not yet. I also write short stories."

"That's wonderful. I hope you keep it up."

Adrien coughed. "Um, I will."

I elbowed him in the ribs and whispered, "Liar."

He looked down at his hands. I caught a half smile but his eyes looked sad.

"You look so much like my husband. You could be his twin. He was a good man. He fought in the war. He never came home." Mrs. Watkins looked wistfully at Adrien.

"I'm sorry to hear that. You must be lonely without him."

A single tear escaped her eye. "Very lonely. It's been a *long* life without him. It feels like a hundred years since I last saw him walk out that door." She gestured to the front door.

Surprised, I said, "You've lived here that long? Since he left for the war?"

"Oh, yes. Yes. We moved in here as newlyweds."

"Wow," I said, picturing a young Mr. and Mrs. Watkins kissing each other goodbye at that door.

We sat, enduring several minutes of small talk. Normally I enjoyed our little chats, but today I felt restless. There was so much I wanted to ask Adrien, so much I wanted to know. The incessant ticking of the grandfather clock combined with the fog of stale perfume made it worse. My leg kept jerking—I felt like a junkie in need of a fix—but then I'd force myself to keep still, not wanting to appear impolite. Mrs. Watkins seemed oblivious to my unusual mood. Today I was practically invisible. She looked straight past me, eyeing the handsome stranger she swore was a dead-ringer for her husband. Adrien seemed to have her in a spell.

"Adrien, I have something for you," the elderly woman said, surprising us both.

"For me, Ma'am?" He placed a hand on his chest.

"There's something I want you to have. In that coat closet there." She pointed a shaky finger at the closet still covered in last year's Christmas cards plus a couple of baby announcements and school photos of grandkids, I presumed.

Hesitantly, he got up and opened the closet door, which was jammed full of stale coats, many of them decades old. A vacuum that looked old enough to be displayed in a museum was crammed into the corner next to a sparkling aqua bowling ball peeking out of a bag. He paused, waiting for further instructions.

"In the back you'll find Ned's jacket—one of his old military jackets."

Adrien raked through various sweaters and coats before pulling out a jacket from the very back. A subdued green, it boasted four pockets and a few patches.

"This is really cool."

"Try it on."

He paused, eyeing Mrs. Watkins in amazement.

"Try it on, boy." She clasped her bony, liver spotted hands together in excitement.

He slipped into the jacket. It fit him perfectly. And, I'll confess, I've always had a weak spot for a man in uniform.

"Wow, this is a nice jacket. But it belonged to your husband. I couldn't take this, Mrs.—"

"I want you to have it. It's even a perfect fit. Ned was tall like you."

"But I don't deserve it."

"It's green. Your color," I teased. I couldn't resist.

"Of course you do. You're a warrior, Adrien. Just like Ned. He fought until the very end. Just like I know *you* will."

It could be my imagination, but I could have sworn I saw her eyes cut into his, almost accusingly. But then her face softened and she simply smiled a warm smile. Was Mrs. Watkins psychic? An angel? How did she seem to sense his dark secret?

"If you insist. Thank you. I'll take good care of it." He looked away, but not before I caught his eyes watering.

I stood. "Well, Mrs. Watkins. If there's nothing else…"

"No, no. You do too much for me already. Thanks for dropping by. Nice to meet you, Adrien."

"It was a pleasure to meet you. Thanks again for the jacket."

"Take care, you two." The way she said it gave me chills. I knew a deeper meaning intertwined the casual phrase.

"We will."

Adrien waited in the hall as Mrs. Watkins handed me an envelope filled with cash for next week's groceries. She whispered to me, her face so animated, she looked like a Saturday morning cartoon, "September. You really met someone. He's special, I can feel it. Don't let this one go."

I smiled in reply, unsure how to respond. "See you next Tuesday."

As I closed her grungy apartment door, I turned to Adrien. His face was screwed up, his eyes troubled as he ran a finger down the front of his new jacket.

15

"What do you want to do now?" I asked after mailing my photos to three online customers. One to a woman in London, England another to a doctor in Nampa, Idaho and the last to someone named Harry Loveless in Austin, Texas.

"That's so cool that you sell your art to people around the world. I must say I'm impressed," Adrien said, stopping to tie his shoe.

"Yeah, I guess it is. I think of it as getting paid to play. Someday I hope to make enough doing just that. As much as I love scrubbing urinals…"

"I have the same dream. For writing." His eyes met mine for a few seconds and he bit his lip when he realized what he'd said. We both chuckled, as if sharing an inside joke. It was funny—in a sad, twisted way—how much of what came out of his mouth sounded off, knowing he was leaving in a few short days, which meant not only his death, but the death of all his plans, hopes and dreams.

Of course it made me sad, but I had to push those thoughts aside, sort of be in denial. It was the only way to cope with such a tragic thing.

Plus, I refused to give up. There had to be a way to stop him. There *had* to be.

As we walked past a few coffee shops and restaurants, the

aroma of sizzling burgers and Chinese food made my stomach growl. "I don't know about you, but I'm starving. Let's grab some lunch."

"I could definitely go for some lunch. But what do you want to do—after we eat?"

"I don't know. It's your thirteenth-to-last day on earth. I'll let you call the shots."

"I like that idea." He grinned. "I want to see some of your photos," he said, grabbing my hand and playing with it. His hand was soft and warm and the touch of it made my heart flutter. I felt like I was in junior high all over again.

"Really?"

"Absolutely."

Then I had an idea. "Will you model for me?" I asked, suddenly excited.

"Excuse me?"

"You have the most...interesting face." *Your eyes, your jaw,* I thought to myself. "I would love to photograph you."

"Really? You think so?" His innocent surprise caught me off guard. Was he really that oblivious to his good looks? Did he not happen to own a mirror? He continued, "Would I be in one of your fancy art shows?"

"Most definitely. So is it a deal?"

He laughed his classic laugh. "Okay, deal. But I'm starving."

"Me too. I'll make us something at my apartment—we're almost there. Sound okay?"

"Whoa, you met me a day ago and you're already taking me up to your apartment?" he joked.

I shrugged. "I guess I am, but don't get any ideas—I'm *just* making you lunch. Oh and I have to warn you. I have a really weird roommate."

"Weirder than you?" He squeezed my hand, shooting a jolt of

electricity up my arm. He shook his head. "Impossible."

✳✳✳

"Adrien, meet Mary. Mary, this is Adrien."

"Whoa, September, he's hot," Mary said, as if he wasn't there in the room. Mary was like that—very blunt. Sometimes even rude. She sat Indian-style on the purple velvet couch, playing with a rubber band with one hand and dinking around on her phone with the other. Her long blue hair was twisted in a knot, a pencil holding it in place. She wore her usual dark colors and rose-red lipstick.

"Hi Mary, nice to meet you," Adrien said, disguising a laugh with a few forced coughs.

"Are you sick?" Mary said, throwing him a mocking scowl, threatening to shoot the rubber band at him.

"Nope, I'm well, but thanks for asking. Must be allergies."

I stifled a giggle. "And this is Tiger," I said, gesturing toward our orange-and-white cat balled up next to Mary on the couch. The cat, bored of the whole situation, gracefully jumped down and left the room.

"You know ancient Egyptians shaved off their eyebrows to mourn the death of their cats," Mary said, eyeing Adrien up and down.

I threw her a warning glance, knowing that she was already thinking of how she could steal him from me (not that he was really mine). She shrugged at me in reply.

"I didn't know that. Good to know, though." He nodded politely.

"This is our living room," I said, feeling silly for stating the obvious.

"Cool place," he said, looking around, his gaze resting on our endless collection of board games.

"I know," I said. "We're kind of nerdy. No one actually plays board games anymore."

"I think it's kind of cool," he said. "Battleship? I haven't played that in years."

"Maybe we'll have to play it sometime. Let's have lunch. Do you like macaroni and cheese?"

"I *love* macaroni and cheese."

"Good. I happen to make some serious mac. Four-cheese mac to be precise." I led Adrien into the kitchen. The kitchen echoed the rest of the trash-to-treasure house, with an ugly vintage refrigerator covered in magnetic poetry, a table painted a metallic turquoise (Abby and I had spent a Saturday morning painting it together) and mismatched bar stools.

Adrien played around with the magnetic poetry as I rummaged through the fridge for various cheeses.

"Do you have a bucket list?" I asked, placing a pan of water on the burner.

"A bucket list?" He raised an eyebrow.

"You know, like a things-to-do-before-you-croak list. Like your biggest goals. Your dreams."

"Yeah, I guess I do. I mean, I did before…But there's nowhere near enough time now."

"What do you mean there's not enough time?" Mary said, still sitting on the couch playing with the rubber band.

"Mary, mind your own business."

"Oh wait. Are you like dying or something? Let me guess. Cancer? Did you know cancer is the second leading cause of death? But just barely. Heart disease is only slightly—"

"Shut up, Mary," I said. Then, turning to Adrien, "Tell me anyway." I dumped the macaroni noodles into the boiling water. "We might be able to do one or two before…"

He rattled off a long list while I sliced the jack cheese. Some of it was the usual stuff: visit Europe, go sky-diving, swim with dolphins, learn Taekwondo. Some of it not so common: try Ethiopian food, live in a treehouse for a year, meet his favorite writers, kiss a girl at the very top of a Ferris wheel. He smiled a little as he said the last one, making me fight a blush. Then, after a moment, he added, "And of course it's been a longtime dream to have a book published."

"That's a great list. Have you thought about self-publishing? It's pretty common now."

"I have, but..."

But it's too late now, I thought.

When the macaroni was finished, I pulled a bag of romaine salad and a bottle of ranch out of the fridge. "Do you want something to drink?" I asked. "Crap, we're out of soda. There's a vending machine in the hall downstairs—"

"I'll grab some," Adrien said, rummaging through his pockets, fishing out some loose change.

"That would be great," I said, grabbing a couple of heavy ceramic plates.

"Be careful Adrien, thirteen people are killed by vending machines every year," I heard Mary say as he slipped out.

***

"I've never modeled before," Adrien said, laughing as we climbed several flights to get to the rooftop of my building. I was a little out of breath. All the lying around grieving didn't exactly help my cardiovascular health.

The neglected rooftop had sun bleached wooden tables and chairs, a long wicker-style bench with faded navy throw pillows and plants that were on their last legs. The graffiti on the walls and the cracked tile floor underfoot were nothing to brag about, but Abby and I loved coming up here to sunbathe and read the latest paranormal fiction.

"You don't have to do anything fancy. Just be yourself," I said, touching his arm. Our eyes locked and I let my hand linger for a moment. The way he looked at me—it was almost penetrating—it was so intense I finally had to look away and unfortunately, I let a childish giggle slip. After I composed myself, I pulled my Nikon out of the bag, adjusted the aperture and began shooting.

He lifted a hand to shield his face. "Wait, you're already taking pictures?"

"Of course. The candid ones are always the best."

"What do you want me to do?" He bit his lip. I snapped another picture.

"Let's try a few with you sitting here on the ledge."

"Sit how?"

"However you like."

Obediently, he sat, shifting back and forth until he found a comfortable position. My heart sped up when I saw how dangerously close he was to falling off the fifteen storey building.

"Careful," I said. "You're not supposed to kill yourself for another two weeks."

"Ha, ha. You're quite the comedian," he shot back. He scooted forward a few inches. The muscles in my face relaxed.

It was a mild early fall evening. Big mashed potato clouds hung in a cobalt blue sky. A gentle breeze combed through my hair, caressed my face and tugged gently at my shirt. The weather couldn't have been more ideal for a photo shoot.

We could hear the usual bustle of the city below. Cars honking, people laughing, a woman shouting in Chinese.

I studied every square inch of his face as I snapped hundreds of photos. I have to admit: this was the perfect excuse to stare at him for as long as my heart desired.

His eyes. The way they'd reveal such sadness, an aching, haunting sadness one minute, then light up full of sheer joy and child-like wonder the next. His coveted bone structure—his prominent cheekbones and perfectly sculpted jaw. The way his lips curved downward when he was deep in thought, but broke into a huge sloppy grin when I made him laugh. The subtle cleft in his chin. The teeny, tiny scar just below his left ear. His messy chestnut hair. His hands. I couldn't get enough of those hands.

"You have a little cheese in the corner of your mouth," I said, flat-out lying. He used his right hand to brush the side of his mouth and I took several shots.

"When's your next show?" he asked, resting his elbows on his knees.

"I have one this Wednesday," I said. "Actually, it's my first solo exhibit. But don't be too impressed. I have connections. My aunt's best friend owns the gallery."

"That's cool. This Wednesday? Where?"

"Red Street Gallery. At seven. You're more than welcome to come. If I can get these printed and framed fast enough, I'll probably use a couple of them," I said, pausing to admire my last shot on the camera's screen.

"I'd love to come," he said, watching me so intently, it made my stomach do a couple of flips. "So, how long have you been taking pictures?"

"Since I was eight. My parents bought me a cheesy princess camera for Christmas. It was bright pink."

"I'm trying to picture you as a little girl." He smiled a smile that lit up his whole face.

"I still have that camera. I have this quirk—I can't get rid of any of my cameras. They're like my babies. I just get so attached.

You'd think I'd given birth to the little beasts."

He laughed, clearly amused. "How many of them do you have?"

"I think I have thirteen now."

"Thirteen cameras? Wow. I get it, though. I feel equally passionate about writing. I have these notebooks. A whole box of them. I can't bring myself to throw any of them away. Although maybe I should. Some of my older stuff is terrible."

"What do you put in them? Poems?"

"Yeah, poems. Thoughts, ideas. Ideas for books, for characters and plots. Doodles."

"Do you think I could read one of your stories?"

His eyebrows rose. He pursed his lips. "Sure. Someday."

Someday? What did that mean? For Adrien, there wasn't going to be a someday.

We were quiet for a while as I snapped photos of him from different angles and perspectives, catching a variety of moods with contrasting lighting. We did some with the graffitied brick wall as a backdrop, some with the sky above him, some with the city below. After a while I had him remove the jacket Mrs. Watkins had given him earlier.

"Do you want me to take off my shirt, too?" he asked, winking at me theatrically. My cheeks burned like hot coals as I admired his sinewy body through his green shirt. I laughed and rolled my eyes.

As the sun melted into the cityscape, it painted the sky a brilliant orange-pink. "It's beautiful," I said, taking a few photos of the surreal backdrop.

As Adrien turned to me, the remaining rays of sun casted a warm glow on his perfect face, making him look angelic. I moved the camera upward and took several shots as he studied my face.

"*You're* beautiful," he whispered, brushing a gentle hand through my hair, his thumb tracing the contours of my face. His eyes pierced mine, digging deep, deep, deep into my soul, making me quiver. I sucked in a sharp breath when he placed his hand around mine and gently pulled the camera away from my grip. He took a step toward me, nearly closing the gap between us and turned, throwing his arm around my waist, his hand brushing my hip. Turning the lens on the two of us, he pressed the shutter button, immortalizing our brief moment together in this earthly experience, this thing we call life.

16

"You're late, Missy," Chris said in an animatedly stern voice, waving a finger at me. I busted out laughing. Chris acting stern— well let's just say it doesn't work.

"I know. I'm sorry," I said, noticing he had already cleaned the toilet and sink. Some of the restrooms were pretty big and had several stalls, and some of them were meant for single occupants. I grabbed a mop and dunked it into the soapy water.

"It's so unlike you. You're never late," he said, fingering a stack of paper toilet seat covers.

"It's true. I'm never late." I couldn't hide the goofy smile on my face.

"Ahhh…You were with that guy, weren't you? What's his name? Julian? Aidan?"

"Adrien. And yes, we spent the day together." And it was a near-perfect day, I added mentally. Probably the best since Abby died.

"Sounds like you're getting serious. What did you do today?"

"We ran some errands and then we had lunch at my place. I made my mean four-cheese mac—"

"Not the famous mac. You must really like this guy."

I bit my lip. "I think I do like him. He's really great. He wanted to see my work. He loved it. He couldn't stop raving. And then he agreed to model for me, so we did a shoot. On the

127

roof of my apartment, actually. We sort of lost track of time."

"He modeled for you? Oh yeah, I remember. He's super hot. Ughhhh." Chris stopped wiping down a wall to make a face.

"Oh, come on. Correct me if I'm wrong, but you've been acting jealous lately," I stopped mid-mop to watch for his reaction.

"I'm not jealous. No way." He rolled his eyes and threw his dirty rag at me, hitting me in the face.

"Hey, not cool." I began swinging my wet mop at him, splattering soapy water everywhere when my phone rang. "Hello?"

"Tem-Tem?" It was my sister April. She was the only one who called me that.

"Hey April, what's up?" Knots began forming in the back of my neck like they did every time we spoke.

"I was just calling to ask you to bring a dish to Mom and Dad's party. Oh, bring your spinach quiche. You make the best spinach quiche. In fact, I was just telling John that."

I cringed. I hated hearing her say his name. She sounded so possessive of him. I guess he did belong to her now, but that didn't make me feel any better. I tried to keep my cool. "Spinach quiche. Done. Should I bring a dessert?"

"No, the dessert is taken care of. Oh and Tem-Tem? I need to know if you're bringing a date. It would be helpful to have a head count." I heard a condescending note in her voice. She loved it. She loved that, as far as she knew, I haven't dated since John. And she loved being the one John wanted. The one he chose.

"My boyfriend might have something that night. I'll let you know soon." I bit my lip. I hated lying—and I usually wasn't the lying type—but I couldn't stand it when she was so smug.

"Your *boyfriend?*" Her voice rose an octave. There was a long pause, followed by a laugh. "September, you and I both know you don't have a boyfriend."

"I guess we'll see, won't we?" I hung up, rage mounting inside. Hot, angry tears tumbled from my eyes. I pushed them away, hoping Chris wouldn't see.

"September, are you okay?" he said, hovering over me, looking cute and awkward.

"I'm okay." I shook my head. "No, I'm not okay."

"What's wrong?" He lifted his arms. They formed an oval shape for a second. Apparently, he was debating on whether to come in for a hug or not. That's something we hadn't done yet—hugged. Well, except for one or two awkward side squeezes. And then he dropped them.

I turned away, embarrassed by the tears. I hated crying in front of an audience. Chris had only seen me cry one other time.

"September, come on, what's wrong?" I managed a moan. Suddenly his strong arms snaked around me. I caught my breath. It felt amazing just to be held, for the first time in ages, but especially by Chris. Maybe it was because we were becoming best friends. Maybe it was that weird sexual energy between us—that mutual attraction we had to ignore. I wrapped my arms around his waist and sobbed violently into his shoulder. He smelled of residual shaving cream mixed with heavy-duty cleansers. And he was warm. So warm.

"Is it about the anniversary party?" he asked, pulling away, brushing my tears away with his thumb.

"That's a big part of it. I just can't bear the thought of showing up alone. Chris, I can't."

"Remind me why this boyfriend of yours can't go."

"He's not my boyfriend. I just said that to April to get her off my back. He has something pretty big that night." I blew my nose on a scratchy paper towel.

"I wish I could take you." He looked so helpless.

"I know. It's okay. I'm going to be okay," I said, hoping if I said it enough times, it would be true.

"Is there something else?" He lifted my chin. I was surprised by the tenderness in his touch.

I looked away. I hated lying to him about Adrien. "It's a lot of stuff. Knowing I'm going to have to see John again. Last time was torture. I wanted to die…And well, girl stuff," I said, unable to tell the whole truth.

"You've been through a lot," he said, squeezing me, holding me close again. I nodded, tears filling my eyes again. Would I ever stop crying? I was turning into Niagara Falls. "But you're a tough girl. You're going to be fine. I promise." He brushed my hair away from my face and kissed my forehead.

A kiss? Another first with Chris.

***

Abby,

Remember when you went to junior prom with Eric Barley and I didn't speak to you for two weeks? I couldn't believe you'd agree to go with the guy I'd been crushing on our entire junior year. You knew it would hurt me, but you went anyway. And I was forced to go with Timothy Smith. Ughh. I still remember his slimy wet hands and the way he burped in my ear while we slow danced. And then remember when I lost your parakeet—what was his name? Bernie? I agreed to take care of him while you and your family went to Florida and I let him out of his cage and he flew out the front door? I remember you were so upset you didn't talk to me for a week. Well now I would do ANYTHING to take those three weeks back and spend them with you. Time is precious. I know that now. Can't we bend the rules and spend those three weeks together? Can't you be with me for just a little while?

Okay, I guess this is also supposed to be a gratitude journal.

Ten things I'm thankful for.

1. Sunsets. I saw this AMAZING one tonight (with that cute boy I was telling you about).

2. Chris. He's my new best friend. I mean we're not as close as you and I were—there's no contest—and no one could ever take your place, you know that. He's my closest friend these days. He's really been there for me since you and John deserted me. Not that I'm blaming you for leaving. I know it wasn't your fault.

3. Indian food. Mmmm…

4. Cameras. That's a given.

5. You and every minute I got to spend with you.

6. Q-tips. Only you know how much I secretly love cleaning out my ears.

7. Rock music. 1980s rock music specifically.

8. Tiger. Don't worry, Abby, I'm taking good care of him.

9. Mac and cheese.

10. Forgiveness. I'm finally starting to forgive the man who killed you. I'm reading this powerful book on forgiveness. Actually, Chris loaned me a few books on forgiveness. He snagged them from his mom's library. (She was molested by her dad, apparently, so she had a lot of forgiving to do of her own.) I don't know how, but I'm finally forgiving. It's something I need to do. To heal my wounds before they take over and fester—I'm not going to let this ruin my life. I mean, it's going to take time—it's not an overnight process. It's not easy, but if it gives me some peace, it will be worth it. Happiness is a choice. I'm doing it for me…I'm doing it for you.

***

That night I dreamed of Abby. In the dream we sat on her leopard-print bedspread, laughing, thumbing through a _Rolling Stone_ magazine, listening to U2.

At first I was happy to see her. I tricked myself into believing she was somehow alive again. It was sunny. The sky unusually blue, the clouds a glowing orange-pink. Strange for midday. It was surreal. Salvador Dali surreal.

"Abby," I said, "I miss you so much. Don't ever leave me again. Promise me."

"You know I can't make that promise," she said frowning, touching my arm.

Her words slashed through me like a razor. I ached to be with her. To spend the rest of our lives together, eating frozen burritos, fighting over clothes and boys, going to rock concerts—even when we're eighty. Just like she said we would. *Nothing would change us,* she'd said years earlier. *Best friends forever.*

I reached out to touch her. I grabbed one of the braids of her fiery hair. "I miss everything about you. Even the annoying things. Even the things I once hated."

She laughed. "So you've forgiven me? For stealing John?"

I shook my head, confused. "You didn't steal John. April did."

"Are you still mad at me for leaving you? For dying?"

As she spoke, she morphed into Adrien. He sat on the bed, inches away from me, his face screwed up, turmoil and despair in his green eyes. "I love you, September, but love is not enough." He reached across the bed and slid open the nightstand drawer. Inside was a black handgun. He picked it up and cradled it for a moment. A scream stuck in my chest as he placed it under his perfect jaw. "Goodbye, September," he whispered before pulling the trigger.

17

"Hey September, wake up!" I heard someone say as they shook me out of my sleep. Reluctantly, I half opened one eye, overwhelmed by the lacerating sun. Above me I saw Mary's amused face, her ink-blue hair swinging as she shoved me around. Still in her gray striped pajamas, she looked as grumpy as I felt.

"Ouch. You're hurting me. Leave me alone, I'm tired," I grumbled, shoving my pillow over my head.

"You have to get up. That hot guy is here."

I sat up abruptly. "Adrien?"

"Yeah, him."

"What's he doing here?" I looked at the glowing red numbers on my alarm clock. 9:40.

"I don't know, but he looks all *happy*. It's kind of annoying. And anyway, *who* just shows up at 9:30 in the morning?" she said as she left the room. Like me, Mary was not a morning person. In fact she usually rolled out of bed at eleven or noon.

My heavy eyelids protested as I forced myself out of bed. What was Adrien doing here? Did he want to hang out again? Maybe he enjoyed our day together as much as I did. Mary said he looked happy. That was a good sign, maybe my plan was working. I grabbed a change of clothes and headed for the shower. I called out, "Mary, tell Adrien I'll be out in a minute."

"Okay, whatever," she said, not bothering to hide her

exasperation.

"No need, I heard," Adrien called from the other room. I laughed as I stepped into the shower.

After a quick rinse off, I spent an extra fifteen minutes primping. I put on my favorite blue-green top which complimented my fair skin and a casual brown skirt that matched my brown eyes. I flat-ironed my hair to perfection, brushed my teeth twice and carefully concealed the zit growing on the side of my nose.

"You look nice," Adrien said when I greeted him in the kitchen. He wore my frilly ladybug apron over a lime green t-shirt and moss green pants. What was it with this guy and green?

"What are you doing?" I asked, confused.

"He's making us waffles," Mary said, beaming. She was still in pajamas, traces of yesterday's makeup smudged around her eyes.

"I hope that's okay," he said, giving me one of those smiles that made me liquefy like candle wax inside. He did look happy. Happier than I'd ever seen him. His whole countenance was lit up like a bright summer day.

I took a seat next to Mary at the table. "No, by all means. I've never had a guy make me breakfast. This is—wow."

Mary and I sat in awe, watching Adrien pour thick batter over the sizzling waffle iron. She scooted toward me and whispered, "He's a keeper." I half-smiled. If only that were true. If only keeping him was an option.

"So September, what was all that screaming about? Did you have another one of those nightmares?" Mary asked, grabbing an orange from the fruit bowl, rolling it around on the table. The scent of fresh waffles and homemade syrup permeated the room, making my stomach bellow like a cranky grizzly.

I cleared my throat. "Smells great." He turned and grinned a boyish grin.

"Was it another Abby dream?" She persisted.

Adrien threw me curious glances over his shoulder. I looked away, trying to act nonchalant. He presented me the first hot waffle, the steam dampening my face. He watched me take the first bite.

"Adrien, this is heaven," I said, my mouth still full of buttery waffle.

Mary eyed my food jealously until he slid a plate toward her. She said thoughtfully, "You know, people have *died* choking on waffles. It takes only four to six minutes for the brain to start dying once the oxygen's been cut off."

"Good to know," I said, rolling my eyes for Adrien's benefit. He laughed.

She continued, "And I for one don't know the Heimlich Maneuver. Does anyone here know the Heimlich Maneuver?" I nodded as Adrien raised his hand. "Good. Then as long as you two don't both start choking at once…" She nodded her head once, looking satisfied.

"She *is* weird," he mouthed. He chuckled as he joined us at the table with a waffle of his own.

"These are the best damn waffles I've ever had," Mary said, fluttering her lashes at Adrien.

"Thanks. I'll have to make them again sometime…" he trailed off, probably realizing there may not be a sometime. "September, what's this recurring nightmare about? Who's Abby?"

"The accident," Mary said, looking matter-of-fact.

Adrien dropped his fork. "What accident?"

Great. I'd hoped to get through these next few days without him finding out. He had enough to deal with, without me adding my own sob story. I threw Mary the meanest look I could muster then sucked in my breath. It was out now—there was no way I could hide it any longer.

I opened my mouth, ready to explain, but Mary beat me to it. "September's best friend was killed."

"Really?" he said, his brows meeting in the middle.

"Really," she said, reminding me of a bratty little sister. I scowled at her again. She got the hint and left the table, but not before licking the syrup off her plate, like a dog. Adrien and I sat in awkward silence as we heard her plop onto the couch in the living room and begin humming some song I've never heard.

I let out a shaky breath. "Yeah. I got into a car accident a few months ago. A very, very bad accident. I…"

"You don't have to talk about it," he said, looking uncomfortable, staring at his plate of food.

"No, no. It's okay. You deserve to know. I was with my best friend, Abby. My very best friend. We were on our way home from a road trip. Someone in a brown van—I never found out who—sped across the freeway and nailed us. My yellow Beetle flew off the freeway, turning over and over. Abby was…" I swallowed, still finding it hard to form the words, "killed almost instantly. I guess I was the lucky one. I left with barely a scratch."

He buried his face in his hands. "What happened to the person who hit you?"

"I don't know. He just took off. It was a hit-and-run." His face paled as he clutched his stomach with one hand. "Are you okay?"

"I'm okay," he said, forcing a smile.

"Needless to say, it was the worst day of my life. By far. Abby's passing just about killed me…She was my world. She was like family to me." I laughed. "Better than family."

"I'm so sorry to hear that, September." He shook his head in amazement, his eyes deeply pained, empathetic.

"I know what it's like to hurt," I said, touching his hand. "I know all about pain. I'd be lying if I told you I didn't, at one point, feel like ending it all."

He nodded, but he seemed troubled. He studied the table, running a finger across the smooth surface. "But are you okay now?"

"Surprisingly, yes. I mean it was really bad for a while. I still miss my friend like crazy. But the funny thing is I'm sort of happy now. Maybe not *happy*, but I'm surviving. I have my days, but I get through them." I drew in a deep breath. "I got through the impossible and somehow I'm still here."

"I don't know what to say. I'm sorry you had to go through that." I watched his Adam's apple slide up and down as he swallowed several times.

"Adrien? Are you all right?" I asked, arching a brow.

"I'm sorry. I'm not feeling well. I have to go." He stood so abruptly, his chair fell over.

I watched him leave me all over again.

18

"Your work is brilliant. Absolutely brilliant," a middle-aged man with a deep scar running the length of his left cheek said in a thick Irish accent. He wore a crazy tie containing every color of the rainbow. He extended a hand and I accepted it. His skin was as smooth as gravel.

"Thank you," I said, feeling a blush touch my cheeks.

"The way you capture your subject's soul. It's utterly amazing." He peered into my eyes, as if for a few seconds glimpsing into my own soul. He studied me the way I'd seen him studying my art. I counted the seconds. One...two...three...four... five...I had to look away on six. He took a sip of red wine, winked and then rejoined his lady friend wearing a lacy black shawl.

Relieved to have a moment to myself, I scanned the area. I was pleasantly surprised by the turnout. The place was swimming with people. My blown up photos popped against stark white walls. Food and drinks were offered on a table in a corner. Soft electronic music was barely discernible above the hum of voices and the squeaking of the ancient hardwood floor.

I was excited—this was a dream come true—but that was nothing compared to the intense feeling of vulnerability I felt. People went out of their way just to see my work. *My* work. Mine. The silly girl just out of high school who knew so little about the real world. What if they didn't like it? What if they realized I wasn't so great after all, that they had come for nothing? What if they figured out I was really a big fraud (after all, it's not like I really earned this—I was just lucky to have family connections)?

I played with my simple ruby necklace as I watched strangers examine my photos—my offspring.

Not only was this my first solo exhibit, this was my first art show of any kind since Abby died. She used to be a huge source of comfort at times like these, always there to hold my hand and make fun of the critics and the people who had little appreciation for art. The ones who'd show up for the free almond mushroom pate and a glass of ten-year-old wine.

Thirty minutes into the evening, Mary made an appearance. She wore a black spider web-looking dress which resembled the witch's costume I wore when I was eleven. Her stop sign red hair coiled atop her head, exposing a snake tattoo on the back of her neck. To finish it off, she wore a black velvet choker. Could she look any more *Addams Family*?

"Mary," I said, giving her an uncomfortable side hug.

"I was able to get off work after all. Thought you could use some moral support." She threw her eyes around the room. "Where's Hot Waffle Guy?"

I laughed loudly, even snorting a little. "Is that his new nickname? Adrien is…I doubt he's coming."

"That's a shame. He won't get to see these ultra cool photos of himself." She chewed on a lock of stray hair as she studied the two pictures of Adrien. One, a huge black and white, zoomed in on his face. His eyes bore an intensity that made me shiver. His messy hair flopped into his face, hiding part of his right eye. His lips turned downward, giving a slight pout. His moodiness gave it a James Dean meets Kurt Cobain feel. Vivid, punchy colors saturated the second photo. The exaggerated red of the brick building behind him complemented his green shirt. His glowing face, half in shadow, contrasted the fluorescent pink-orange sky behind him. I'd caught him in mid-laugh. His whole face contorted in a moment of pure bliss. If it weren't for the same striking, unusual features, one would never guess this was the same guy as the one in black and white—the contrast between the two photos was stunning.

Against my will, my mind wandered back to Adrien.

What if I never see him again? The way he left so suddenly had me perplexed. Was it something I said? Something Mary said? Would he come wandering back like a lost kitten, or was that the end of it? I shuddered when I thought of him hurting himself and began to whisper a prayer for him when a hand touched my shoulder. My pulse accelerated. *Adrien?*

I spun around. The gallery director, Kerry Perry, stood cradling a glass of wine, her lips curled slightly upward. She wore Princess Leia buns and a slinky violet dress, her body unusually trim and sculpted for a woman nearing sixty. "I've said this before, but I must say it again, your work is just fab-u-lous, September."

"Thank you, Kerry, you're too kind."

She lowered her voice now. "You've sold four pieces already and the show's not half over."

"No kidding," I said, surprised.

Behind her I saw my Aunt Sara wearing a dark suit, her hair cut short around her ears. She had that classic professor look. She bore little resemblance to my mom, but the two shared the same gray eyes that crinkled when they smiled. "September, come here, kiddo," she said, pulling me in for a bear hug, her short hair prickling my cheek. "I'm proud of you. You're going to be the next Ansel Adams—I can feel it."

I laughed. "Right. Thanks again for hooking me—" My heart hammered in my chest as a tall man with chestnut hair entered the room. His hand momentarily hid his face, but as it dropped to his side, I realized it wasn't Adrien. I felt my heart plummet into my stomach. "Excuse me," I said, pushing my way through the wall of admirers. My eyes began leaking as I made a mad dash for the restroom.

"September," I heard someone say. I stopped mid-step when I felt a strong, cold hand wrap around my arm. I swept the tears away before turning around.

"Chris," I said, smothering him with a hug, feeling comforted by his familiar scent.

These days Chris returned my embraces—almost too enthusiastically—but to my surprise, he gently pushed me away, peeling my arms from his body. I was hurt until I saw a pretty girl standing behind him with a nasty scowl and arms crossed over her chest. I then understood Chris's odd behavior.

"Um, September, meet my girlfriend, Megan," Chris said, apologizing to me with his eyes.

"Oh," was all I could say at first. "Nice to meet you, Megan."

She was much prettier than I'd expected. Beautiful, even, with big blue-gray eyes and a long curtain of blonde hair framing flawless tanned skin and lips so full and pouty, they should be illegal. Plus, she looked like she could be Chris's sister—they looked so alike (minus Chris's less-than-perfect skin). I had to resist wrinkling my nose as I saw what a gorgeous couple they made, with their identical long butterscotch hair and similarly slanted blue-gray eyes.

"Nice to meet you, too, September. Chris has told me all about you."

I smiled weakly. Of course he hasn't told her *everything*. He practically had to lie to her about us. To Megan, I was simply the female co-worker. She would never allow Chris to see me again if she knew how close we'd become, how Chris snuck behind her back to spend time with me, to occasionally grab a late night burger (a veggie burger for me, of course) and talk. And one Saturday he took me to see the dogs at his shelter. I felt somewhat bad about sneaking around, but not too guilty, as there was nothing romantic going on. Chris was *clearly* in love with Megan.

"You're just so talented," Megan said, draping herself all over Chris. I wasn't sure why, but seeing another girl cemented to my closest friend made me want to vomit. I had to pry my eyes away from her perfect size zero thighs that peeked out of a much-too-short dress, long enough to thank her.

"It's very nice of you to come."

I followed Chris and Megan around the room as they admired my work.

"I love this one," Megan said, squeezing Chris's hand. "Who is this?"

"That is my best friend, Abby." I didn't feel like explaining her passing. The three of us studied one of the very last photos I'd taken of her. Her indigo eyes peered out defiantly from under thick mascara. The wind had blown her blazing orange hair around her luminescent freckled skin. She wore a ratty black tee and shredded jeans, exposing fishnet tights. The silver charm bracelet I gave her for her birthday so long ago dangled on her delicate wrist. I closed my eyes. I could almost smell her jasmine perfume, hear her throaty laugh.

"That's Abby?" Chris said. "I pictured her differently. It's nice to finally see her. She was very pretty."

"Was?" Megan said.

"She passed away a few months ago," Chris whispered.

"Oh, I'm soooo sorry," she said, touching my arm.

"Hey!" Mary said, appearing out of nowhere. She slapped Chris on the back. "You must be the infamous Chris."

"Infamous?" He turned to me, an eyebrow raised.

"Don't listen to her. She's a complete weirdo. I've said nothing but good about you," I said, rolling my eyes.

"It's true. Lots and lots and *lots* of good. It's ultra nauseating," Mary said.

"Shut up," I said, hoping to murder Mary with my eyes. My cheeks burned as Megan eyed Chris curiously and he laughed nervously.

We shuffled to the left. Chris said, "Is this…?"

"Adrien," I finished for him.

He wrinkled his nose. "He really *is* a pretty boy."

"There's a lot more to him than—"

"Where is he?" he asked, scanning the room.

"He couldn't make it," I said, trying to hide the disappointment in my voice.

"Adrien makes a really mean waffle," Mary said stroking her belly in a circular motion.

"He does," I agreed, ever amused by my roommate.

"Wait, how would you know?" Chris asked, his eyes questioning me, a hint of jealousy registering on his face. "Are you…? Did he…? Is there something you're not telling me?"

"Oh relax, Chris. September's not that kind of girl," Mary said. "He just came over *early* Monday morning. Woke me up. I mean, who comes over at 8:30 in the morning?"

"It was 9:30," I said, laughing.

"Okay, like that's any better. Speaking of waffles, did you know that Lincoln and Kennedy's wives both ate waffles the morning their husbands were assassinated?"

19

On the morning of September twentieth, I was never more tempted to stay in bed. Not only was I falling for an incredibly handsome suicidal guy who I may never see again, but I was now facing my very first birthday, in eleven years, without Abby.

My birthday was just not my birthday without her.

But life moved forward regardless, like The Little Engine That Could.

My mom and dad, plus April and even John called to wish me a happy birthday, taking turns with the phone (they stopped throwing parties for me after my sixteenth). April was unusually sweet. She even said she loved me but passed the phone to my dad before I could respond. John spoke to me briefly. For a short moment, it almost felt like the old us, the old John and me, before April pulled the phone from him mid-sentence. Mom told me to look for a birthday check in the mail today.

Mary was feeling generous and made us blueberry-banana smoothies for breakfast. When I took my final sip, I said, "Hey, thanks. That was the best smoothie I've had in months."

"I'm glad you enjoyed it because by the time you're sixty, you'll have lost half of your taste buds," she said, grabbing our blueberry-stained glasses and tossing them in the sink.

I laughed. "Good to know."

"Not to mention your nose and ears never stop growing.

You'll look like Pinocchio and Dumbo all at once."

"Something to look forward to," I said, shaking my head.

***

Abby,

It's my birthday. Where are you? I can't face this day without my very best friend. If you're there, give me a sign.

***

"I have something for you," Mary said, straightening her pink waitress uniform, about to leave for work. She worked at this hole-in-the-wall restaurant a few blocks away that apparently had the worst coffee around. How it stayed in business was beyond me. Anyway, it was the only time she ever wore pink. I didn't know what I found more entertaining: Mary in her uniform, or Mary's discomfort in her uniform. She handed me a small, flat present in confetti wrap.

I was touched. She and I had come a long way, but I didn't expect this. "Mary, you didn't have to—"

"Open it." I caught her smiling before she looked away.

With the enthusiasm of a six-year-old on Christmas morning, I ripped away the colorful wrap. Inside I found a letter addressed to me. My heart began thumping like a rock concert when I recognized Abby's handwriting.

"I don't get it."

"Abby wanted me to mail this to you, but I never got around to it. You know me—flaky as pie crust. It's a letter she wrote you last year when we were at that stupid leadership camp my mom forced me go to—and Abby tagged along so I wouldn't lose my mind and kill everyone there. I stuck it in my backpack and forgot all about it. I found it under the passenger seat of my car last night. Right before your birthday, can you believe it?"

"You're kidding."

"I had to use ultra self-control not to rip it open and read it myself. You'll have to tell me what it says. I'm late for work. Happy birthday, September," she said, squeezing my arm. "Do something fun today."

"Thanks. I mean it." I bit my lip.

I sat down next to Tiger on the couch and waited for Mary to go before carefully opening the letter. I took three deep breaths to calm my racing heart before reading.

Hey September,

   This place sucks royally. If I hear words like "assertiveness" and "effectiveness" and anything ending in "ness" again, I'll have to be committed. Seriously. I'm losing it. Do yourself a favor and never go to one of these stupid things. There are a couple of hot guys here, though, so I'm not completely miserable. And Mary and I play cards and listen to tunes on her phone whenever they give us ten seconds to breathe.

   Can you believe I've been gone for two whole weeks?? We've never been apart this long. I miss you like crazy. Thanks for believing in my dreams when no one else has. I now know that <u>anything</u> is possible. I have my whole life ahead of me.

   I love you so, so much. You mean the world to me and then some. See you in a few days!

   Your friend forever,
   Abby
   xxxxxxx

I spent the next two hours in bed, rereading the letter at least a dozen times, reminiscing, laughing and crying and laughing some more. It was my first birthday in eleven years without my best friend, in the flesh. I wasn't sure where I stood on the whole life after death thing, but I felt Abby near. Could it be a coincidence Mary found that letter the night before my first birthday without Abby? I also thumbed through her scrapbook. It was probably just my mind playing tricks on me, but I could've sworn I saw Abby smiling at me—for a fraction of a second—in one of the photos.

I also thought about Adrien—I couldn't help myself. I was beginning to wonder if I'd ever see him again. The way he just left after I told him about the accident was weird. I couldn't stop replaying it in my head, the way he just took off like that. Was he so shallow he couldn't deal with someone with a little baggage? Or was it that he was just in too much pain to share someone else's burden? Whatever it was, I knew I had to see him again. I was beginning to have Adrien withdrawals. But the question was how? This time it wouldn't be so easy to find him—he quit his job. I just had to hope he'd get bored and come over to hang out again. It was unlikely we'd run into each other a second time—not in a place as massive as New York.

I slid Abby's letter into the book I was reading about forgiveness and took a short birthday nap.

***

"Happy birthday, Tember," Chris said, giving me a vise-grip hug, smelling like minty shampoo and shaving cream.

"I can't breathe," I said and it was partially true.

"I have to admit, I forgot it was your birthday." He raked his butterscotch hair into a ponytail and secured it with the elastic on his wrist. "I was planning on giving you something great. Rain check?"

"Sure, no big deal," I said, rubbing my sore ribs. Chris was even stronger than he looked.

"Meanwhile, I hope this will do." He pulled about a dozen bags of Reese's Pieces out of his bulging jeans pockets, handing them to me, one by one.

"Ooh, you remembered. My favorite," I said, shoving them into my purse.

"Good old reliable vending machine. I bought all the ones they had—on each floor."

"On each floor? You are too sweet." I shook my head in disbelief. He really was the nicest guy, like, ever. "But are you trying to make me fat? Because it took a lot of lunges to undo the damage all those Twinkies did me," I joked.

He shook his head. "You females and weight. You could never be fat."

"I beg to differ," I said, "You should've seen me my freshman year of high school. It wasn't pretty."

"September—not pretty? Impossible," he said, looking at me in a way that caused me to blush. "Do you have fun plans for tonight?" He unlocked the janitor's closet and pulled out his blue jumpsuit.

"You mean besides scrubbing urinals with my favorite guy?"

"I would never let you do such a thing on your birthday. Go home, I've got you covered."

I was touched. "Really?"

"Really," he said, his big hands cradling my head as he kissed my hairline. "Happy birthday. I love you. In a friend-who-already-has-a-girlfriend sort of way, of course," he added, blushing.

"I love you, too, Chris." It was the first time we'd exchanged the words. I looked away before he could see my eyes wetting.

"Go out to dinner with that boyfriend of yours or something.

Just promise me you won't spend the evening alone."

It wasn't a promise I could keep. Who would I celebrate with? Chris and Mary had to work and Adrien was, well… "Like I mentioned—he's not my boyfriend."

"Then he's an idiot." His eyes cut into mine for an intense moment before we both looked away.

"Well I'm off, then," I said, studying the ground, still unable to make eye contact with my friend.

"Happy Birthday—again." He laughed an awkward laugh as he filled the cart with rolls of toilet paper.

"Thanks—again," I said, also laughing, turning to go.

"No problem."

"And thanks for the candy," I said over my shoulder as I headed out.

"Ah, forget about it."

***

As my dingy apartment door greeted me, I let out a heavy sigh. The day had turned out much better than I expected, but now I had the evening to face alone, with more than enough time to mope and miss Abby. I combed through my purse until I found my keys and unlocked the door. It was when I started kicking off my shoes that I heard: "Happy birthday, Beautiful."

I dropped the keys and just about catapulted out of my skin. "Who is that?" I palmed the phone in my purse, ready to call 911 and with my other hand, flipped the light on.

I couldn't have been more surprised to see Adrien sitting on the couch, cradling a chocolate birthday cake, which had my name neatly written in yellow icing across the perfectly smooth surface. Little flames danced atop handfuls of tall, white candles.

"Wait, how did you know?" I asked, still a little shaken up.

"I heard you coming up the stairs. I have superior candle lighting abilities. A perk that comes with being a pyromaniac," he said, smirking a little.

"How did you know it was my birthday? And how did you get in here? You didn't break in, did you?"

Tiger greeted me with a curious meow.

"Sit down first, blow out your candles. Then I'll explain everything."

Obediently, I sat beside him. Although we'd spent a lot of time together, the fact that I hadn't seen him for a few days—combined with how gorgeous he looked tonight—made me feel all sorts of things at once: excited, relieved, flustered. Weak all over. This guy had a strange and powerful effect on me and I wasn't sure how much I liked it. He wore one of his usual green ensembles, this time a fern green button down shirt with Brunswick green pants and the green Converse he wore the day we met at Tim's Coffee.

I giggled as he sang *Happy Birthday*. His voice was about as horrible as Aunt Number Two's at Abby's funeral, but the gesture was incredibly sweet.

"Make a wish."

I squeezed my eyes shut. I didn't have to think long before knowing exactly what I wanted. I blew out the candles in one forceful breath. "Wow, um, this is quite the surprise."

"I bet." He laughed. "Your expression—when you first walked in—was priceless."

I shifted in my seat. "You really didn't have to go to all this trouble. You barely even know me."

"It's nothing, really. And anyway, I have to admit I'm developing a little crush on you." He reached out and grabbed my hand. His comment, combined with the warmth of his hand, shot electric currents through my body. I felt heat rising to my cheeks.

"I don't even know how to reply to that," I said, my voice quivering.

"Sorry, you shouldn't have to. In fact, I slipped. It wasn't fair of me to say that, considering…" His eyes wandered down to our clasped hands and he pulled his away.

For a moment we sat and listened to the hum of the refrigerator and Tiger clawing at one of his toys making jingling sounds in the hallway. I broke the uncomfortable silence. "Now explain how you got in, how you knew it was my birthday."

"Yes, ma'am," he teased. "Mary told me it was going to be your birthday that day I was making waffles, while you were in the shower. I told her I wanted to surprise you tonight, so she gave me a spare key."

"Mary gave you a spare key?" I didn't know what surprised me more. Mary playing a part in a nice birthday surprise or her giving a stranger our spare key, allowing him free reign of our apartment. The truth was we didn't really *know* this guy. Adrien could be a thief or a rapist or a killer—or a combination of all three. He could be anyone. Ted Bundy, Freddy Krueger, Hannibal Lecter. And here I sat in the apartment all alone with him.

No, I thought, shaking my head. I hadn't known this guy for long, but I somehow *knew* he was a decent human being. I had a gut feeling about him. He might be capable of hurting himself, but he was too gentle and sweet to do anyone else harm.

I felt surprisingly safe with him.

"So how did you know I'd be coming home just now? I had work tonight—"

"I called Chris to ask him to cover for you. He was more than happy to. In fact, he said he was planning to do it anyway." He pulled a candle from the cake and licked the frosting off.

The night was full of surprises. *"You* called *Chris?* Where did you get his number?"

He pulled at his collar. "Mary, um, let me use your phone."

"Wow." I was stunned. Three people had plotted and schemed to make this work. I felt loved. And then amused— Chris and Adrien spoke to each other over the phone. The two guys I had feelings for, I realized just then.

"September, I also wanted to apologize for the way I left the other day. I didn't plan—I didn't mean—"

I touched his knee. "Don't worry about it."

He looked down at his lap. "The thing is I've been through a lot. Much more than most people go through in a lifetime."

My interest was piqued. Maybe I could finally get him to open up to me. "Do you want to talk about it?"

"No," he said, avoiding eye contact. "I'm sorry, but...I can't."

We sat in silence for another endless moment. Tiger made another appearance, stretching and yawning before rubbing his body against Adrien's legs, leaving orange and white hairs on the bottoms of his green pants.

He brushed them off and gave me one of his sly grins, making me weak as an infant tree again. "Are you ready to celebrate? I'm taking you out for your birthday."

20

"What do you want to do? It's *your* day," Adrien said as we hopped onto the L train. We squeezed into plastic seats next to an elderly man wearing a Hawaiian shirt and trench coat. I could faintly hear him humming Cat Steven's *Peace Train*. My grandma used to sing it a lot. She passed away when I was fourteen. Whenever I hear Cat Stevens I think of her and the delicious glazed donuts she used to make her grandchildren.

"Pizza sounds really good," I said, just now realizing how hungry I was, hearing my stomach grumble.

He grinned. "Pizza it is."

He turned to face me, now sitting so close I could study his baby grass green eyes, feel his breath on my face. He squeezed my knee for a brief moment and it felt like a dozen ice cubes slid down my spine. His eyes were beautiful. I spotted small gold flecks I'd never noticed before. He bit his lip and studied my own eyes just as intently. The part of me that was afraid to be vulnerable wanted to break eye contact but I held my breath and dared to look deeper. For a moment I felt like we were dipping below the surface, like we were diving headfirst into each other's souls. The water was so warm and inviting. For a fraction of a minute his walls were down. Completely. The sorrow, the despair. All gone. His truest self was, well, beautiful. Kind. Sensitive. So gentle. Vulnerable, meek and humble. While also strong and stubborn and passionate. And the way he looked at me. No one had ever looked at me—*really* looked at me—like that before. His eyes held me with such tenderness, like the gentlest palm cupping a new caterpillar. But there was an intensity there, too.

Like he wanted me as much as I wanted him.

But I didn't dare hope it was true.

My eyes strayed to his shapely lips and I wondered if I'd ever taste them. My heart knocked against my chest as I imagined what our first kiss would be like. Knowing we would probably never take our friendship to that level made him forbidden fruit. Made me want him that much more.

But I was also scared. He wasn't the only one with a protective brick wall—or two—up. I didn't know his story but I sensed we both had experienced heartbreak and loss.

When the soul gazing became too awkward, we laughed and turned away. Pretended to find other people or things around us fascinating. I people watched while he played with a string he'd found in the pocket of the jacket Mrs. Watkins had given him.

We listened to the hum and clatter of the train along with the obnoxious beeping of a little boy's video game.

"So how old are you turning?"

"Nineteen," I said, realizing it was the last year of my teens, surprised by how fast it all went. Like a vapor. In another nineteen years I'd practically be middle aged. How depressing. What is the point of all this? This life could be so damned depressing if you let yourself think about stuff enough.

"How old are you?" I'd wanted to ask him for a while now, but the right moment never came up.

"I'm twenty."

"So how are you liking your twenties?"

He took his time answering, twisting the green thread around his index finger. He shrugged. "I'm not the person to ask. I haven't been happy in years. Actually, I don't remember when I was last truly happy." For a second his green eyes became stony, which caught me by surprise, made me shudder. Adrien was one of the moodier guys I've met. He'd go from intensely happy, giving me a smile that made my head spin like a merry-go-round, to a place so dark it scared me. I couldn't even begin to imagine what he's had to go through. I've wondered about it a lot these last few days.

"That's really sad." I swallowed, turning in my seat to face him. "Is that why you're…?"

"This subject keeps coming up," he said, shaking his head, half smiling. "Do you think for just a while we could pretend I never told you—that thing—the first day we met?"

"I don't know if that's possible—"

"Please try." His eyes pleaded with me. "I know I'm not being fair. I shouldn't be hanging out with you, subjecting you to any of this—"

"I *want* to spend time with you," I stammered.

"I don't see why," he said, unraveling the thread.

I didn't know how to answer. Even I wasn't entirely sure why I wanted to spend his last days with him. I guess I still had a sliver of hope that I'd be able to get him to change his mind.

***

We decided on Eddie's Pizza, a hole in the wall joint that smelled of cigar smoke, tomato sauce and garlic, an eyesore with barn red walls and lime green vinyl booths that should've been reupholstered years ago.

Adrien and I talked on and on about music. I was shocked to discover, like Abby and me, Adrien also had a passion for 1980s

New Wave/alternative.

Could the universe be screaming any louder that Adrien and I were soul mates?

"Okay, name your top five favorite bands," I said, nibbling on a piece of slightly burned crust.

"Don't do this to me. I couldn't possibly narrow it down to just five," he said, leaning forward, really getting into the conversation.

I giggled. "Try."

He took a long sip of Coke. "Okay, let's see. Echo and the Bunnymen, The Cure, Psychedelic Furs, The Smiths, U2 of course and...The The."

"Cheater. You named six," I said, kicking him under the table. He shook his head. "But five was just too tough."

"You have excellent taste. I love them all, especially The Smiths and The Cure. The The's one of the most underrated bands, don't you think?"

"Totally. The sad thing is none of my friends have even heard of them," he said, grabbing another slice of pepperoni. We ordered a half-and-half. Half veggie for me, half pepperoni and mushrooms for him.

"Yeah, well most kids haven't heard of any of these bands, except for maybe U2. It's just the oddest thing, you and me loving the same stuff. I mean, what are the chances? I think you'd love Abby's band, The Striped Goat," I said, my mouth full of artichoke.

He almost choked on his food. "Abby was the singer of The Striped Goat? You're kidding me. I love that band. I hear them all the time on college radio."

"Seriously?" I was shocked, because one, I hadn't realized her band was getting regular radio play. She would've been over the moon. And two, what were the chances Adrien was a fan? "You like The Striped Goat?"

"Do you need proof?" he asked, pulling his iPod from his jacket pocket.

I laugh. "Who still uses iPods?"

"Shut up. This thing is my baby. I cuddle with her every night. She always lets me be the big spoon." He winked at me and scrolled through a million different '80s and indie bands until The Striped Goat filled the screen. "I have their CD in my car, too."

"You have a car?"

Adrien laughed. "Of course I have a car. I am—was a car salesman, after all. It's in the shop getting worked on. It's a beater and it breaks down on me all the time. I really should get a new car." Cradling his Coke, he searched my face for a moment. "Tell me more about Abby. If you want to, I mean. I don't want to make you sad on your birthday."

I sat my half eaten slice of pizza down. "It doesn't make me sad. I love talking about her. We met in second grade. She saved me from being the constant target of the school bully and we were best friends ever since. She was amazing. She had such a zest for life. She had big plans for the future, *huge* dreams. One of the things I loved most about her was she didn't doubt them for a second, even when everyone else did."

"That's awesome."

I nodded. "She was very sweet natured. A little flighty, too. We got an apartment together before she died. It was a big plan of ours to room together the second we graduated from high school. The tragic part is she was killed two weeks after our lives were really just beginning. And her band—they were on their way. That was her dream, you know, to be a professional musician, to see the world."

"I'm so sorry, September. Sounds like she was pretty

amazing." He dropped his eyes and picked up his empty straw wrapper, rolling it into a ball.

"She was amazing. There's no one else quite like her." I sighed, nibbling on an olive left on my plate. "Enough about Abby, tell me about you. Where did you grow up?"

"Vegas."

I chuckled. "Las Vegas? You don't hear that every day. What brought you here?"

"I moved here to go to film school, but I found I enjoyed writing books more than screenplays. Less interaction with people that way." I raised an eyebrow. "That came out wrong. I'm not a hermit or anything. I just...crave time alone." He averted his eyes from me and I wondered if he was hiding something. "My parents are divorced. They split up when I was nine. My dad was a security guard at a casino—he's retired now—and my mom runs a bakery. I have an older brother who's coaching high school basketball in Dallas." He grabbed a third slice of pizza. "What about you? Where are you from? Tell me about your family."

"I grew up in Queens. My sister, April, still lives there with my folks. My dad is a podiatrist; my mom chose to stay home to raise us. She loves gardening. It's crazy how much she loves to garden. She's like, the plant whisperer. Me, I seem to kill a plant by just *looking* at it. Anyway...My family, they're really normal—and incredibly boring."

"Then it must not be genetic because you're far from boring," he said, gazing at me until I had to look away.

We sat saying nothing, taking in the ambiance. The jukebox played a sappy love song. Something from the '40s or '50s.

An elderly couple stood and danced. The woman wore sexy heels and a smile so big I wouldn't have been surprised if it broke her face. The man with pit bull skin wore plaid pants high on his waist, almost reaching his armpits. The romantic way they gazed into each other's eyes rivaled any Jane Austen book. I'd never seen a couple look so in love. I turned to Adrien, realizing he'd never grow old and sadness poured into my soul like a heavy rain.

***

"After you," Adrien said, opening the door for me as we exited the diner.

"Thank you," I said, delighted by his chivalry.

"You look really nice tonight, by the way."

I smiled in response. I wore a mock leather jacket I scored from the thrift store a few days ago with a camel colored sweater and my favorite black jeans. I decided to wear Abby's Dr. Martens to find a way to feel close to her today.

We watched a toothless, greasy homeless man pushing a cart of dirty wool blankets and trash bags full of who-knows-what walk by, followed by a cute artsy couple in their early twenties sucking face. Adrien and I made quick eye contact and laughed.

The smells of tar and cigarette smoke and sizzling meat from a nearby restaurant wafted through the evening air. I love the smell of the city. There is something exciting about it; I never tire of the various scents. Each unique aroma is a time machine that takes me to different treasured moments of my past. Skipping school to get falafel at Taïm and record store hopping with Abby. Searching for the best chimichangas with John. Visiting animal shelters with Chris.

Creating a new memory here and now with Adrien.

We simultaneously looked up at a halo of pink, orange and yellow clouds hovering over New York.

"Beautiful," I said, suddenly overwhelmed with joy, happy to be alive. My belly was full of good food and I was spending the evening with the most handsome, sensitive and mysterious boy I'd ever met.

"Do you like the Phantom of the Opera?" he asked, flagging down a yellow taxi.

"I *love* the Phantom of the Opera." I'd always wanted to see it but never seemed to have the money to buy tickets. Abby and I watched the movie version over and over.

"Good," he said, grinning really big. "Because I have fourth row tickets."

***

After the show, which was everything I'd hoped it to be and more, we went for a walk to enjoy the perfect early fall night. My nose was a little cold but I felt cozy in my thick jacket. The golden moon dangled in a midnight blue sky. A gentle breeze rattled colorful leaves above us. The scents of fall and Mexican and Chinese food filled the night air. We could hear faint rock music from inside a nearby bar.

Adrien grabbed my hand, making my pulse pick up and my stomach muscles tighten. For a while we wandered aimlessly, telling jokes and swapping stories and laughing, stretching out the magic of my birthday, not wanting the evening to end.

The streets this time of night were practically empty. Occasionally we'd cross paths with a random person or two. A gangly woman jogging. A troll of a man staring at his phone, tripping over a curb. A hip couple in their forties carrying groceries in paper bags.

Adrien stopped us at a street corner in front of a store with a window display of faceless mannequins wearing ear muffs and tweed coats. I turned to face him. He looked at me thoughtfully as he tucked a strand of hair behind my ear. He hesitated. He exhaled audibly before finally speaking.

"September, I…" He squeezed his eyes shut.

"What is it? You can tell me anything."

"When I'm with you, September, you make me remember the good things. Sometimes I almost forget…the pain I'm in." He gripped my hand. "There's something about you." I studied his face which was glowing under a yellow street lamp. He looked so sweet tonight, like a little boy. "I feel strangely drawn to you. It's almost…other-worldly." As he said this, I got the chills.

He was right. There was some mysterious connection between us, besides physical chemistry, which we obviously had. If I believed in previous lives, I could've sworn I knew him from before. This was all so very déjà-vu.

His brow furrowed and he hesitated for several long seconds. Finally, he said, "I…I think I could fall in love with you, September…but I'd be an egocentric, selfish pig if I let this go any further than it already has."

For a moment I forgot how to breathe.

"Adrien—I don't know what to say."

"Ask me to leave. Ask me to never see you again," he said, his tone pleading, but his face full of conflict.

"I…I can't."

"You deserve so much more than this. So much more than me. And after all you've been through. I don't want to hurt you, September. It's the last thing I want to do."

I bit my lip. He was right. Our spending all this time together wasn't helping either of us. At least not in the long run. But I couldn't bring myself to ask him to leave.

Suddenly I wanted to kiss him—like mad.

But I refrained. I didn't want to get hurt again. I didn't want to fall hard for someone I wouldn't get to keep.

I'd suffered enough loss. I didn't know what to do. There was no manual for this, no how-to guide for girls who found themselves falling for devastatingly handsome suicidal guys.

So I changed the subject.

"Knock knock."

He shook his head and laughed, catching on, fully aware that I was avoiding this hard conversation, shoving it in my back pocket, saving it for another day. This was my birthday and I wanted it to end as perfectly as it started. He let out a shaky breath and grinned a grin that made me melt right there into the sidewalk.

"Who's there?"

21

The day after my birthday Adrien came over first thing in the morning and took me out for breakfast. We ordered eggs and cheese on multigrain bagels and freshly squeezed orange juice at Tim's Coffee, where we had our first real conversation, when Adrien had asked me out.

Last minute we decided to order everything to go and had a picnic on a red plaid blanket on the roof of my apartment building.

As the early morning sun rose, it cast an orange glow on the world below, setting skyscrapers ablaze. Despite my sweater, the chilly morning air gave me goose bumps and made me shiver.

"Cold?" Adrien asked, scooting closer to me and wrapping his warm arm around my shoulders.

Words could not express the relief I felt seeing him again. I missed him. So much. More than a girl should ever miss a boy in such a short time.

I knew I was being stupid. Stupid for starting something that was going nowhere. Stupid for putting my already broken heart on the line. Stupid for loving Adrien a little more every day. Stupid for still hoping I could change his mind and choose me over death.

But I couldn't help myself. Adrien had cast a spell on me.

I was a goner.

We chatted about this and that, but mostly we enjoyed each other's company in silence, hearing cars whiz by below and Middle Eastern music playing somewhere in the distance.

We laughed as we watched greedy birds fight over the bread crumbs we would toss in their direction. A bigger bird kept bullying the smaller ones.

"You have a little cheese," he said, gesturing to his chin.

"Right here?" I brushed the center of my chin.

"No, right here." He used his thumb to rub it off. He left his fingers under my chin for a few seconds and studied my eyes, his face so close, I could smell the bagel on his breath. My lips burned and again, I ached for a kiss.

"What's your favorite color?" he asked, finally dropping his gaze, crumbling the bagel wrapper and tossing our empty cups and napkins into the paper bag.

"Why do you ask?" I hadn't been asked that since grade school.

"It says a lot about a person."

I eyed him in his current clashing get-up. A tea green button-up shirt with hunter green pants. His favorite green sneakers. My gaze moved up and I took in his kind eyes, which were emerald in the morning light.

"Green. My favorite color's green."

***

"Hi. How's your day going?" I asked Chris when we arrived at work at the same time. He opened the door for me and I thanked him. We crossed the lobby which was sleek with pale wood paneled walls lined with royal blue Mid Century Modern chairs and potted palm trees. I was always tempted to steal one or two of the plants for my living room. We waved at a couple of fellow janitors who were sweeping and cleaning windows.

"I got a new foster puppy," he replied as we headed for the janitor's closet. "He's a handful but you'll never find a cuter face." He fished his phone from his back pocket and showed me a picture of an English bulldog puppy, a velvety wrinkled ball, with the saddest look on his face.

"I'm dying!" I said, throwing my hands over my mouth.

"I know. I'm keeping him if they can't find him a home. Never mind if he eats my furniture." He chuckled.

"Heck, I would take him if I didn't already have Tiger."

"How was your birthday?" Chris asked, pulling his hair back into a ponytail, eyeing me in my tight t-shirt as I climbed into my jumpsuit.

"Surprisingly wonderful. I didn't think I'd survive the day without Abby. She always spent my birthday with me, glued to my side, literally morning till night. We were like conjoined twins."

"It must be a big adjustment."

"You played a major role in making the day amazing. If it weren't for you, Adrien wouldn't have..." I trailed off when I saw Chris catch his breath and look down at the floor. "I'm sorry. Did I say something...?"

"It's nothing. I guess I'm a little jealous you have a new guy in your life. It's stupid, though. Why should I be jealous? It's not like I don't have a girlfriend or anything."

"Oh," I said, zipping up my jumpsuit.

"Not a big deal," he said, zipping his own. But I knew he was lying for my benefit.

"Just so you know, no one can replace my Sunshine Boy. In fact, you and Adrien are practically opposites."

He didn't seem to take any comfort in this.

We filled the cart with toilet seat covers and fresh rags. Chris refilled a container of toilet cleaner while I swapped out an empty bottle of Windex.

"What did you end up doing?" He locked the janitor's closet and pocketed his keys.

"We went out for pizza and then he took me to Phantom. Something I've always wanted to see. He made me a chocolate cake. That's it." The memory alone gave me butterflies but I tried to downplay the night for my friend's benefit.

"Are you two getting pretty serious?" he asked, pushing the whistling cart toward the first restroom.

We passed a sharp looking man in a business suit who nodded a quick hello.

I thought for a moment, unsure what to say. Was I falling for Adrien? Yes, I think so. Was I in a real relationship with him? Not really. Not a lasting one. And anyway, we haven't even kissed or anything. "I don't know. What do you mean by serious?"

Chris opened the restroom door. "After you."

"Thank you."

He dropped the rubber doorstop and kicked it under the door, then pushed the yellow cart inside. The room reeked of rotten eggs.

"Do you see yourself with him six months from now?"

The question, although not unreasonable, was like a punch in the stomach. How could I answer that? I busied myself with some Windex and a rag and said, "You've got to hear what Mary gave me. She found an old letter from Abby."

***

After work, when I opened the apartment door I didn't expect to see Mary making out on the couch with a guy, or Adrien sitting at the kitchen table eating an apple, reading *Crime and Punishment*. Had he even gone home today? Nag Champa incense burned on the side table next to the monkey lamp. I could smell a hint of Tiger's litter box, too. Time to change that. Adrien turned to me and smiled. Oh man. His smile did things to me you wouldn't believe. He stood and gave me a quick half hug, a peck on the cheek. He let his arm linger around my waist.

Our eyes wandered over to the oblivious couple molded into a big lump on the couch. I wanted it to be us. I wanted it to be Adrien and me doing that on the couch. I glanced at him, wistful. Was he thinking the same thing? Did he want to kiss me as much as I wanted him to kiss me? Or did his depression and lack of will to live suck those desires out of him? And then it made me wonder: Has he ever been in love? If he dropped his defenses and let himself really fall for me, would I be his first?

We continued to watch the mound on the couch, amused. We started snickering simultaneously. Starting to laugh at the same time made us laugh even harder. And of course Mary and the boy she was slobbering all over were oblivious.

Okay, I wanted to be them, only not so gross. Mary was nearly sucking the poor guy's face off. And then it hit me: was that Keaton she was kissing? Abby's Keaton?

As we approached them, I theatrically cleared my throat. After a second try with no success, I grabbed an empty beer can and threw it at Mary's head. My aim was perfect. A few remaining drops of brown liquid splashed onto Mary's black jeans. Adrien made a failed attempt to stifle another chuckle.

"What?" she said, finally pulling away. She looked up at our surprised, amused faces. Lipstick was smeared around her mouth, giving her a clown face. "Oh."

"What do you think you're doing?" I said, placing my hands on my hips. "What are you thinking, Mary?"

"What do you mean?"

"You're with *Keaton* now? *Abby's* boyfriend?"

"She's dead, September." The way she looked at me, one would think *I* was the crazy one. Keaton rested his elbows on his knees, studying the edge of the Oriental rug on the floor. It was strange seeing him again. I hadn't seen him since the funeral and having him around brought a funny feeling into my stomach and a prick to my heart. It made me miss her all over again, with a fresh intensity.

"Keaton and Abby were together for years," I said. "It's not *weird* for you...?"

"I've always had a thing for Keaton," she said as if he weren't in the room. She chewed on a black fingernail. "And now there's nothing stopping me from—"

"You speak of Abby like she was some—some—"

"You know I loved her every bit as much as you did. Of course I'm still sad she's gone. She was our best friend." She shrugged. "But life goes on."

I couldn't believe what I was hearing. "Yeah, I guess for *you* it does." I crossed my arms over my chest. "Mary, Abby would be—"

"Maybe I should go," Keaton said, standing up, his handsome face turning red faster than an electric burner. He wore a Muse t-shirt and his black pants were tucked into tan army boots.

I shook my head. "No, Keaton. Stay. It's actually really nice to see you again. It's been waaaay too long."

He rocked back on his heels and let out a quick breath.

"It totally has," he said, throwing his arms around me, giving me a bear hug that nearly knocked us both to the floor. His eyes became glassy as he pulled away. I gave him an understanding look, communicating: *I miss her, too.*

"Chestal is *not* a word, Mary," I said, not bothering to hide my exasperation. I got up to grab Adrien and myself another ginger ale. "Anyone else want more soda?" I asked, opening the practically empty fridge. Mary and Keaton shook their heads. Abby's ginger ale was almost gone. The thought of it made me a little sad. It was one more piece of evidence that my best friend was gone and never coming back.

I plopped on the floor beside Adrien, Indian-style and handed him the soda.

"Thanks," he said, touching my knee.

"Chestal is too a word," Mary said, protecting the Scrabble tiles with chewed away fingernails as I tried to slide them off the board. "Okay, let's ask the writer." Mary, Keaton and I simultaneously turned to Adrien.

He shrugged. "I've never heard of it. What does it mean?" he said, taking a big bite of licorice, turning his teeth red.

"You know. The chest area. Like 'He has a lot of hair in his chestal area'," Mary said, gesturing to her own chest.

"Okay, we don't need the visual," Keaton joked.

"Yeah, right, you made that up. You're always breaking the rules," I said, opening my ginger ale and taking a swig, the initial taste intense and sour from the carbonation.

"Rules are made to be broken," Keaton said, balancing an empty soda can on one finger.

"It's not in the dictionary," Adrien said. "I'll bet you a hundred bucks."

Mary made a face. "Chestal *is* in the dictionary. The diction-*Mary*."

"Cute," I said, rolling my eyes. "Just because you made it up doesn't make it a word."

"All words are made up by someone. Why can't I make some up?"

"She has a point," Keaton said, letting out a loud burp.

"You guys are impossible," I said, growling. "I quit. I can't bear any more of Mary's cheating."

She stuck her hands up. "I don't cheat."

"You always cheat," I said, making a face.

"Who's up for a movie?" Keaton asked, stretching. "Does Abby—do you still have *Harold and Maude*?"

"Of course," I said, standing up. Abby had a killer movie collection. Mostly cult classics and 1980s stuff.

After filling a bowl the size of the Grand Canyon full of buttery popcorn and ordering Korean takeout for a late-night dinner (it was already past eleven and we'd forgotten to eat something other than junk food until now) we all settled into the couch, except Mary who snuggled up to Keaton's legs and rested her head on his lap. He stroked her hair like a cat. She purred in reply. Adrien raised an eyebrow and I shrugged. I sat a few inches away from him until he pulled me closer and casually threw his arm around me. His delicious scent overwhelmed me and made me feel weak all over.

"You have strange friends," he whispered.

I groaned. "Tell me about it." Although I loved how entertaining they were.

I wouldn't have it any other way.

***

I fell asleep during the end credits. Well, I was half-asleep. I wasn't sure how or when it happened, but I found myself lying on the couch, using Adrien's lap for a pillow. And Tiger was using my legs for a bed. I heard Mary walk Keaton to the door and whisper goodnight. There was a long drag of silence. Kissing?

"It was nice to meet you, man," Keaton said, keeping his voice down for my sake. "September's lucky to have found you."

"Oh, we're not..." Adrien said. "We're just friends. Nice to meet you, too. Sorry for your loss."

"Thanks. You would have really liked Abby."

"That's what I hear. Take care, man."

"I'm going to bed," Mary said through a yawn after she closed the door.

"Okay, goodnight," Adrien whispered. "Sweet dreams."

Her bare feet made soft patting noises on the hardwood floor. She hummed a song I vaguely recognized as she left the room.

After I heard her bedroom door snap shut, Adrien got up, cradling my head as he slid a throw pillow underneath where his lap had been.

The thoughtfulness might have made me swoon a little.

He cleaned up a bit, tossing the empty Korean food boxes in the garbage, putting the soda and beer cans and bottles in the recycle bin under the kitchen sink. I heard his sneakers squeak against the floor as he pulled a soft blanket over me (picking up a protesting Tiger and gingerly placing him back on my legs) and tucked it carefully around my shoulders. I felt his warm hand brush the hair away from my face and moist lips press against the side of my nose.

"Goodnight, September," he whispered.

I must've been pretty tired because I don't remember hearing him leave.

22

"You seem really distracted lately," Chris said, carving out a big chunk of pork burrito and shoving it into his mouth.

"What?" I said, unfolding a paper napkin and placing it on my lap.

He shook his head and laughed. "That's exactly what I mean."

"I was kidding, Chris. But you're right. I do have a lot on my mind lately."

The smell of sautéed onions, sizzling meat and fresh flour tortillas filled our lungs as Chris and I soaked up the late September afternoon sun. A gentle breeze caressed our skin as we ate on the outdoor patio at Chris's favorite Tex-Mex restaurant.

It was the first time we'd spent quality time together, outside of work, since I'd met Adrien. We used to do this a lot, well, as much as Chris could get away with without making Megan jealous. Megan didn't really know about us—about how close we'd become. He felt bad about lying to his girlfriend, but the girl was impossible. She smothered him like a needy boa constrictor. If it were up to her, he'd have no friends. No social life at all.

I looked Chris up and down as I chewed on my yummy black bean salad, the tangy cilantro lime dressing tingling my mouth in a pleasant way. He looked especially handsome today. I'd forgotten how good he looked in jeans and a shirt—I was so used to seeing him in that silly blue jumpsuit. I hadn't noticed in ages the cute way his hair sometimes fell into his face and how endearing it was when he shoved it away in an angry sort of fashion.

But Chris angry? Impossible. He was the sweetest guy I'd ever met.

I smiled at his defined forearms that reminded me of Popeye, his long eyelashes and the way he'd gaze at me through them with his kind gray eyes.

A bullet of guilt shot through me as I realized how much I'd taken him for granted lately. I loved Chris. He was the closest thing to family since Abby died. I didn't deserve him, the way I neglected him, like an ever-growing stack of unopened mail. My insides melted and formed puddles as I thought about how much he meant to me, how he was one of the best things to happen to me in years. I took another bite, barely getting it down, feeling so laden with shame.

"I'm so sorry, Chris. I haven't exactly been a good friend lately."

"You're forgiven," he said, half-smiling. "But I won't lie. I miss you, Tember. I'm glad I was able to catch you today."

I frowned. The only reason I made time for Chris was because Adrien had his godson's birthday party to attend (I know— Adrien had a godson? There was still so much I didn't know about him). He'd be gone all day. "I miss you, too." And it was the truth.

Chris studied my face. "You look good. I'd swear you're happy, because you kind of have this glow lately, but then sometimes your eyes are sad. Like they were when we first met. Is everything okay?"

I pulled away from his gaze, feeling exposed. "Yeah, I guess."

I didn't feel ready to tell him the truth about Adrien. Would I ever feel ready?

"Come on, Tember, you used to tell me everything," he urged, smoothing out a clump of guacamole on his burrito.

"I know, I know." I picked at my food, feeling increasingly slimy, like a worm on a sidewalk, fated to be stepped on.

"What's going on? Are you still seeing what's-his-face?"

I laughed nervously. "Yes."

He stabbed his burrito with his plastic fork. "Are you…falling for him?"

"No. Well, yes, actually…I don't know…It's pretty complicated."

I couldn't meet his gaze. I could see in my peripheral vision he was crushed. It was then I knew for sure I wasn't the only one falling in love. Chris seemed to have a thing for me and I was stupid not to have caught it before. I mean, I knew he had a little crush on me, but this was a whole different ball game. But why? Wasn't he in love with Megan? And if he really did have a thing for me, why didn't he dump Megan ages ago when the door was wide open? I would've had him, no hesitation, if the choice was there. Before I met Adrien, that is.

I lifted my gaze. Our eyes locked and there was an intensity shared between us that took my breath away. The way he looked at me—if there wasn't a table between us, if we weren't in the middle of a crowd, if everything wasn't so damn complicated—I knew he would've kissed me. And a part of me would've let him. I did love Chris. I always have. He was sweet and cute and funny. He could do no wrong. Probably not even intentionally hurt a bug. And he cared for me—more than I deserved. But I loved Adrien, too, with a more desperate urgency. I was falling for him harder, faster. But with Chris it was a slow, steady burn. A safer, more familiar love.

Why did life have to be so complicated? Why did I have to fall for two guys at once? And right after John dumped me and my best friend died, right when I swore to never let anyone back into my heart, ever again? The timing of everything was so off. But that's the funny thing about life. It has no respect for silly things like plans or timing. It does its own thing, no apologies.

"Can I ask you something?" I said, regretting it as soon as I opened my mouth.

He put his fork down. "Anything."

I choked on the words. "Are you in love with…Megan?"

"No. Well, yes, actually…I don't know…It's pretty complicated." Almost like a tape recorder, he mimicked me perfectly. We both laughed nervously. "Honestly? I'll always care for Megan. Deeply. But I haven't been *in* love with her for a long time. I'm not sure I ever did love her that way."

I was stunned. "Why—then why—?"

"Her dad's sick. He's dying. He has Huntington's. His body and mind are deteriorating. Shutting down. Megan is devastated. She's a daddy's girl. I can't leave her…I can't leave her in the middle of all this."

"Oh," was all I could say.

Why was I surrounded by so much tragedy? Only last year the world seemed to be a much simpler place. I was so young and innocent. So carefree. But ever since Abby died, I seemed to draw sadness into my life like a magnet. Or maybe this was just part of growing up—realizing there were equal parts of joy and sadness.

"She took a test a couple of months before I met you. She found out she has it, too, but it could take years for it to kick in."

"Oh, wow. I'm so sorry."

"I've been planning on breaking up with her for a while. She's a special girl, but she doesn't let me *breathe*…When I finally gathered the courage to end things, she broke the news." He raked his hands through his hair. "How could I, September? How could I dump a girl who's going to die?"

I shook my head. "It must feel like an impossible situation. I'm so sorry, Chris." I laughed, but only because it was so *Chris* to want to do the right thing. "You're just too nice for your own good sometimes." He sighed, his face screwing up, reminding me of a little boy. I continued, "But does that mean you should stay with someone you don't love because she's sick? Because her father's sick? Is that fair to her, to live a lie? I know I wouldn't want someone—no matter how much I loved him—to sacrifice everything, including his own happiness to be with me."

"I hadn't thought of it that way," he said, studying his food. Suddenly, against my will, tears filled my eyes. "What's wrong, Tember?" He reached across the table to touch my hand.

I pushed my half-eaten food away. "I'm not going to lie to you anymore."

He seemed hurt and confused. "What? Lie about what?"

I struggled to talk through a lump in my throat. "Megan's not the only one who's going to die."

Chris's eyes moved around my face, searching for clues. "What's going on?"

"Adrien. He's…he's going to kill himself in eight days. The night of my parents' party."

He laughed nervously. "Adrien's *killing* himself?"

"Yes," I whispered.

"Wait. Why? Why would a guy who has it all—who has September Jones—want to kill himself?"

I shook my head. "I'm flattered, but it's more complicated than that. He was suicidal before we met. In fact he told me he was the first day we met. Actually, it was the second day," I said, remembering we'd first crossed paths when I worked at that art supply store.

"Why, though? Is he depressed or something?"

I bit my lip. "He won't tell me the reason. And he refuses to get help."

"I want you to break up with him. Right away," Chris said through his teeth. I was taken aback. I'd never seen him angry before. "I can't *believe* this guy. Does he know about your recent breakup? About the accident? Does he know how much you've suffered already? You don't need this, September. You don't need some wallowing loser pulling you down like this."

"It's not his fault. I practically begged him to spend time with me. I basically stalked him until he agreed to hang out with me."

"But why? Is he that good-looking? Or is it the whole moody, bad boy thing he has going for him?"

I laughed. "Oh, come on. You know I'm not that shallow. I just felt this responsibility to save him. To keep him from hurting himself. And then he wasn't anything I'd expected. I started…falling for him."

Unable to meet Chris's gaze, I studied the edge of my plate, fully aware I'd stabbed him in the heart—again—with those words.

After a long silence, he said, "Okay, but if he refuses to get help, if he's going to *kill* himself in a week…wouldn't it be better for you both if you just walked away?"

I swallowed. "Maybe…Yes."

"Okay then," he said, frowning, standing up.

"But—"

"Leave him, September. This will only end badly. You were just starting to find some happiness. I don't want to see him crush you. Please. I'm begging you to leave him."

23

"Did you know, on average, people with mental illnesses die twenty-five years earlier than normal people?" Mary said as we climbed out of Adrien's ancient silver Nissan. Keaton had offered to pay for a cab, but Adrien insisted we ride in his car, which was finally out of the repair shop.

"Mentally ill people are normal, too, Mary," I said, watching Adrien as he locked the car. Was he mentally ill? I was certain he was depressed. Why else would he...I let the thought trail off. No use dwelling on the inevitable. It was something I couldn't think about too much. In fact, I pretty much had to be in denial because there was no other way I could enjoy my limited time with him.

"That's pretty random," Adrien said, laughing, raking a hand through his hair.

"And anyway, what *is* normal?" I said to Mary. "You certainly aren't."

"Ha!" she said to me. She then turned to Adrien, "Abby was mentally ill. She was bipolar."

"It wasn't a serious case," I said. "I barely even noticed her lows. She was pretty happy most of the time. It was her highs that got her into trouble."

Keaton laughed, adjusting his fedora. "She really thought she was invincible." He said it wistfully and with affection. I frowned. Poor Keaton. He really did love Abby. They'd made a really cute couple, too.

It was a chilly afternoon. Despite the bright, clear sky and the sun directly overhead, an icy wind still managed to bite the skin underneath our clothes. The crisp, earthy smells of fall permeated the air. I almost hated fall. It wouldn't be so bad by itself, but cold, bitter winter always followed.

"Cold?" Adrien asked, wrapping his arm around me.

"Are you sure you want to do this?" Mary asked. It was my first time visiting Abby's grave since the funeral. The visit was long overdue.

"I'm sure. Adrien, you really didn't have to come. You're the only one here who didn't know Abby," I said, snuggling up to him to keep warm. I wasn't sure what made my heart race more—anticipating seeing Abby's grave again or Adrien's strong arms encircling me.

We wandered through a maze of headstones, trying to find hers. Cemeteries always freaked me out. It was so abnormal to be standing on rotting corpses. Okay, not directly *on* them, but *over* them which wasn't much better. But, unlike Mary, I was definitely not comfortable with death. Morgues, coffins, crematoriums, all of that. Even an approaching hearse on the road unhinged me. Every time I saw one, I'd get this sick feeling in my stomach and wonder if it held a dead body and then, of course, my imagination would get the best of me and I'd start making up tragic stories about the poor dead guy in the back. How did he die? Strangulation? Drowning? A black widow bite? Who was he leaving behind? His soul mate? A paraplegic mother? Five children?

"Here it is," Keaton whispered. Alarmed, I stopped so fast I stepped on Adrien's shoe.

"Sorry," I said, feeling like an idiot.

"No problem," he said, stealing a kiss from my cheek. What did all these touches and stolen kisses mean? Was my plan working? Could I change his mind?

When I saw her name engraved in the granite headstone, it felt like being punched in the stomach by a world champion boxer. I wasn't ready for this. Why did it still catch me off guard, all these months later? When would I finally realize she was really gone?

We stood in silence, listening to chirping birds and leaves being rattled by the wind, before Mary said, "Death is so beautiful."

I shot her a look. "Death is *not* beautiful," I said. "Are you *crazy*?"

"I'm just saying—"

"How can you *say* that?" I nearly spat the words out.

Mary's eyes darted left and right. "Wait, I—"

"You weren't in the car with her. You didn't see all the blood. You didn't watch her take her last breath. You don't know *anything*," I said, nearly shouting.

Adrien cringed before taking my trembling body in his arms and holding me tightly, soothing the anger and hurt away.

"I'm sorry, I shouldn't have said that," Mary said, clutching her black velvet jacket tightly over her chest, looking down at the ground.

"No, I'm sorry. I just—I guess I freaked out there for a minute. This is all so fresh for me still. I thought I was getting better, but sometimes it just hits me all over again."

Keaton, who seemed oblivious to the rest of us, began singing Abby's favorite song, *Lovesong*, by The Cure. Surprised, the rest of us stood in silent wonder, carefully listening. Keaton had a pretty decent voice. He'd sometimes sing backup in The Striped Goat, his smooth falsetto perfectly complimenting Abby's deeper voice.

Mary hid her face in her hands, on the verge of hysterics. I couldn't tell if she was laughing or crying, or maybe both. Keaton took her hand and squeezed it. The last lines of the song got the best of us and we were all in tears. Even Adrien's eyes became glassy and I felt him trembling, too.

After a few intense moments of silence—which I was sure were going to kill me—Mary spoke up first. "Abby, you were the most beautiful soul I ever knew. My very best friend." She placed an iridescent silk butterfly atop the tombstone. Abby loved butterflies.

Keaton was next. He set a paper origami bird next to the butterfly and whispered, "Now you're free…Free as a bird…I will always love you, Abby."

It was my turn. I opened my mouth, unsure of what to say. I managed to get out a frog-like croaking noise.

Adrien pulled his arm around me tighter and said, "I've never met you, Abby, but I've heard nothing but good. I—I'm sorry your beautiful life was cut short." His face crumbled in pain. "I'm so sorry."

Finally, I said, "Abby, you're my best friend, my sister, my soul twin. Death cannot keep us apart. Somehow, I feel you near me. Somehow I know you'll always be around. I love you."

Mary did that laughing-crying thing again. I pulled a handful of gourmet ginger ale bottle caps from my jacket pocket and sprinkled them, like dirt, over the grave. "She loved ginger ale," I explained. This struck everyone as funny and we all laughed. Really, really hard.

On our way back to the car, I started feeling funny. Tired, weak, nauseous. Like my stomach turned inside-out. The grave. Mary and Keaton. Chris. Adrien. John and April. It was all too much.

"Are you okay, September?" Mary asked, her heavily made up

face concerned. "You don't look too hot."

Keaton nodded. "You do look a little pale."

"I'm always pale," I said right before I threw up all over some poor guy's grave. My half-digested black bean salad slid down the center of the headstone.

"Poor Jonathan," Adrien said, struggling to read the victim's last name, "Jonathan Bacon. He never saw it coming."

"Ha, ha," I said, feeling increasingly miserable by the second.

"You're running a fever," Mary said, feeling my forehead with the back of her hand. "Let's get you home."

***

"September, you have a visitor," Mary said, yanking me out of a rare good dream. I dreamed Adrien, Mary, Abby and I spent a perfect day at the park, playing on swings, eating strawberry ice cream.

I moaned. "Leave me alone."

Not unlike a dentist extracting a tooth, Mary yanked open the curtains. Cruel, ruthless sunlight blinded me. My eyes slammed shut in protest.

"Wakey-wakey. Hot Waffle Guy is here."

"What time is it?"

"3:27."

"What day is it?"

"It's September twenty-sixth. Two days after you puked all over the cemetery," she said, running a damp cloth over my face. "Sit up."

Obediently, I struggled to get into a somewhat seated position on the bed. She pressed a glass of room-temperature water to my lips. I sipped carefully, afraid if I drank too much, I'd throw up again. Some of the water wandered and dribbled off my chin, wetting the front of my shirt.

Mary smiled at me affectionately. How did I ever hate her? Every day I understood a little more why she meant so much to Abby. She grabbed a brush from her back pocket and began running it through my hair.

"Wait. What are you doing?" I asked, confused.

"You want to look good for Hot Waffle Guy, don't you?"

It finally clicked. I panicked. "Adrien's here? I don't want to see him. I mean, I don't want *him* to see *me*. Not like this. I'm a wreck."

"Calm down, you actually look kind of cute, in a half-dead sort of way," she said, yanking on a knot in my hair.

"Ow! I don't want to see him. Not today. Send him home."

A quiet tap on my door informed me it was too late.

"September?" It was him. Great. How much did he hear?

I groaned. "Come in, if you must." When he opened the door I wanted to hide under my covers and never come out again. I felt naked without makeup and my hair was a stringy mess. Did I have B.O.? My breath could probably kill anything within a ten mile radius.

"I'll leave you two alone," Mary said, in a mocking tone. I shot her the look of death before she slipped out.

Adrien entered the room, looking around for a moment, admiring Abby's 1980s band posters.

"Good ole Morrissey." He gestured to the one I had torn earlier.

His eyes rested on Abby's photo, the one of her on the fifty cent kiddie ride, before he sat on the edge of my bed. He placed a single sunflower in a simple blue vase on my nightstand and a mysterious paper bag on the floor. He noticed the pile of books on forgiveness and flipped through one of them.

"Are these working? Are you forgiving the man who killed

Abby?"

"They're helping a lot. I didn't think I could, but I'm starting to." I felt my cheeks burning like fire pits, not entirely comfortable with my crush seeing me looking like a total slob.

"What if he doesn't deserve your forgiveness?"

I laughed. "Maybe he does, maybe he doesn't. Forgiving him is more for me and my own happiness than for him."

He thought about that for a few moments before asking, "How are you feeling?"

"A little better," I said, aiming my offensive breath away from his general direction.

"Good," he said. "I missed you."

I chuckled. "We've been apart for like two days."

"I guess I'm used to spending every day with you. The past two days have felt endless. I'm having September withdrawals. The truth is you should be illegal. You're like a drug."

I couldn't help but smile. "That's what all the guys say," I joked. I explored his face. He looked tired. The whites of his eyes had red rivers on the surface. His usual vibrant skin had become dull. His green shirt looked as disheveled as his hair.

As if he could read my thoughts, he said, "I haven't been sleeping much lately."

I opened my mouth to ask why, but I knew why. He had six days left before…No. I shouldn't think about it. I was going to get him to change his mind. Somehow.

"I brought you something," he said, opening the big brown bag.

I sat up straighter. "What is it?"

"A flu survival kit," he said with a goofy, proud look on his face. "Let's see…vegetarian chicken noodle soup." He pulled it out. It was in a foam To-Go container with a plastic lid.

"No way. Where did you find vegetarian chicken noodle soup?

You're my hero." My stomach rumbled. I'd been living on saltines for the past couple of days.

"There's this little veggie café I'll have to take you to sometime. And of course, some orange juice." He pulled out a carton. "With 300% of your daily allowance of vitamin C. You can never have too much of that." He reached into the bag. "A Sesame Street coloring book, with the ever coveted set of ninety-six Crayola crayons. *With* a built-in sharpener."

"I've always wanted this. I never had anything bigger than the sixteen count."

"Well it's about time all your Crayola dreams came true."

"And I love Sesame Street. How did you know?"

"Who doesn't like Sesame Street?"

"Mary, for one. She says the show creeps her out."

He laughed. "You're kidding. Okay, I also brought you some short stories." He pulled out a manila file filled with white paper.

"Wait. *Your* short stories? You're going to let me read them?" I asked, eager to finally get my hands on them.

"Yes, but if you hate them, promise me you won't keep reading just to be nice," he said, holding the folder out of my reach until I agreed.

"Okay, I promise." I flipped through a few of the pages. A smashed fly decorated the title of one of the stories.

"And, last but not least, an '80s mix CD."

"You made me a mix CD?" I said, wanting to cry. "No one's ever made me a mix CD before." Cute doodles of spaceships and weird little aliens decorated the CD insert. I knew he'd put a lot of thought into it and it was probably the sweetest thing any guy had ever given me.

He looked surprised. "You're kidding. If I'd met you earlier, I would've made you a hundred of them."

24

The day after Adrien's visit, I began feeling like myself again. A little weak and tired, but more restless than anything. I took a refreshing lukewarm shower, washing my hair twice.

I'd just finished reading his short stories. He was a quirky and inventive writer and he came up with the most unusual metaphors. One story was about a geeky high school student (wearing a dorky dinosaur shirt) trying to gather courage to ask his longtime crush to the prom. I wondered if it was autobiographical and just picturing Adrien in a dinosaur shirt made me bust out in laughter. Another story was an eerie dystopian. A third one was about human-like aliens secretly living among us. Obviously, he was exploring different genres, trying to find his style.

As I ran a comb through my chaotic wet hair, I heard muffled voices coming from the front room. I assumed it was Mary and Keaton until I pressed my ear against the bathroom door. I recognized his voice immediately. Adrien was here. Their voices remained obscure until I flipped off the bathroom fan and opened the door just a sliver. I heard Mary say, "September's sister actually stole John away from her. She never saw it coming. It surprised everyone. We never thought John was the cheating type. We thought he was smitten with September. Well, he seemed to be at first. Abby had told me September was pretty crushed when he dumped her…September said John and April weren't remorseful in the least. They justified the whole thing and accused September of blowing things out of proportion. They felt *entitled* to cheat. Like they were meant to be together and September shouldn't get in their way."

I struggled to catch Adrien's reply. "I had no idea. Anyone would be an idiot to let September go…"

I hurried and put on some mascara and a little lip gloss.

Mary continued, "Even if April and John *were* meant to be, like soul mates, or whatever, they should've handled it better."

"Definitely," Adrien said.

"Can you imagine? September was in love with him and now he's going to be her brother-in-law. I mean, gross."

"That would be really awkward."

There was a long pause before Mary said, "Are you sure you can't go with her to her parents' anniversary thingy? She's ultra dreading showing up solo."

"I wish I could be there for her," he said. "I have an important commitment to keep."

I swallowed twice and squeezed my eyes shut. The words "important commitment" rung in my ears. Again, I pictured a young Adrien in a dinosaur shirt until I felt genuinely happy. I marched out of the bathroom, determined to enjoy what little time I had left with the boy who I couldn't help but love. But first I grabbed a CD from my room and shoved it into my back pocket. I thought the mix CD he made me was so sweet, I made him one yesterday. Like his, mine was also purely '80s bands. I put on some of my favorite love songs. I was sneaky and included a few songs with messages of hope and even squeezed in a couple of guilt trips. Actually, all of the songs' lyrics were messages to him, things I would say if there were no consequences.

"Hey, Adrien," I said, twisting my wet hair into a bun. "What are you doing here?"

He smiled, making my insides soften like a Tootsie Roll left in the car on a summer day. "Rumor has it you're feeling better. I wanted to spend the day with my favorite girl."

"Sounds good to me," I said, fiddling with the sleeve of my red blouse. "I have something for you." I handed him the CD.

"Oh, wow. Thanks." His eyes trailed the long list of tracks. "Kate Bush, OMD, Corey Hart, The Human League...Good stuff! I can't wait to listen to it. I've heard most of these but some of them are new to me." He slid it into his jacket pocket. "I still can't believe we have such similar taste in music. No one our age listens to this stuff."

"I know. Very strange."

Adrien was sprawled on the couch with the cat while Mary was sitting on the Oriental rug stretching her legs, like she was about to do a workout or something but she was dressed more like she was about to go trick or treating.

"So why didn't you tell me about John and April? That's a pretty big deal," he said, stroking Tiger's back. Blissful, he hummed like a diesel, his eyes two slits.

I plopped down on the couch next to them. "Careful, you're going to spoil him. Just like you spoil me. Soon you'll find us both at your doorstep and there will be no turning back."

His lips curled upwards. "That wouldn't be so bad. Seriously, though. I had no idea. Now I get why you need a date to your parents' party. What happened with your sister and your ex is pretty awful."

I shrugged, trying to appear unconcerned. The last thing he needed was another thing to feel bad about. Of course I wanted him to come with me, but I wasn't going to press the issue. Not again. Not when his impending suicide was such a delicate subject and my asking might push him away.

But I knew I still hadn't tried everything I could to stop him. I couldn't let him destroy himself. Couldn't he see how *wonderful* he was? What was there left to do? Was there any hope? Rose's words bobbed to the surface of my mind. I could always call his parents. Maybe he could be hospitalized. Forced to get professional help. There may be drugs for this. Anything to keep him around.

"And speaking of parents, I want to hear more about yours. They still live in Las Vegas, right?" Adrien nodded. "Remind me of their names."

He laughed. "Why would you want to know their names?"

Okay, this wasn't going to be that easy. Maybe if I found out where he lived, I could find a phone number and talk to one of his roommates. He had to have roommates. No one our age could afford living alone unless they were rich. "So...Just out of curiosity, where do you live?" I said, keeping my tone light and casual. "I feel like we've known each other forever and I've never even seen your place."

He studied my face carefully. I knew then he'd figured me out. He was too smart. Thankfully, he didn't get ticked this time. He let it go and changed the subject.

"Did you get around to reading my stories?"

"Yes, I read them all."

"All of them?"

"You really kill me," I said. "You're funny, but in a subtle, clever way. I love your dry humor. It's refreshing. And your metaphors. You're very talented. I'm surprised you're not published yet."

He pursed his lips as his brows rose. "Wow, was I fishing for compliments?"

"I'm being honest. You really have what it takes. You're going to be a hotshot writer someday! It'll all go to your head and you'll lose your endearing humility. Ugh. It'll be tragic." I laughed. "So forget what I said. I love you the way you are: humble and self-deprecating—"

I stopped cold, realizing I'd slipped and confessed my love for him. Did he catch that? My flushing cheeks betrayed me again. Wasn't there a magic pill for this? An anti-blushing ointment?

"I love you, too, September," Adrien said so softly, I wondered if I imagined it. For a few seconds I could've sworn he was going to kiss me. His soft warm hand inched up my arm, giving me instant goose bumps. It trailed over my shoulder and stopped and rested gently on my neck, his thumb toying with my throat, my cheek, my jaw. His green eyes—his beautiful, beautiful baby grass green eyes—caught and held mine, then wandered down to my mouth and back to my eyes. My lips were on fire as he began closing the gap between us. At that point I was aching to feel his mouth on mine. A dizzy rush came over me. He was so close I could smell his soapy sandalwood scent.

For a moment I forgot Mary was in the room and I could've screamed at her for her rotten timing.

"Yahtzee anyone?" she said, an eyebrow raised, her lips in a twist.

I settled on hitting her in the face with a throw pillow.

***

I promised to get off work early to meet Adrien and Mary at Blue Moon to see Keaton's new band, Foolish Thing Desire, perform. I dressed up for the occasion, going for a boho-meets-rock look, wearing a paisley burgundy dress, cat eyeliner and stylish edgy black boots.

It was really strange to see all of the members of The Striped

Goat—everyone but Abby—in a new band, with a new lead singer, some guy I'd never even met.

But weirder than that was the way Adrien behaved after our almost-kiss. Distant wouldn't be a strong enough word. Maybe more like aloof. Although originally he wanted to spend the day with me, "his favorite girl," he'd said, he apparently had something "important" come up. He did agree to meet with me after work for the gig, but I almost wish he hadn't.

Blue Moon, an all-ages club and popular hangout for hipsters, punks, goths and artsy types, was just a couple miles from my apartment. The Striped Goat played there a lot on weekdays. The inside, a small hole in the wall, or more like a dark cave, smelled of sickly sweet Italian soda, sweat and e-cigs. Unstable blue cocktail tables, along with mismatched stools dotted the room. A few people sat at the bar, including a guy who reminded me of Chris and a touchy-feely couple sharing an Italian soda. Only a handful of people were here to support the band, including Tyrone's parents, which was a surprise. They'd always frowned on his dreams of being a musician and thought of it as a silly phase he'd eventually grow out of. His parents' haute couture apparel looked out of place in the seedy club.

The band played a slow song that dripped like sap as I walked in. Their guitars nearly collided on the minuscule stage, which was framed by heavy blue velvet curtains. A glittery half-moon hung low over the band, almost knocking Marcus's top hat off. I was surprised to see how everyone had changed. Marcus had finally chopped his sparse ponytail off. Tyrone wasn't so skinny anymore. He'd been working out. Keaton looked about the same, but his eyes gave away sadness, something I'd never seen in The Striped Goat days. The accident had forced us all to grow up too soon. The new lead singer was impressive, although I didn't want to admit it. His voice was low and powerful. He was annoyingly attractive and charismatic, too. I'd hoped he'd be horrible because it was painful to see Abby so easily replaced.

No, no one could replace her. We all knew that. But life marched on without her—a bittersweet fact.

I spotted Mary and Adrien at one of the tables in the front. Mary wore a black corset dress with a lacy choker. Her hair was a shocking pink now. Adrien dressed up for the occasion and wore a vintage black (gasp!) leather jacket, combat boots and an olive green felt hat. A green scarf was the cherry on top that made him look like a stylish European.

"Hey," I said, sliding in between them, sitting on an empty stool with a crack in the vinyl.

"Hey, glad you made it," Mary said, squeezing my hand.

Adrien's gaze met mine briefly and he smiled, but it didn't reach his eyes. He looked more troubled than I'd ever seen him.

"Are you okay?" I asked him.

He shrugged and rubbed his nose. "I'm fine."

We exchanged fewer than a dozen words for the rest of the night. Adrien sat as stiff as an overly starched shirt, his arms folded, his jaw tight. He kept his eyes mostly duct taped to the band, letting them wander over to me only a couple of times.

Previously, I was in a great mood. At work Chris was unusually silly, acting like a drunk stand-up comedian. We'd joked around the whole time. I left with sore stomach and cheek muscles from laughing so much. But a superhuman-sized steel-toed boot squashed my spirits as I watched the band play brilliantly without Abby and on top of all of that, Adrien was giving me an Arctic shoulder.

Had I made the whole thing up? The almost-kiss? The confession of love? He did say it rather quietly. It was more than possible I misheard him, had misread the whole thing. I thumbed through our past several days together. Had I said something wrong? Was it because I tried to find out his parents' names and where he lived?

I realized it could be something else entirely. Maybe he was pulling away because he *did* love me and it hurt too much when he knew he couldn't follow through. He knew he wasn't sticking around.

Thoughts turned around and around in my head like a washing machine gone haywire. I *had* to let this go—I was going to make myself sick again. I sucked in several deep breaths until I began choking on my own saliva. I thought I was going to die coughing when Mary started pounding on my back and then finally Adrien fetched me icy cold bottled water from the bar and escorted me outside, where we were greeted by crisp night air.

When I started shivering he took off his leather jacket and draped it around my shoulders.

"Thanks."

For the first time tonight he finally noticed my outfit. "You look really good tonight. I love your dress."

I was going to say that he did too, but I was feeling too grumpy now. Instead I stared at pink gum smashed into the concrete and played with the zipper of his jacket.

"You okay?" he asked, concern and amusement molding his face. The club's sign cast a strange electric blue glow on us both. We could smell liquor and cigarette smoke coming from the club next door. Music from the two clubs blended together in a chaotic mess that only amplified my bad mood.

"I'll be fine," I snapped, pulling his jacket around me tighter.

He took several deep breaths, opened his mouth then snapped it shut. He shoved his hands in his pockets, threw his head back in frustration and peered at the coal black sky before finally meeting my gaze. "September, we need to talk."

"Oh really? You say that now after practically ignoring me all night," I said, unable to mask the irritation in my voice.

"Look, I'm sorry—"

I shook my head. "I've gotta go."

He gestured to his car across the street. "Let me give you a ride home."

"I'm more than happy to grab a cab," I said, stubbornly raising an arm. And as if fate was on my side, an eager taxi with an older Indian man immediately pulled over. I hopped in and slammed the door before Adrien could protest. Upbeat Indian music filled my ears, reminding me of our first date and how Adrien ditched me in the end.

He waved goodbye, worry and frustration written all over his handsome face.

I looked away, pretending the glare on the window obscured my view.

***

Abby,

I'm really losing it. I'm allowing myself to really, really like this Adrien guy. Okay, actually, I love him, too. If you were here, I'd ask you to talk me out of it, wake me up, shake some sense into me. Maybe this will have to do:

Ten Reasons Why I Don't Love Adrien Gray

1. He has major commitment issues.

2. He talks with his mouth full (of food), especially when he gets excited.

3. He eats meat. You ate meat, too and so did John, but that's NOT the same.

4. He's a tease. He almost kissed me a couple of times. He never follows through.

5. Which brings me to this: he never finishes what he starts. Okay, maybe he does, but not where kissing's involved.

6. He smells TOO good. Why is that a bad thing, you ask? (See numbers 4 &5).

7. He's Baggage Boy. He could fill an entire train with his baggage. He needs some serious psychological help and refuses to get it.

8. He wears green all the time. So what if it's my favorite color? It's WEIRD.

9. He's moody.

10. He is, I mean, was a car salesman. So there MUST be some tacky side of him he's hiding from me.

25

"I'm sorry I was so moody yesterday," Adrien said, grabbing a Phillips screwdriver out of his rusting metal tool box, trying to make sense of the slabs of wood in front of him.

It was a yucky overcast day, making my apartment look dark and gloomy. New Order was playing softly in the background. A warm, soft Tiger was curled up on my lap. I stroked the smooth hair between his ears, where he liked it the most. His claws expanded and contracted, a sign of contentment.

"Moody is an understatement. Try unfriendly. Standoffish. Indifferent," I said, pulling an Erasure record out of its soiled sleeve after Tiger tired of being touched and strolled into the kitchen.

That morning Hannah brought over two big boxes of Abby's vintage vinyl collection she'd found while cleaning out their garage. Apparently, they'd forgotten all about them. She thought she'd swing by to see if I wanted them before she made a trip to Goodwill. Adrien enthusiastically agreed to assemble a bookcase that would house the enormous collection. Afterward, we'd clean and organize them alphabetically.

He laughed. "Okay, the first two may be fair, but I promise you I'm not indifferent. Not even close. I care about you and your feelings."

"Then why were you…?"

"Being such a jerk last night?" He squeezed his eyes shut. "Because I almost *kissed* you, September. Because I said…some things which could be irresponsible and hurtful in this type of situation. I don't want to hurt you. It's the last thing I want to do."

"The I'm-going-to-off-myself-in-four-days type of situation?" I said so bitterly, I tasted poison in my mouth.

His hands shot up in defense. "Hey. You knew who I was the day you met me but you asked me out anyway. I laid it all on the table. It's not my fault you find me so charming and irresistible," he added to lighten the mood.

"Ha, ha," I said, pulling out a Celebrate the Nun record.

"Whoa. Celebrate the Nun? That's pretty rare. Some of this stuff has got to be worth a ton," he said, admiring it for a moment.

I stood and jerked open the front room window. "It's getting dusty in here."

Cool city air drifted into the room. We could hear a dog barking and an old man swearing from the sidewalk below.

I sat down, cross-legged on the tired Oriental rug running a finger over the remaining boxed records.

"What are we going to do then?"

"The right thing to do is go our separate ways—as much as I don't want to. I don't want to hurt you anymore than I already have. I shouldn't be spending so much time with you. It's not healthy and it's definitely not fair. I guess I've put you in a hard spot."

"That's the understatement of the year," I said. "Maybe you *should* go. Maybe that would be best."

"If that's what you want, I'll honor your wishes," he said, getting up.

"Come on, you know I can't stand to be away from you." I

grabbed his pant leg and pulled him back down.

"I feel the exact same way. You're annoyingly bewitching. You've cast some creepy spell on me, woman," he said, sighing theatrically.

What I wanted to say was: "Okay, prove it. All your words, your declaration of love—they're meaningless because you are choosing death over me. Prove you really mean it. Stay, Adrien. Stay." But a promise was a promise. And I learned the hard way what happens when I say the wrong things, when I push.

So instead I said, "Then we're back to the beginning. What are we going to do?" And the stupid frustration grew inside like a noxious weed.

Adrien frowned. "Enjoy each other while we can?"

***

"Too frilly," Mary said, scrunching her nose. "I liked the black one better."

"I'm going to have to agree with Mary. Too frilly," Adrien said, giving me an exaggerated thumbs down.

"You're right. It is a little girly for my taste," I said. "What would I do without you two here?"

Adrien and Mary insisted they come with me dress shopping. Plus, Mary needed to find a new winter coat and Adrien wanted to check out a couple of used bookstores. He said he wanted to find his favorite childhood book to leave for his godson (yes, he was really going through with this—he even wrote an unofficial will). Then the three of us would try out a new local Ethiopian restaurant, something on Adrien's bucket list. We'd already hit a few outlet stores in SoHo (I never like paying full price for anything), without any luck. I needed to find the perfect outfit to wear to my parents' party. If I was going to show up alone, at the very least I'd show up looking hot. I wanted John to get down on his knees, groveling for my forgiveness, wishing he'd never let me go. Or at the very least, I wanted there to be some proper gawking.

Ducking into the dressing room with new carpet smell, I began feeling a mounting frustration. I'd already tried on at least a dozen dresses. Many of them looked "good", but I wasn't looking for "good." I wanted a dress that wowed. I had only one more left to try on—a small brown one.

"Okay little brown number. Please be the one," I whispered, feeling more than ready to move on with my day. Unlike my sister, I was not a self-proclaimed shopaholic. As I pulled the froufrou dress off, someone tapped on the door, making me jump.

"Try this one on," I heard Adrien say. He tossed a red chiffon dress over the door.

"Adrien! What are you doing in the women's dressing room? You could get arrested or something," I said, covering myself up with the frilly dress I'd just taken off. My cheeks were on fire, my heart pelting my ribs. Did he see me through the crack on the side of the door? Today wasn't a good underwear day. I wore my last resort pair, the boring white ones with a hole in the hip, due to my neglecting the towering pile of laundry at home. (How could I possibly think about laundry at a time like this?)

"You're right. I'm leaving now. But try on that dress."

"Fine! Just go!"

"Cute underwear."

"I hate you!" Did he really look, or was he just teasing me?

It took me a few moments to regain my composure and slip on the red dress. I didn't breathe as I turned around and caught my image in the full-length mirror. The dress had a plunging V-neck with an A-line knee-length skirt. It looked like something from an old movie, something Marilyn Monroe or Audrey Hepburn might wear during a night out on the town. The cut flattered me perfectly, showed just enough skin to be sexy but not desperate and the crimson red played up my brown eyes and fair skin. I felt beautiful. Adrien was right. This was the one.

Feeling self-conscious about modeling the dress for Mary and Adrien, I considered slipping back into my jeans and t-shirt. But I knew they wouldn't go for that. Mary, especially. She was stubborn, that girl. And Adrien would be disappointed he missed out on seeing me in the dress he picked out. So I sucked in a breath and wandered out of the dressing room and greeted my friends, who were sitting on a bench just outside the dressing room, waiting.

Mary whistled so loud, it put a flirty Italian man to shame. Everyone in the store turned to look, including a couple of men. One, who was old enough to be my grandpa even winked at me. Certain my cheeks matched my dress, I was tempted to dig a deep hole in the floor and stay there until closing time. Okay this was weird. I was definitely not used to all this attention.

"September, you look hot. Ultra hot," Mary said, nodding in approval.

"You do look good," Adrien agreed, standing up to get a better view. I was perfectly aware of his eyes trailing up and down the dress.

"You have to get it. It's the one," she urged.

I contorted my body to find the price tag. "I don't know. This one's a little out of my budget."

"I picked it out, let me buy it," Adrien said, his eyes still cemented on me.

"I couldn't let you—"

"Please. I insist."

"Adrien, I—"

"It's not like I'll be needing the money," he said, reminding me again of the thing I was trying so hard to forget.

"Come on, Tember, let the guy buy it for you," Mary said.

"Okay, okay. Thank you, Adrien. Really, I mean it," I said, turning to him, my face probably blood red now. I started for the dressing room when he called after me. I turned around.

"September, you're beautiful," he said, his eyes smoldering.

***

At work I felt like my head would explode from thinking too much. My heart had had better days, too. It had already been broken twice this year, but now, what remained of it was being beaten, stabbed and thrashed and then tossed in a garbage disposal for good measure. I felt a canker sore coming on, too. The words Adrien and I exchanged while going through Abby's vinyl, ran over and over in my head like a wind-up toy. The truth was I had only three days left with Adrien. *If* I couldn't stop him from self-destructing.

Three short days.

I knew as each day passed, it would hurt a little more to be with him. As I drew closer to the end, I stupidly fell deeper and deeper in love with him. There was only one thing I could do. I had to stop him. I had to change his mind. But how? He said he loved me, too. Wasn't that enough? Wasn't our evolving relationship reason enough for him to stick around?

Apparently not.

Logically I knew I should stop seeing him. But the more I thought about it, the more I realized I wanted to stay by his side as long as he'd let me. If I'd known in second grade, the day I met Abby, our friendship would end abruptly and tragically eleven years later, would I have still chosen to befriend her? And would I have loved her any less, knowing our days were numbered, knowing in the end I'd be faced with almost unbearable heartbreak and grief? Her death just about killed me. This was no doubt the hardest year of my life—times a million— but I'd do it all over again. It was worth it, every single minute of it because I can't even begin to imagine what my life would've been like without her.

The same applied to Adrien. Maybe I was crazy. Maybe I'd feel differently after he was gone. Maybe it was a tiny smudge of hope which kept me anticipating his visits every day—hope he'd get some help and choose to stick around for a while.

"Are you okay? You're pretty quiet tonight," Chris said, emptying the garbage, concern etched all over his lovable face.

"Oh. I'm fine. I just have a lot to think about I guess," I said, working on a stubborn brown spot on a blue tile wall.

"You know you've been working on that same spot for the last ten minutes, right?"

I looked up, stunned. "Have I?"

"You're not still going out with that suicidal guy, are you?"

He made it sound so ridiculous.

I tossed the rag I was using onto the yellow cart. "That's none of your business."

"I thought so. Why are you doing this to yourself? Do you *like* to be miserable?"

I tossed him a dirty look but he didn't notice. "Of course not. It's...you wouldn't understand."

He lined the trash can with a new plastic bag, knotting the corner. "Try me."

I picked up a bottle of Windex and a fresh rag and started wiping down the mirror, cringing at the squeaking sounds the damp rag made against the glass.

"Actually, maybe you *would* understand. I'm not the only one who's not in an ideal situation, who is maybe sabotaging my happily ever after," I said, remembering his confession about Megan. "You don't love her. And yet here you are, still dating her, living a lie. To me that's worse."

"It's not the same at all. I was genuinely in love with Megan at one point. And *happy*—before she started smothering the life out of me. But what are you doing with this guy? You've known him for a couple of weeks—or less than that—and you really have no obligation to be nice to him. He's probably just using you. Having his way with you before he—"

"That's not true. I'm not the kind of girl who—I wouldn't even let him try—Chris, Adrien hasn't even *kissed* me. He's been a perfect gentleman."

He seemed genuinely surprised—and relieved.

"And anyway," I said, "I still have hope I'll somehow be able to convince him to get some help. There still may be a way. There's *got* to be. I mean, he can't be in his right mind. And I'm not doing this to be nice. It's so much more than that. Adrien's a really special guy. He's so talented and sensitive and generous and—"

"Don't make me puke," Chris said, obviously joking. Or at least half-joking. He exhaled. "Okay."

"Okay what?"

"Okay, I get that you gotta do what you gotta do. Just keep in mind there are other men out there. Other more *deserving* men."

26

We spent Adrien's last night together at Coney Island.

Originally he was going to kill himself in two days, the day of my parents' party. But, much to my dismay, he pushed the date up a day. He'd finished the note early, plus he said it would be better for both of us if he didn't draw things out and left earlier.

I was stunned when he told me. And really angry. I thought I'd have two full weeks with him and now he was cutting our time together short.

The thought of losing Adrien, the thought of this being our final time together was hard to comprehend. Unbearable to think about. So I did my very best *not* to think about it, not to think about cruel reality following me around like a lunatic jester. It stalked me, pointing and laughing, mocking me for being such a reckless fool. *You should have never agreed to spend time with this guy*, the voice said. *Now you're losing someone you love all over again. You stupid, stupid girl.*

I saw it in Adrien's eyes, too. He didn't have to speak. I saw the anguish, the being torn by two choices: life with me, or an eternal, sweet sleep, away from the pain and suffering that preyed upon him for so long, that had made his life unbearable enough he felt ending it was the only solution.

I hadn't been to Coney Island in years. My parents brought April and me here every summer when we were growing up. I tasted the familiar salty sea air on my lips, inhaled the nostalgic smells of hot dogs, popcorn, pizza, cotton candy. But there was a thickness in the air that pulled my heart down into my stomach, an empty feeling despite the bustling crowd.

We distracted ourselves for a while trying different rides, some of them for the first time since I was too short to meet the height requirements when I was little. The nearly one-hundred-year-old rollercoaster, The Cyclone, stole my breath away. We rode it three times. We played carnival games. Adrien, who was highly skilled at Whac-A-Mole it turns out, won me a giant stuffed banana wearing a bowtie and a goofy grin. I thought the gesture was cute and planned to keep the banana forever. I kicked his butt at skeeball and used my tickets to buy Adrien Pop Rocks and a dinosaur eraser. He shared the candy. We laughed as the tart strawberry candy exploded in our mouths, bringing us back to a simpler time. We did silly poses in the old-fashioned photo booth.

"Look," Adrien said, pointing to the gorgeous orange and purple streaked sky, which made a perfect backdrop for the majestic Ferris wheel (AKA Deno's Wonder Wheel) ahead.

"Pretty," I replied.

Dancing lights framed the rides and game tents of my childhood. Emotions whirled inside me as I took in the surreal landscape around me. It was like I was in a dream. A really, really strange dream. It was a magical night. And it was a terrible night. Charles Dickens' words echoed in my mind: *It was the best of times, it was the worst of times...*

"Let's go on the Ferris wheel," I said, grabbing his hand, pulling him forward. I hoped the impending night would camouflage my crimson cheeks. I remembered it was on his list, the things he wanted to do before he died: "Kiss a girl at the very top of a Ferris wheel," he'd said. I touched my lips, anticipating the kiss I ached for. Would he kiss me tonight? I wanted him more than anything.

"Okay." Adrien shrugged. Maybe he'd forgotten the list. Or maybe kissing was the last thing on his mind. He played with my hand and answered my questions about Las Vegas and what it was like growing up there as we waited in line. For some reason I pictured Vegas as just The Strip—one long row of casinos. He assured me that it was like any other place to live, with home improvement stores, malls and everything else you'd expect a city to have.

When it was finally our turn, he grasped my elbow, helping me into the rocking seat first before sliding in next to me. My heart started to race; I have a mild fear of heights. I hugged my stuffed banana for moral support, rubbing its fur under my chin. Adrien casually threw his arm around me, protecting me against the clammy autumn air.

"You cold?" he asked when I shivered.

"Yes," I said.

He slid in closer until our sides touched. We sat saying nothing, watching the shady-looking Ferris wheel operator with tightly coiled hair load people into the other seats as we inched higher and higher into the darkening sky.

To anyone around us, we might've appeared to be two young people newly in love, the perfect couple, the kind you see in those cliché romantic comedies or on Instagram. But no one could know the truth—that this would be our last night together.

That things were ending before they really had a chance to begin.

On the outside looking in, this could be a page in a fairytale book. I'd finally found my handsome prince, my soul mate. We were young and healthy and beautiful. The night around us couldn't have been more magical. But...I wanted Adrien, more than anything. And Adrien wanted death. It was an intriguing love triangle of sorts. An ugly, twisted love triangle. I felt a kaleidoscope of emotion turning inside. I was angry at Adrien for choosing death over me. Bitterly angry. But more so, angry at myself for being more than willing to be a part of this. I was heartbroken. After losing Abby, I didn't think there was anything left to break. But my heart had grown bigger, doubled in size and now there was twice as much heart to be trampled on.

All of that aside, I was burning up with love. (Or was it lust? Honestly, it was probably a little of both.) The intensity overwhelmed me, sucking all of my pride, all of my energy. I was determined. I was going to kiss Adrien Gray tonight on this Ferris wheel, whether he liked it or not. Nothing would stop me. And maybe my love would be enough. Maybe Adrien would wake up, snap out of this dark spell and realize there was something to live for. But it was more than I could hope for and knowing Adrien, there was nothing left I could do to change his mind.

At the very least, I wanted a goodbye kiss.

He gazed at me, sadness etched all over his perfect face, as the huge wheel lifted us higher and higher. I met his gaze, here and there and then looked away. Just as we were approaching the top, I opened my mouth to ask for the one thing I wanted the most, other than Adrien himself. A kiss. But he spoke first.

"I'm so sorry, September. I really shouldn't have let you be involved in all this. I don't know what I was thinking. I'm hurting you just like I hurt them. I'm doing it all over again."

"Shhh. Adrien—"

"Wait, let me finish. If there was any way I could take these past days back, I would. Not because they weren't some of the best days of my life, because they were. Not because I don't love you, because I do. But because I was wrong to let you be a part of this. If there was any way I could make it up to you, I would. I don't regret meeting you, September. I only regret the hurt I caused you…and will yet cause you."

"Anything?" I bit my lip, feeling sick with longing. Confused, his eyes swept my face. "You said you'd do anything to make it up to me," I said, feeling my cheeks burn again.

"September, you know I can't cancel my plans." He said it so nonchalantly, like he was speaking of travel plans or a reservation to a nice restaurant.

"I—I didn't mean that. You know I want more than anything for you to change your mind—now more than ever. But I know I can't talk you out of it. I tried everything I could think of, apart from tying you up and locking you in a closet."

He smiled, apparently amused by the thought. "Then what do you want?"

"I want—I—I want…"

He gently nudged my arm. "Come on, just say it."

I let the words fall out. "I want you to kiss me."

His eyes grew into the size of ping-pong balls. "What?"

I swallowed twice. "I think you heard me."

"*I* want to kiss you, September, more than anything. Believe me. I've wanted to for days. But it wouldn't be fair. I don't want to hurt you anymore than I already have."

"Please. I love you. This is torture." Now at the very top of the Ferris wheel, my hope peaked. I pleaded with Adrien with my eyes. His lips seemed to have a lunar pull on mine. His face was sheer heaven in the moonlight. The view around us didn't compare to the boy sitting beside me.

He whispered, "I wasn't planning this. I didn't think I'd fall so hard—so deeply in love with you."

"Then stay with me. Don't leave me."

He hesitated. I counted the beats of my throbbing heart,

waiting. One...two...three...

Hope began dwindling as the perfect moment passed. We began moving downward, back to earth.

"I wish I could. I promise you I would if I could. You're the best thing to happen to me in years. Well, ever, actually. But there's something you don't know, something that would change your mind about me."

"Nothing could change my mind about you. Adrien. Please. Stay."

"Even if I did, even if you knew the truth and accepted it, it wouldn't change the fact that I'm a monster. I destroy everything I love. Everything I touch. I'll destroy you, too. It's better for us both if I leave. Trust me on this one."

"I want to trust you. I do trust you. But things are rarely as bad as they seem. Five, ten, twenty years from now you won't see any of this the same way." He shook his head. "Tell me what it is. We'll deal with it. Together," I pleaded.

"I can't." He turned away from me.

My eyes welled up. "Then...at least...kiss me."

"I can't hurt you. I love you too much to hurt you anymore." He smiled sadly, lowered his head, letting his eyes fall to the balled-up fists in his lap.

Before I could open my mouth, the machine operator opened the side of the seat. "This way please," he said, guiding us off the ride.

***

Adrien offered to buy me dinner, but I wasn't hungry, although I hadn't eaten since breakfast. Food was the furthest thing from my mind. So he bought himself a corndog and scarfed it down. How could he eat at a time like this?

Without fully realizing it, we wandered away from the lights, away from the people, onto the beach, which was quiet this time of year. Only a small family dipping their toes in the water and a few teenagers making out on beach towels were in the area. We found a private spot and kicked off our shoes and let the wet, gritty sand enclose the bottoms of our feet, sucking us into the earth. We could hear the water softly lapping and seagulls chattering. Adrien threw his arm around my waist as we strolled along the edge of the shore.

"Did you really finish your note?" I asked, feeling defeat creep up on me like a jungle cat.

He nodded. "Yesterday."

"Then why didn't you...?"

"I had to say goodbye first. You would've killed me otherwise."

I rolled my eyes. "Very funny."

"*I* wanted to say goodbye," he said, tightening his grip around my waist.

"How very thoughtful of you." I didn't bother to mask the sarcasm in my voice.

"I'm sorry," he whispered, stopping mid-stride and turning to face me. He enclosed my hands in his, his skin warm to the touch.

"I am, too." I studied his tormented face, consuming every detail. This would be my last chance to see it—in the flesh. "How are you going to...do it?" My voice trembled.

"I'd rather not say." He pursed his lips. "You don't need to live with the image in your head." I was thankful for that. I guess it was better not to know.

"Are you scared?"

He laughed nervously. "Scared as hell. Scared of right be-fore—how much pain will I be in before I go? Scared of what's after. Heaven? Hell? Or maybe nothing. Maybe when I'm gone, I'm just…gone."

I squeezed my eyes shut, swallowing back tears. Heaven. I wanted to believe in heaven. I wasn't religious, but it was a kinder, more bearable thought than the alternative. "Tomorrow then?"

"Tomorrow."

"Morning? Noon? Night?"

"I haven't decided."

We stopped to watch the moon paint the ocean a vibrant yellow-gold. We could hear kids laughing and faint carnival music playing in the distance. The music seemed to be taunting us. Cheerful music for a far from cheerful evening.

I wanted to leave then. I had nothing left. Like fireworks, emotions erupted then fizzled inside of me for too long and now I was just tired. So, so tired. I was ready to pull away, free myself of Adrien's gentle grasp. Sleep. I wanted to sleep for days. Months. Wake up when things stopped hurting so damn much.

"I think I'm going to go home now."

This seemed to surprise him. His eyes bored into mine, his lips parted slightly. "If that's what you want," he said, although he kept holding my hands.

I shrugged. "I think there's nothing left to say."

"September…you're right," he said, his shoulders sinking. "Nothing left to say."

I took a shaky breath and collected the courage to say what I've wanted to say for days. I didn't have to keep my promise anymore. Screw promises. "One last thing. You say you don't want to hurt me. You say you don't want to hurt anyone anymore. And suicide's your solution?" He looked at me expectantly. "If you kill yourself, you'll be hurting *everyone*. Everyone who loves you. Your parents, your brother, your friends, your co-workers. Your godson. Probably me the most."

He dropped my hands. "What do you want from me?"

"You know what I want. Change your mind. Get some help. Choose life. Choose me."

"You promised, September. You promised you wouldn't try to talk me out of it," he said, his eyes pleading.

I growled. "I'm past caring about stupid promises."

"You don't know what it's like for me. You don't know what I'm forced to live with every day, who I see when I look in the mirror. I'm a monster."

"You're not a monster. You're sweet and gentle and funny. You're beautiful, in every sense of the word."

"I've...I..." He shook his head. "Will you settle for a kiss?"

"The moment's passed." I crossed my arms. "It's too late for—"

Before I could say anything more, he caught me by the small of the back and pulled my body close to his. He hesitated, our mouths inches apart. He was so close I could feel his hot breath on my lips.

"I really shouldn't do this," he whispered so softly, I strained to hear him over the crashing waves. I squeezed my eyes shut in anticipation, my breath labored, my body trembling.

He kissed me wildly, passionately, like I'd never been kissed before. I could faintly taste the corndog on his breath, but I didn't mind. I returned the kiss, hungry and eager. After a while, his mouth trailed down to my jaw, to my neck and back up to earlobe. I got chills on top of chills. I clung to his back, pressing him closer to me. I couldn't hold him tight enough.

I wanted him to be mine—forever.

Just when I thought I'd collapse from the intensity of the moment, he pulled away. I saw he was trembling, too, as he searched my face frantically.

"Wow. That was…" I touched my throbbing lips, stunned.

He laughed, hooking his thumbs into the belt loops of my jeans. I liked it. It felt like a very boyfriend thing to do.

"Wow is right. I should've kissed you a long time ago."

We watched an older couple walking a Border Collie pass by, leaving three sets of prints in the sand. The white haired man winked at us, making me flush in embarrassment.

When we were alone once more he cradled my face and kissed me a second time. This kiss was more deliberate, more tender. It was so gentle, so sweet, I could almost cry. The way he held my face, so carefully, made me feel like I meant everything to him.

I wanted to kiss him forever. I could've kissed him forever, but my mind forced my body to pull away. I didn't want this to hurt anymore than it had to. Reluctantly, I pulled away.

"I better go now," I said, feeling a little dizzy, stumbling like a drunk in the sand. "Goodbye, Adrien."

"September?" I froze, a drop of hope, like a butterfly, fluttered inside me. Adrien frowned. Looking defeated, he shoved his hands in his pockets. "I'm sorry. About everything."

I was out of words—and the last of the hope dissipated, disappearing into nothingness. I peered at him one last time, drinking in his glorious face in the moonlight, before turning to go.

I walked away, dragging heavy feet in the sand—hot, bitter tears burning my cheeks.

In the morning I stayed in bed for hours, clinging to the banana Adrien won me at Coney Island last night. I drifted in and out of sleep, being plagued by strange dreams. Each time I'd awake, I'd hope the part about Adrien possibly already being dead was just part of one of the bad dreams. Each time reality struck me like a punch to the gut, knocking the air out, all over again.

I considered staying in bed for the rest of the day. What reason did I have to get up and face the day? The boy I'd fallen fast and hard for was ending his life—if he hadn't already—and there was nothing left I could do about it.

I thought about calling the cops, but Adrien never gave me his number or address. I'd tried other things earlier in the week: Searching for his parents online. There were too many Grays in Las Vegas. Following Adrien home. But instead of heading home, he walked into a bookstore. I waited outside for two hours until closing time. The oddest thing happened. I never saw him leave. Had he slipped out a back door? Did he know I was following him? I went back to Mike's Okay Cars to ask for Adrien's number, his address, any clue to help me find him, but it was closed. A sign taped in the window, written with a sharpie, read: *Closed for a family emergency*.

I hadn't slept much the night before. I bawled like an injured toddler until Mary threatened to take me to the hospital to have me sedated. "What's wrong? Is it Hot Waffle Guy? Did he break up with you?"... "Is it John and April? I'll beat them up for you, I swear I will. Just say the word."... "Is it Abby? I miss her, too. *So much.*" I said nothing in reply, too worked up to tell her the story. Mary finally climbed in bed beside me and held me like my mom used to until I fell asleep.

When I finally did get out of bed, I could barely shovel a few spoonfuls of soggy Cheerios into my mouth. Between my trembling hands and my stomach feeling like it'd become home to dozens of snakes, I didn't even bother with lunch. Horrifying images of Adrien shot through my mind, a slide show gone awry. The images stalked me throughout the endless morning like the paparazzi. Images of him killing himself in every possible way— ODing, slitting his wrists, hanging himself, carbon monoxide poisoning, jumping from a bridge or tall building—the list was endless. Thoughts of him being all alone in the last minutes of his life. Images of his long body lying in a coffin.

And then there were the memories. I thought about the day we met at Anderson Art and Frame. The day we formally introduced ourselves at Tim's Coffee. Our first date. The morning he made Mary and me waffles. Our photo shoot. Dress shopping. His flu survival kit. The mix CD he'd made me. His smile that turned my insides into mush. The carnival. I thought about our kiss more times than I'd care to admit.

I tried busying myself, attempting to keep my mind off of him, but nothing worked. I scrubbed every square inch of every tile in the bathroom. I organized the Tupperware. I spent the better part of the afternoon watching *Friends* reruns on TV, but my mind kept roaming back to Adrien.

At three I took a shower. By then I was so exhausted, I could barely raise my arms to wash my hair. Like an unsupported clay sculpture, my wobbly legs gave out. I finished the shower sitting on the floor of the tub, bawling like a baby.

The thought that Adrien could already be dead made me sick. Sick, sick, sick.

He could be gone. Now. Forever.

I fell onto my bed, clutching my chest and suffered through a full-blown panic attack. Or could it have been a heart attack? At this point I no longer cared.

I threw up three times as I dressed myself for work, once on my foot, once on my poor cat. The third I managed to get in the toilet.

"You look *horrible*," Mary said, frowning at my bloodshot eyes, my red-and-white crazy quilt skin. "September, please just tell me what's wrong. Maybe there's something I can do to help."

"I'm okay," I lied, smiling weakly. I never got around to telling her about Adrien's impending suicide.

Mary, who was playing with her keys, sat them down on my nightstand. "I have work in twenty minutes, but maybe I should stay here to take care of you. You've never looked worse, not even when you barfed up a lung at the cemetery."

"Don't worry about it. I'm going to work, too," I said, running a comb through my wet hair. I *had* to see Chris. I had to do *something* to get my mind off Adrien.

"But you look like hell, like the angel of death is hovering—"

The comb slipped from my fingers when the doorbell rang. Who could that be? Chris? Mrs. Watkins? One of Mary's friends?

"You sit. I'll get it," she said, shoving me lovingly onto the bed.

"Mary, who is it?" I called from my bedroom, wiping puke off Tiger—who was glowering at me—with my damp bath towel. I pulled myself off the edge of the bed and stumbled into the hall, tottering my way to the door.

When I saw him at the door my heart nearly stopped.

"Adrien?" I said, confused. For several seconds I wondered if I was delusional or dreaming. This was a dream within a dream.

I bit down on my finger and yelped in pain.

This was real.

He was here. Adrien was here. Alive. In the flesh. Here.

"September?" he said, his face contorting in pain. "What have I done? You look like you've been to hell and back."

I laughed, or actually, a strange noise resembling laughter escaped my throat. I took three steps forward and collapsed in his arms. Never mind that my hair was sopping wet and I wasn't wearing even a speck of makeup. He clutched me—tight—preventing me from crumbling to the floor. His strong arms felt like heaven around me. I took in his amazing scent, the scent I never thought I'd experience again.

"You're alive," I said, delirious. I held him so close, I was probably crushing his ribs, but I didn't care. I wanted to hold onto him and never, ever, let go.

"What have I done?" he echoed, pressing his lips into my hair.

"You broke her," Mary said matter-of-factly, sliding into her black velvet jacket.

"I broke her," Adrien agreed. He shook his head. "I'm a monster."

"I don't know what you did, but after seeing her suffer like this—yeah, you're pretty much a monster," she said, half-joking. She remembered she left her keys in my room and fetched them.

Adrien quickly stole a kiss.

I cringed when I remembered that I probably had puke breath.

"Can I trust you to take care of her while I'm gone?" she asked, slipping her keys into her pocket. He nodded. "Whatever you did—don't even *think* about doing it again," she threatened, kissing me on the cheek before leaving for work.

With ease, Adrien picked me up and carried me to the couch,

dropping me into his lap. He gently palmed the side of my face before saying, "September. I'm *so* sorry. I..." He squeezed his eyes shut, trying to find the words.

I wanted to say something, but I was paralyzed. So I settled for placing my hand on his.

"Can we go somewhere? I need some air," he said, his voice urgent. "We need to talk."

***

I endured what felt like several eternal minutes of silence as Adrien collected his thoughts. What could he possibly have to tell me? And more importantly, is he still planning on...? I squeezed my eyes shut and shuddered.

It was a crisp afternoon. For whatever reason, Adrien chose Cooper Park of all places to talk. Why a park? Why not Tim's Coffee or someplace warm? Maybe he felt this would be more private. We had a better shot at not being overheard.

Adrien and I sat shivering on a cold wooden bench. He'd grabbed a plaid blanket from his trunk which was now thrown around our shoulders. In silence we watched bundled up dog owners playing with their little fury companions a few feet away.

The air smelled of car exhaust and hints of early fall.

"What is it? You can tell me anything," I finally said, feeling exhausted from anticipation and dread. I grabbed his hand and squeezed it to encourage him.

"I'm ready to tell you why I'm..." he trailed off. My heart fluttered. I'd been waiting two weeks to hear this. But it felt much longer than that. Like almost a lifetime ago. "Remember when you asked me about my family?"

"Yes," I said weakly.

"I told you I have a brother, but what I didn't tell you was...

that I had a sister."

"Had?" I said, turning to face him.

He wouldn't meet my gaze. Instead he stared at a patch of grass near his feet.

"When I was a kid I had this huge fascination with fire. I started fires all the time. With matches, lighters, magnifying glasses. Anything I could get my hands on." He stopped, looking at something off in the distance. He swallowed a few times and collected the courage to continue. "When I was seven I snuck into my Aunt Lora's purse and borrowed a book of matches. Later when my mom and aunt ran to the grocery store, my sister and I found ourselves alone. Mom usually took us with her on her errands, but she was having a bad day and needed a break. Aunt Lora talked her into leaving us alone, telling Mom I was an unusually mature seven-year-old.

"It started out so innocent. I was just lying on my bed, striking each match, one by one, watching the flame flicker and then blowing it out before the flame could hit my fingers. But when the phone rang, I must've dropped a match because by the time I got back, the entire room was up in flames. At first I froze. I stood and watched the flames consume my room with fascination and horror. I knew I had to call 911, but I panicked. I didn't want to get in trouble. I was a *good* boy. I *never* got in trouble. Desperate for my parents' approval, I couldn't stand to see them unhappy with me. So I ran outside and hid in a bush. I didn't think my sister would be in any danger. She was napping in her bedroom. I didn't realize the fire could spread to another room. I swear I thought she'd be safe. I sat in the bush crying like a baby, spinning the wheels of my toy truck. A neighbor must've called emergency, but when the firefighters got there, it was too late. My sister was gone."

By now he was in tears, his body trembling.

"Adrien, I'm so sorry." I shook my head and squeezed his hand.

"They don't know what got to her first—the smoke or the flames."

"That's awful."

"She was four years old, September. She was so innocent, so pure. She had her whole life ahead of her. There's so much she'll never experience."

"What was her name?"

"Lily," he whispered, anguish painting his face.

"That's a beautiful name."

"It killed my parents. It was unbearable to watch. My mom blamed herself for leaving us alone. She kept saying, 'I shouldn't have left them alone, I shouldn't have left them alone.' She sunk into a deep depression, never fully recovering. My father blamed me. He couldn't *look* at me anymore. He barely spoke to me. They couldn't take it any longer; the grief destroyed their marriage. They got a divorce a year and a half later."

"I'm so sorry."

"I *killed* her. I killed my sister," he said, holding my hand so tight, it was cutting off circulation. "I tore my parents apart. I destroyed my family."

I touched the stubble on his cheek. "It's not your fault. You were just a *kid*. You need to forgive yourself."

"I don't deserve forgiveness. I can't let it go." He shoved the tears from his face.

To our left, several yards away, a young boy of six or seven missing his front teeth struggled to get his homemade blue kite to catch the wind. We watched his determined face as he encouraged his handiwork to take flight. When a gust of wind shot the flimsy paper upward after several failed attempts, his triumphant face made us chuckle.

"Would you forgive *him*? If he accidentally harmed his sister? Would he deserve a life sentence of guilt and punishment?"

"Of course not," Adrien whispered.

"You were just a *kid*," I repeated, pleading with him with my eyes.

He nodded but dropped his gaze again. "But there's something more. It's so much more than that."

I sucked in a breath and braced myself. "What is it?"

"I…can't say," he said, kicking a pebble.

"Just tell me," I pleaded, tired of secrets. I wanted to finally know the truth—all of it. Now.

He shook his head. "Later."

"Later? There are no laters for us. There are no laters! I hate you," I said, acting like a three-year-old, dropping his hand, scooting away. "I wish we never met."

Adrien winced, his green eyes pained. "I deserved that."

"I don't hate you," I whispered, my mood turning like a leaf in the wind. "You know I don't hate you. I just want you to stay. There's so much I want to say to you—*need* to say. If you'd only stick around a while longer you'd see that time has a way of healing things. Life can be beautiful, Adrien, you just need to push the dark clouds away and you'd see. If you'd just stop being so stubborn and get some help—"

"Okay," he said flatly.

"What?"

"Okay." He turned to me and grinned.

I held my breath for a moment. "I don't get it."

"My suicide plans are canceled," he said, scooting closer, tucking a strand of hair behind my ear.

"Canceled? Not postponed?" I was suspicious. It was too easy.

He shrugged. "Canceled."

I bit my lip and examined his face. "Just like that?"

"Just like that. It's why I had to see you. I couldn't get to your apartment fast enough." I was dumbfounded. I studied his face more carefully, looking for signs of lying. "I'm in love with you, September. I just can't bring myself to leave you."

What I did next surprised me as much as it did him. Before I realized it, my hand curled up into a fist and I punched him in the gut. Alarm registered on his face before he doubled over, the breath knocked out of him.

"Oh, Adrien. I'm so sorry. I didn't mean to do that, I swear," I said, laughing. "But you don't have a clue what you put me through last night, today. The last two weeks. It was pure hell."

As soon as he caught his breath, he smiled a guilty, tortured smile. "I don't deserve you, September. I'm a selfish creep. I promise you I'll *never* put you through that again. I'm here for good. If you'll have me, that is."

Tears cascaded down my face. "Of course I'll have you. All I want is you."

My whole body quaked as Adrien took me in his arms. He held me for a long time as we both cried. His soapy sandalwood scent was intoxicating. He stroked my hair and kissed me softly, over and over, making me feel drunk and dizzy. (Thankfully, I had taken a moment to brush my teeth and put on some concealer and mascara before we left.) He bit my bottom lip and tickled the back of my neck, driving me crazy. I buried my face in his shoulder as his arms pulled me in tighter. I hooked my leg over his knee and traced the lines in his palm, wondering what each crevice meant. Was I carved into his palms? Were we destined to be together? I'd never felt this way about a boy before.

I wanted to stay on this hard wooden bench forever. I wanted to freeze this moment, with our bodies entwined, our shoulders sheltered by a warm blanket.

When, if only temporarily, everything was okay.

Everyone around us sort of disappeared. Sounds blended together. The sun peeked out from behind a cloud and warmed us for a little while.

"What made you change your mind?" I asked, my voice muffled by his shoulder. I pulled away to study his face. He bit his lip and searched for the right words.

"I thought about what you said last night. That if I followed through with my plans, I'd hurt my family and friends. And I'd hurt you." He gazed at me lovingly for a moment. "I don't want to hurt anyone, anymore. I know I can't always help it. I'm human. People hurt people—that's life. But this is something I *do* have control over."

I nodded.

He continued, "I was still unsure about things this morning. As much as I love my family, as much as I love you, September…" He paused, searching for the right words. "Love isn't always enough. Love won't fix things. *You* can't fix me. I need to do this for myself…When I woke up this morning despair crept in. Darkness filled every inch of my body and soul. I thought about ending it all, right then and there in my bed. But something strange happened. A bright light—the sun, I presume—an overwhelming light, whiter than I'd ever seen in my life, came through my window and poured its warmth on me. On my face, on my chest. The warmth felt like pure love." His green eyes watered. "Then I heard a whisper. At least I thought I heard a whisper. I swore I did, but it sounds crazy now. The voice said, 'You're going to be okay.' That's it. Nothing too profound, but the light and the words bore into me, saturating me and then I just knew. I knew eventually I would be okay, that I'd pull out of this. I haven't made up my mind about God— whether he's really there or not. But this thing, this experience this morning…was much bigger than me."

"Wow," I whispered, getting goose bumps.

"It's not going to be easy. It's going to take a *lot* of work. It could take months. Years. But if you could get through losing John and Abby and find some happiness, I will—somehow—get through this."

"I know you will," I said and believed it with all my heart.

We sat saying nothing for a moment, listening to leaves flittering in the wind and distant laughter. I had a lot to digest. I still couldn't believe that I'd get what I wanted most—Adrien. He was mine. Mine to keep. I never wanted anyone the way I wanted him. But as I studied his face, I saw anxiety written all over it. There was something else. Something he wasn't telling me.

"What? What is it?"

"It's nothing."

"You're lying."

"There's something I have to tell you, September." His troubled eyes and furrowed brow worried me. "But I can't…"

"Tell me," I urged. "You can tell me anything."

He shook his head. "It's complicated."

"Come on. You told me your deepest, darkest secret. It hasn't changed the way I feel about you. If anything, I love you more."

Adrien raised an eyebrow and squeezed my knee.

We watched a little puffy bird frantically eating an old French fry plastered to the ground. Adrien tickled the inside of my arm. It felt great, but I knew it was only a ploy to distract me.

"Tell me," I repeated. He sighed, folding his arms. "You're a very stubborn man, Adrien Gray."

"I could say the same about you. Only you're not a man, thankfully," he added with a laugh.

I watched a devilish smile creep up on his lips. "What is it?" I asked, perplexed by his sudden change in mood.

"Let's play a game."

"What?" How could he want to play Scrabble or Monopoly at a time like this? He was always surprising me, but that was one of the things I loved about him.

"Starting tomorrow you have to be completely honest with me."

I pulled my brows together. "I'm *always* honest with you—"

"Here're the rules. One," he began, raising a finger. "I get to ask you whatever I want. You have to answer *all* my questions with pure, unadulterated honesty. Two. You don't get to ask any questions in reply. Not even one."

"But—"

"No buts." He placed a finger over my lips. "And then I'll tell you...the thing...after your folks' party."

"Why can't you tell me now?" Chills shot through me as his finger moved away from my mouth and traced the outline of my jaw. His green eyes bore deeply into mine.

"You'll understand later. Is it a deal?"

I moaned, frustrated and confused. I hated secrets. I knew I could make myself sick tearing it apart, analyzing it. But I was more relieved than anything. Relieved that he was here. Here to stay. Mine, hopefully for forever.

"It's a deal," I said, shaking my head. "You're a complete weirdo—and I love that about you, by the way—but it's a deal."

When we got back to his car, the sky turned to a murky, dish-water gray. As he opened the door for me, I grabbed the back of his head and pulled him in for a kiss. We kissed enthusiastically, but there was something sad about the kiss, like it would be our last one, like we were saying goodbye. I finally pulled away, catching my breath.

"Why do I get the feeling you're still leaving me?" I asked, searching for answers in his baby grass green eyes.

He was quiet for a time, his lips turned downward. Finally, he said, "I won't leave you. Ever. I promise." He said it with confidence, but a flicker of pain in his eyes had me doubting. I never could've predicted in a thousand years what he'd say after that: "But after tomorrow tonight, *you're* going to leave *me*."

***

"Is everything okay? You've been unusually quiet tonight," Chris asked as I worked up a foam on the restroom counter. Standing behind me, he watched for my response in the reflection of the dirty mirror. Tonight he wore a man bun and looked like he hadn't shaved for a couple of days. The look was becoming.

"Huh?"

"What's going on? You've scrubbed that same spot for like a year now."

"Oh. I guess I'm just worn out. Long week. Long couple of weeks. No, actually, long three months. The longest three months of my life." I sighed, wishing I could make an early date with my pillow. I was so tired. Utterly wasted. I couldn't remember a time I was more exhausted.

"You've been through a lot. With your stupid ex dumping you, with Abby. And now you're wasting your time with that loser." I heard a toilet seat slam.

Normally I would've argued, defended myself. I would have explained how everything was different now, but I didn't have even an ounce of energy left to explain the turn of events. I would tell Chris everything. Later. All I knew was that I desperately needed a good night's sleep, then tomorrow I'd get to spend the whole day with the boy I loved, the boy who'd chosen to stick around—in part to be with me. I was too worn out to let it sink in that I'd be bringing a boyfriend to my parents' party. (A boyfriend! Did that mean Adrien was my boyfriend now? I liked the sound of that.) I'd have plenty of time to feel smug tomorrow.

"What is it?" Chris asked after our ten minute break. I'd spent the break resting on a stiff sofa in the lounge, making a failed attempt to take a nap. Usually Chris and I spent our breaks together, playing cards, watching funny videos on his phone. But my relentless thoughts wouldn't leave me be. I was dying to know the final secret Adrien kept from me and why he was certain I would leave him. *Of course* I wouldn't leave him. I was too gone on him now to leave. I've never loved a guy more than I loved Adrien Gray. It would take something pretty colossal to change my mind about him. He'd have to be a member of the KKK or a puppy torturer or a neo-Nazi. What made him so sure I'd leave him? Was he really that insecure? Did he not realize how crazy about him I was?

Maybe I'd have to take a sleeping pill tonight. Rose had written me a prescription months earlier when I'd complained of insomnia. It was during the nightmare period, when I was forced to replay the accident over and over each night. I'd only used them twice but held onto the bottle just in case. Tonight might be one of those nights, tonight I may need a little something to barricade these thoughts.

I sighed. I was so tired. I probably should've just called in sick. But I would've felt like a total jerk leaving Chris with all this work to do, especially since I'd been neglecting him more lately.

"Can we talk later? I'm pooped."

Chris eyed me carefully, his face drenched in concern. "Sure. Later."

Tonight was different from any other night. For the first time since we'd met, we worked side by side in silence. Chris gave up trying to start a conversation. He put in his ear buds and listened to the classic rock stuff he loved so much. I felt kind of bad and wondered what would become of Chris and me, now that Adrien was definitely in the picture—long term.

After we finished the final restroom, I pulled off my rubber gloves and tossed them into the garbage, then kicked off my blue jumper.

"See you Monday, Chris," I said, pulling on my jacket, happy the night was over, overjoyed to become one with my bed.

"See you, September." He frowned. "Good luck with tomorrow night. I really wish I could be there for you." He rested a hand on my back for a small moment.

I knew I should've said something. He'd probably worry about me all weekend because he was that way—so sweet and selfless and concerned—and he *was* one of my closest friends. I knew I'd been selfish lately, neglecting our friendship, taking Chris for granted. And I did feel guilty about it. But the image of my snuggly bed pulled me away from doing the right thing, the considerate thing.

One more thing pulling me away from Chris.

"Your all-time favorite song?"

"With Or Without You by U2."

"That's a good one," Adrien said, nodding in approval.

"What can I say? My taste is impeccable," I said, sitting on the living room floor Indian-style, fiddling with my camera while Adrien, on the couch, played with my hair. I closed my eyes from time to time, enjoying the tingles shooting through my body, sinking deeper and deeper into a restful bliss. The apartment was quiet. We could hear the hum of the refrigerator, the ticking of the guitar-shaped clock hanging by the entertainment center. Although it was late morning, Mary was still in bed.

"Favorite food?"

"I think you know this one. Indian."

He twisted a lock of my hair around his finger. "That's right. Vegetable coconut kurma."

"You remembered," I said, touched.

"It was a memorable first date. I'm sorry I took off like that."

"It's over now," I said, shrugging. I let out a sigh. "Why are you spoiling me so much?"

"I've put you through a lot these past two weeks. For which I can't say I'm sorry enough. Favorite time of year?" he asked, his strong hands kneading the back of my neck now, loosening the knots.

"September," I answered. "It's my birth month, after all. And I love summer. Mmm. That feels great. You should consider doing this professionally."

"Hmm, maybe I will. I guess I do need to find a job now. I wonder if Mike would be willing to give me my old job back. Which brings me to the next question: favorite car?"

"Volkswagen Beetle. I have to make a confession: I don't drive—anymore, I mean. Since the accident, it freaks me out. I tried, but I get panic attacks."

His hands stopped mid-massage. "Really? Do you think you'll ever drive again?"

I shook my head. "I don't know. Maybe someday. And maybe if I wore a football helmet and some body armor and drove only on the back roads," I said, partially kidding.

Mary stumbled into the room in her bats and skulls patterned pajamas, her newly dyed purple hair in tangled disarray. Mascara streaks loitered the sides of her swollen face—a big clue she had been crying.

"Bad night?" I asked, laughing nervously.

"Something like that," she said, yawning, scratching her armpit.

"Are you okay? You look like you were crying," I probed.

"Keaton and I had a little fight. Nothing major."

"I'm sorry," I said and I was surprised I meant it. I guess I was okay with Abby's boyfriend moving on now. I mean what did I expect? That he'd wear sackcloth and ashes forever? It's not like I wasn't making other friends—so why shouldn't Keaton be able to date? Abby would always be a huge part of us, but I know she would've wanted us to live our lives.

She shrugged. "Not a big deal. His band is leaving tomorrow for a tour. He doesn't want me to come."

"Why not?" I asked.

"Who knows? This is why I usually try to avoid men," Mary said, rolling her eyes. She poured herself some coffee and got started on breakfast, fishing eggs and cheese from the fridge.

Adrien shrugged, his face amused. He continued our silly game. "Favorite Abby memory?"

"That's impossible. There're just too many," I said, turning around to face him. "Wait, I know. Probably when we went on that cross-country road trip just before the accident. It was magical. Other than to end up in LA, we didn't make any plans. It was all spontaneous. We'd drive until we couldn't stand it anymore and stay at random cheap motels. We stayed up late eating junk food and watching bad cable TV. We'd stop and check out these silly tourist traps, like Olney, Illinois, the mecca of albino squirrels and the International UFO Museum in Roswell, New Mexico."

Adrien laughed. "Albino squirrels?"

"You should go there sometime. They are so cute. Abby and I were tempted to kidnap one and take it home for a pet. Of course Tiger would've probably tried to eat it, plus we weren't sure if we could housetrain a squirrel."

"You're hilarious."

"In LA we practically lived on the beach. We checked out the Hollywood Walk of Fame and Amoeba Music and ate the best veggie burgers in the world. We went to the Getty museum and to the Santa Monica Pier and to Disneyland."

"Sounds fun."

"We fought a little, of course, plus we got some food poisoning from this hole-in-the-wall diner in Texas, but other than that, the trip couldn't have been more perfect. I never, in a million years, would've guessed she'd never be coming home, though. I guess I'm glad things ended on such a perfect note." I sighed. "I only wish we had more time together."

"Do you hate the guy who killed Abby?" he asked, his hands moving to my tight shoulders.

"I used to. But I've had some time to think about it and I'm pretty sure now that he—whoever he was—didn't do it intentionally." His hands dug deeper, softening the knots. "Ouch!"

"I'm sorry. Am I hurting you?"

"It hurts but it's a good hurt. Keep going. Ahhh, you are spoiling me…"

"You were saying?"

"People are basically good, right? I like to give people the benefit of the doubt. You don't know what was going through his head. He could've just—"

"But he just took off. Left you and Abby for dead. The coward didn't even stop to see if you were okay."

"I'm sure there was a reason for all of it. And maybe the guy *was* a total jerk. Or maybe it was an honest mistake. A horrible, awful, but honest mistake. Who knows? I'm not going to let it make me bitter anymore. I refuse to let it ruin my life. I chose to forgive him. It wasn't easy. Those books Chris lent me have helped a lot. Rose, my therapist, is helping me with it, too. It's a lot of work, forgiveness. It takes time. For some people, years. I can't say I'm one-hundred-percent there, but I'm getting there."

"How can you forgive someone you've never met?"

"I chose forgiveness for *myself*. Forgiving the guy who hit us…it isn't saying what he did was okay. Forgiving him, whether he deserves it or not, it's a gift you give yourself. I wasn't going to let this anger—this hate—eat me alive. Life is a gift. I know that now. Even the accident, as tragic as it was, was a gift in a weird way. I've never appreciated anything the way I do now. I don't take things for granted anymore. I don't take the people I love for granted. The accident—it woke me up. And," I took a deep breath, "I'm stronger now. They say what doesn't kill us makes us stronger. I believe that. Do you?"

He paused for a moment. "I don't know if I do. Everything I've been through—it's killing me. Little by little."

I hesitated. "Do you…want to talk about it?"

He answered with a bitter laugh. I decided it would be better not to push my luck. There was a long pause. As he kneaded my back and shoulders, we listened to Mary humming and making herself a late-morning breakfast.

Adrien pulled me up onto the couch, wrapping his arms around me. I rested my face against his shoulder. I was surprised by what he said next. "September, I'm sorry."

I pulled away a little to make eye contact. "For what?"

"That you had to go through all this. You've suffered so much. If there was a way I could make this all go away, I would. If I could take the pain away, I would," he said, his face tightening.

I laughed. "It's not your fault. And anyway, I'm okay now. I'll always miss her…like a *lot*…but I'm okay now. I wish *I* could take *your* pain away," I said, gazing into his lovely eyes.

His lips turned up slightly before brushing my neck. "First kiss?"

"Zach Larson, second grade."

"First *real* kiss?"

"Hmmm. Mart Beesley, tenth grade."

"Your favorite…thing about me?" He tightened his grip around me.

"Okay, this will take a minute," I said, pretending to concentrate.

He laughed. "Don't strain yourself."

After teasing him long enough, I finally said, "I love that you're a writer. A good one, too. I love how generous and thoughtful you are. I love your laugh. I love that you've made it this far after all you've been through, that you've chosen not to give up." I paused before adding, "And I love the way you look at me."

Adrien pressed his mouth against my temple. "Thank you. We should definitely play this game *every* day. Um…First impression of me?"

"I thought you were intriguing. Very moody. And incredibly good looking," I said, feeling my cheeks burn a little.

"You think I'm incredibly good looking, huh? Tell me more about that," he said, tucking a stray lock of hair behind my ear.

"Don't even get me started. Do you have any idea how *gorgeous* you are? First of all, your eyes are *amazing*. Then there's your jaw. And I've always had a thing for your hands."

"My hands?" He laughed, clearly amused.

"Your hands make me crazy," I confessed. "I noticed them the first day we met."

"You're an odd duck. Want to know my favorite parts of you?" I nodded. "Your big brown eyes, your soft, full lips and your…" His eyes trailed down my body, "And your…ears."

I smacked him playfully in the arm. "You and I both know it's not my ears."

He threw me a sexy grin.

Mary, with a plate full of steaming scrambled eggs and a chocolate Pop-Tart in one hand and her giant mug of coffee in the other, plopped down on the couch. She turned to Adrien and me and said, "Did you know that more people are killed by toaster ovens than by roller coasters?"

***

"You look amazing," Adrien said, eyeing me up and down, admiring the red dress he and Mary helped me pick out. "Your ex-boyfriend's going to be having some serious second thoughts tonight."

"I hope so. Not that I'd want him back. You don't look so bad yourself," I said, smiling at his olive green sweater. He'd left earlier to shower and change. His hair was neatly combed for once.

"Ready to blow this joint?"

I took a deep breath, feeling a nervous energy mounting inside me. I hoped tonight would go smoothly, seeing John and April together, introducing Adrien—my boyfriend—to my family. And I hoped the big secret Adrien would reveal to me later tonight wouldn't destroy us. I shuddered when I recalled the tortured look on his face when he predicted I would leave him. I shook my head, pushing the image away.

"Ready as I'll ever be."

Inside his car, which had a faint scent of greasy fast food, the questions continued. "Dream vacation?"

"Backpacking Europe."

"That's something I've wanted to do, too," he turned to me and smiled. I wondered if he was thinking what I was thinking: there was so much we could do together now that he was sticking around. We could cross off everything on both of our bucket lists. "Favorite candy?"

"Reese's Pieces."

"Mmmm. You're making me hungry." His expression changed. "Do you think there's life after death? Do you think you'll ever see her again?"

I knew right away who he was speaking of. "I hope so. I never believed in heaven, in an afterlife, until Abby died. But now I want to at least have a *flicker* of hope that I'll see her again."

He adjusted his mirror and turned the ignition. Outside the sun hung low in the sky and rush hour traffic clogged the streets.

A rough looking man on the sidewalk was cussing out another man.

"Tell me more about your family. Starting with your dad."

I laughed. "As I mentioned before, we're not a very close family. So my dad…What do you want to know?"

He glanced over his shoulder before changing lanes. "Anything. Something random."

"Okay, my dad. Let's see…He likes to clip articles out of the paper. He does it every day. Sort of drove me crazy growing up. That scissors cutting noise and the serious, stern look he'd have on his face. I have no idea what he does with the clippings, or whether he ever rereads them. It drives my mom nuts, too. He used to take April and me to baseball games. Always was a Mets fan. He'd buy us huge, buttery pretzels."

Adrien tapped his horn at someone who cut him off. "And your mom?"

"She's always been a neat-freak. She irons everything—the sheets and her jeans included." I laughed. "I mean, who irons jeans? Ironically, she loves to play in the dirt. She's a gardening fanatic. My dad loves it. He's never had to hire a landscaper and my parents have always had the best looking yard in the neighborhood."

"What about your sister?" he said, sneaking glances at me while still managing to drive carefully.

"April is a younger version of my mom, minus the garden worshiping. She's daddy's little girl. She and my mother are too much alike. They sort of butt heads. She's hoping to get into law school—and knowing her, she will. She's always been everything I wanted to be and then some. Smarter, prettier, more popular. Well, that's how I felt growing up. Now I kinda like who I am."

"I've noticed that about you."

I was surprised. "Noticed what?"

"Your sense of self-worth. Few girls your age have it. It's sexy. And yet you have this vulnerability that drives me crazy. I think the combination of the two—the confidence and vulnerability—is what makes you so appealing."

"Wow." It was all I could say. I'd never heard anyone say anything like that to me before.

He chuckled. "I can't wait to meet the fool that gave you up."

"John?" I said, amused by Adrien's goofy grin.

"Any man would have to be an idiot to let *you* go," he said, his hand brushing my knee. "But lucky for me, he did."

We said nothing for a few minutes, but it wasn't an uncomfortable silence. I felt relaxed and safe with him which was interesting considering I'd known him for such a short time. I've always thought it said something about a relationship: when two people could enjoy each other's company in silence without filling the gaps in conversation with talk about the weather.

Feeling serene, I took comfort in the familiar scent of Adrien's car as I watched the yellow light of street lamps flicker on his arms and face. The rhythm was hypnotizing. He turned to me and smiled that smile which did crazy things to me. In that moment I forgot all my worries. Everything was perfect. I closed my eyes, absorbing the magic that enveloped us.

30

"Everyone, I want you to meet my *boyfriend*, Adrien," I said as we entered the front room, which smelled of potpourri and furniture polish. Mom had redecorated since I'd last been there. Large watercolor paintings of tulips and pansies hung above white leather couches. As usual, the place was immaculate. Throw pillows were thoughtfully placed on each couch and even the magazines and coffee table books were neatly stacked. We could hear classical music playing from another room.

The second the word "boyfriend" escaped my mouth, which I admit I enjoyed saying maybe more than I should've, my family, who had all stood to greet us, was in silent awe. Finally, my grandma giggled in delight. My parents seemed pleasantly surprised. A huge smile crept onto my mother's face, while my father nodded approvingly. My sister gawked at Adrien in admiration, her mouth hanging open like a hungry pelican. (Where was my camera when I needed it?) Other than the goofy expression, she looked flawless as usual, like a celebrity who just walked out of hair and makeup.

"He's cute," she whispered in my direction. "You have a…September, you really have a…?"

"Boyfriend," John finished for her, looking kind of hurt the second the shock wore off. The way he eyed Adrien and me, you'd think *we* were the ones cheating. I had to stifle a petty grin when sheer jealousy molded his face. The moment was priceless and almost worth the pain he caused dumping me, betraying me. John looked especially handsome tonight, all dressed up in nice slacks and an expensive sweater, but I hardly noticed now that Adrien stood next to me.

"Well he seems like a fine young man," my grandma said, licking her lips, eyeing him like a gourmet dessert. I groaned. Grandma was being…Grandma. She'd recently cut her hair. Her steel gray curls were tight against her head now. Her makeup was too bright as usual. She wore fluorescent blue eyeshadow and had fuchsia splotches on her prominent cheekbones.

"Adrien, this is my dad, Ed," I said, gesturing to the serious man who stood perfectly straight. They shook hands. Dad wore his usual stern expression now: tight, searching eyes, mouth a thin straight line across his face.

"My mother, Sue." Mom's eyes crinkled warmly. She wore an expensive gold suit and pearl earrings, her hair in an elegant bun above the right ear. With her hands clasped together over her chest she seemed almost *too* happy to have Adrien here.

"April," I continued.

"Hi Adrien," April said in a flirtatious manner. I shot her a warning glance. She smiled guiltily. She stole a boy from me once and I would never let it happen again—even if it meant moving to Saudi Arabia and taking Adrien with me.

"Hello, April," Adrien said politely, holding back an amused grin.

"And this is John and my grandmother."

Adrien said, "Nice to meet you, I've heard so much about you all. And congratulations on twenty-five years of marriage," he added, turning to my parents.

"Thank you. And what a pleasant surprise," Mom said and I knew she was sincere. She was probably relieved I'd finally moved on from John. Maybe her daughters could finally get along.

"We're glad you're here, Adam," Dad said.

"Adrien," April corrected, her eyes still fastened on my date. John cleared his throat when he noticed, throwing her a hurt look, waking April from her spell.

After Mom informed us dinner was ready, we all took a seat at the long cherrywood table in the dining room. It had also been redecorated, adopting all the latest *House Beautiful* trends. The new color

scheme, "dusty gold", "brick red" and "swimming pool aqua", (these were the actual names of the paint colors—Mom had called me up a while ago asking for color combination advice) gave the room a more modern feel. A massive variety of food and lit candles crowded the long table. Mom proudly pointed out each dish, reminding me of Vanna White.

"We have chipotle grilled filets with mango salsa, gazpacho soup, San Francisco-style sourdough bread, asparagus and three different salads. I hope you all brought your appetites."

"I'm sorry, I totally forgot to bring the spinach quiche," I said, slamming my palm against my forehead. With so much on my mind the past few days, I'd forgotten until now that I was supposed to bring one.

"You're fine, honey. We've got plenty of food," Mom said, winking at Adrien.

"I remembered to bring the Waldorf salad," April said, shaking her head at me, hanging on to John's shoulder in a possessive way.

"You're going to make the perfect little housewife," I shot back, unfolding my napkin.

"Everything looks amazing," Adrien said as we all took our seats at the table.

"So what do you do?" Dad asked Adrien. "Are you a student?"

"I'm a writer." Good answer, I thought, relieved. My snobby parents would be less than impressed if they knew Adrien sold used cars. *Used* to sell cars.

"Oh? What do you write?" Dad asked, unfolding his cloth napkin and laying it in his lap.

"Novels and short stories. Fiction."

"Would I recognize any of them?" Dad inquired, reaching for the asparagus.

Adrien smiled timidly. "Probably not," he said, buttering his slice of bread. I squeezed my eyes shut, hoping he wouldn't confess he hadn't yet been published. That would not go over too well in my family. Respect was won with success. Financial stability and a good name in the community mattered more than friendship and true happiness.

"Where did the two of you meet?" Mom asked, sipping wine from a crystal glass.

We answered at once. I said, "Anderson Art and Frame." Adrien said, "Tim's Coffee."

Blushing now, I cleared my throat. "Adrien was a customer at Anderson Art and Frame. That's when we first *saw* each other. We formally introduced ourselves at Tim's Coffee."

"How long have you been dating?" John asked, watching my face so intently, it made me squirm like a worm in my seat.

"Two weeks," Adrien answered before I could. The red in my cheeks intensified.

"That's not very long," April said between bites of salad, looking skeptical.

Adrien squeezed my hand under the table before saying, "True, but we've spent every day together. And strangely, I feel like we've known each other forever."

April scowled, setting down her fork. John frowned as he played with pomegranate seeds on his plate.

As I savored the gazpacho soup, I realized I couldn't feel happier. This was turning out so much better than I'd ever hoped. For weeks I'd dreaded this night. The smug looks I imagined on John and April's faces, not to mention the twenty questions Mom would've asked to make sure I was doing okay. Now *I* was the one feeling smug. I couldn't help myself.

But then, much to my horror, dad turned to Adrien and asked, "What are your intentions with my daughter?"

"Daaaad," I protested, mortified. John chuckled, probably remembering the time he was the one being asked the question when I first brought him home for dinner not that long ago. Adrien cleared his throat, shifting in his chair. My father had a way of making April's and my dates uncomfortable. But boys who were invited to the house for such special occasions would meet a more severe interrogation.

"I really like September. We haven't known each other for long, but I want to spend as much time with her as she'll allow me to. I'm here for as long as she wants me."

"That's so romantic," my mother said, clasping her hands together. She looked intently at Adrien, then me, then back at Adrien. The way she was studying at us—like we were protozoa under a microscope—kind of gave me the creeps.

Adrien turned to me, smiling. "I think your mom is visualizing future grandchildren," he whispered.

I quietly snorted and mouthed, "I'm sorry."

"Not a big deal," he whispered back, squeezing my hand.

John lightened the mood by bringing up the latest juicy true crime documentaries available on Netflix. Eventually he and Dad got into a heated discussion about whether a certain white trash convicted killer was innocent or not while Mom and April discussed wedding plans. Grandma, who had a piece of lettuce stuck to her chin, started nodding off in her seat. Adrien and I just sat quietly, enjoying the delicious food and listened, finding the scene amusing. Occasionally we'd make eye contact and softly laugh to ourselves. It had been years since he'd been to any family dinner and I always found myself feeling like an implant in my family that I had nothing in common with.

After a while Adrien turned to my mom, interrupting her discussion with April about wedding colors. "Excuse me. Do you mind if I use the bathroom?"

"No, of course not. It's down the hall, second room on the right."

"Thank you," he said, standing up, wiping the corners of his mouth before leaving the table. Everyone watched him leave before attacking me with questions.

"What does his father do?"

"What about his mother?"

"Does he go to school?"

"Are you in love with him?"

Flustered, I sat my spoon down and said, "Slow down. One question at a time."

Just as my father opened his mouth to repeat his question, the doorbell rang, making me jump in my seat. It stirred Grandma, who was now awake and alert.

"What did I miss?" she asked, finally wiping the lettuce from her chin.

"Who could that be?" Mom asked, getting up before my dad could. She discreetly checked her hair and makeup in the mirror in the front room before answering the door. Everyone sat in silence, straining to hear the mysterious voice from outside the front door.

When Chris entered the room, I almost fell out of my chair. A hundred questions surfaced at once, beginning with: *What is* he *doing here?* It only took about five seconds for me to figure it out and then, *Oh no, oh no, oh no! What have I done?*

Chris, who looked unusually sharp in a dark gray suit, his ponytail slicked back neatly, smiled hugely, like a kid bringing home a 4.0 report card. If I wasn't gawking at him, I probably wouldn't have caught the subtle wink he threw at me.

"Who's this?" My father whispered to my mother. She shrugged, taking her seat.

"Chris?" I said. What are you...?"

"Hello, everyone. I'm Chris, September's boyfriend," he said, resting his hands on my shoulders in kind of a possessive way, as if trying to convince them with his body language. "It's nice to finally meet all of you."

I squeezed my eyes shut—mortified.

I turned around and whispered, "Chris, I have to—"

"What's going on?" April and Grandma asked simultaneously.

"Nice to meet you, Chris," my father said politely, his usually tight mouth slack, an eyebrow raised.

Chris took Adrien's spot at the table and I was immediately hit by the pleasant smell of his cologne. He pressed his lips to my ear, whispering, "I broke up with Megan. I hope I'm not too late."

The brief light tickle of his lips against my skin combined with the shocking statement made me catch my breath. "Chris, I—"

"I found your parent's address online."

"That was clever of you. Chris, I need to tell you—"

What he did next probably startled me more than anyone. With rough hands, he cupped my face and before I could protest, covered my mouth with his. He kissed me ardently, surprising me with his passion, stealing my breath away. He kissed me like he didn't care my whole family was watching.

Months of frustration and unexpressed desire were manifested in the kiss. For a few seconds I forgot where and who I was and kissed him back.

I have to admit, I very much enjoyed the kiss. It made me realize I really do have feelings for Chris, the way he clearly does for me.

And he and Adrien could definitely go head to head with their kissing abilities.

My father cleared his throat and the spell was broken and Chris finally pulled away.

I sat feeling stunned, dazed and definitely confused, with my heart battering my chest.

"Can someone *please* tell me what's going on?" April said, toying with her diamond necklace, laughing nervously. I couldn't help but glance at John, whose face froze in astonishment.

I wasn't prepared for what I saw next. Adrien frozen in the hallway—shock, hurt and anger scribbled all over his face.

"Adrien," I said, my heart galloping, my cheeks burning. What have I done? How much did he see? All of it? "Adrien, I…" He shook his head in disgust and turned to go. "Wait, let me explain."

"No, I think I got it," he said, his eyes throwing darts into my heart.

"Wait, you're Adrien?" Chris said, standing up, knocking over a glass of water. Mom stood and began dabbing it with her cloth napkin. Adrien stopped mid-step and turned around. "You're the jerk who's breaking September's heart?"

"And who are you?" Adrien asked, crossing his arms over his chest.

"I'm the one who *really* loves September." Chris threw down his napkin and took several steps in Adrien's direction. Adrien stiffened. His face was stony. It was strange, seeing this side of the two boys I loved. Both were typically so gentle and kind. Even docile. It was like seeing a trusted pet attack, suddenly and out of nowhere.

The room hummed with soft murmurs. Water streamed across the gold tablecloth. Some of it dribbled onto my lap.

Chris continued, "I'm the one who's *man* enough to stick around."

Adrien laughed. "So you love her, too? Wait, you're Chris?" He'd put two and two together. "Ah. I've heard a lot about you. You might find it useful to know that I won—September picked me."

Chris took another step toward Adrien. "If anyone deserves a girl like September, it sure as hell isn't you," he said, his cheeks flushing, his fists balling up. "You have no idea what you've put her through these past couple of weeks. No idea. You're a— you're a selfish coward."

"No, Chris!" I squawked as Chris took a swing at Adrien's face, knocking him into the antique china cabinet. I heard a chorus of gasps and John laughing, apparently amused by two guys literally fighting over me.

Adrien, defeated, laughed a humorless laugh. "I deserved that...You're right," he said, speaking to Chris, cradling his cheekbone. "You're so right. I'm sorry, September." His gaze rested on me, sadness in his eyes. "I really shouldn't be here."

"Adrien, wait!" I left my food and the spilled water and my family in confusion and ran after him. And I left Chris. I knew it would hurt him. But I couldn't think about that right now.

I thought I'd lost Adrien once and I wasn't going to let it happen again.

"September, I think you owe us an explanation," I heard my father say as I shut the front door behind me.

"Adrien, please. Wait," I said as he unlocked his car. "Please, just let me explain."

"You don't need to explain. I get it," he said, refusing to look at me. He was hurt. I could see it all over his face. He was really hurt.

"No, you've got it all wrong," I said. "Please. Let's talk."

31

"Please," I begged, trying unsuccessfully to open the passenger door. "Don't leave. Please, just let me explain."

He dropped his head in defeat and unlocked the door so I could climb in. The street lamp above the car illuminated his face which was contorted in pain. More from witnessing the kiss than being socked in the face, I guessed.

"If that's what you want, September." The way he said it—without even a trace of hope in his voice—frightened me. Despite the mild weather, an arctic chill traveled up and down my spine. Suddenly I realized this was more than about the mix up with Chris. His words from earlier resurfaced: *There's something I have to tell you, September.* And, *Tomorrow night,* you're *going to leave* me.

What was he finally going to tell me? The big secret. So big it had to wait until after my parents' party. So big, he was certain I was going to leave him—after all we've been through together.

"You okay?" he said, resting his hand on my knee. "You don't look—"

"That kiss? That was nothing," was all I could muster up. I'm an idiot. What was I thinking? Letting Chris kiss me like that. Kissing him back—when I knew Adrien would come back at any moment? How could I hurt him like that? Of course the answer was screaming over and over in my head—and in my heart—but

249

I refused to let myself think about it. I refused to let myself feel it. "It was nothing," I repeated lamely.

He laughed. "It didn't *look* like nothing."

"I told Chris you weren't going to make it—to the party. That's before you...well, I never got around to telling him *you'd* be my date. He knew about John and April and felt bad for me. He wanted to help. I didn't know he'd come. I swear I didn't expect him to *kiss* me. He *has* a girlfriend." I bit my lip, realizing I'd lied. Just before the kiss Chris revealed he'd broken up with Megan.

Chris had broken up with Megan. Wow, this was getting more and more complicated.

"He won't have a girlfriend for long. I saw the way he kissed you." His expression hinted at jealousy.

I looked down at my hands in my lap. "Yeah, I guess he has a thing for me. I sort of overlooked that."

His lips curled. "A *thing* would be putting it lightly. And I don't blame the guy. You're quite the catch. What man wouldn't want to be with you?"

"I could name a few," I said, John being the first to come to mind. I laughed nervously. "He's just my good friend. I want *you*, Adrien. I love *you*." I had to use all my self-control to keep myself from climbing into his lap and latching onto him— refusing to ever let go.

He chuckled bitterly. "You won't feel that way after..." He turned to me, his eyes piercing mine with so much intensity, it made me shudder. "I want...you should be with Chris. It's plain he really loves you."

I couldn't believe what I was hearing. A wave of panic and hurt crashed over me, enveloping me. "Don't...you...love me?"

"I do love you. Believe me." He touched my arm for emphasis. "I love you desperately. But how *I* feel and what *I* want doesn't matter. You'll be happier with Chris—trust me. You deserve a good man."

"I don't *want* Chris—I want you."

"I saw the way you kissed him," he said, gripping the steering wheel until his knuckles turned sandy white.

My cheeks burned. His intruding stare wasn't helping things. It was true. I did kiss him back. Why had I kissed him back? "I'm sorry," I whispered, forcing myself to look him in the eye.

"Please be honest with me," he said, searching my face so intently, it made me feel naked. "Are you in love with him?"

I bit my lip. "No. I'm in love with you."

He smiled a tight smile that didn't reach his eyes. "Come on. I'm not buying it."

I swallowed twice before I said, "I guess I might have *some* feelings for him. But they pale in comparison to how I feel about you."

Adrien laughed. "Of course I'm jealous. But I have no right to be."

Surprised, I said, "What does that mean?"

"It's time you learned the truth. I *owe* you that. What you do with it is up to you. I promise you, you can choose…between me and your friend…without worrying about the consequences—or feeling any guilt," he said, gently brushing my knee. I was surprised. He seemed genuine. My feelings were more important to him than his own. How did I get so lucky? To have my choice of two of the nicest guys I'd ever met? "I'm not going to hurt myself when you—" he cleared his throat, "if you choose to leave me. I promise."

He seemed so sure I was going to leave him I wanted to cry. I opened my mouth but I felt too sick to speak. I thought I'd lost him once. Now those feelings of dread and panic saturated my whole body all over again. I was so exhausted I was tempted to become a hermit and live in a cave. Never risk loving and losing anyone—ever again.

He continued, smiling softly, "First let me say that I care about you more than anything. I'm crazy in love with you. I've never felt this way about anyone." He ran a finger down the side of my face, making me almost liquefy into my seat. Why did he have such an effect on me? It's not like I haven't been touched by other guys. But with Adrien...something was different.

I braced myself, waiting for the inevitable *but*. I winced as he said it.

"But I can't lie to you anymore. I owe you the truth. Even though I know it will destroy what I treasure most—you and me—us."

My mind began running a marathon a minute. He already shared what I thought was his darkest secret: that he'd—by accident—killed his sister. What could it possibly be now? Was he married? A convicted felon? A priest sworn to a lifetime of celibacy?

"Go on," I said, almost inaudibly, squeezing my eyes shut, hoping to somehow protect myself from the truth—whatever it was.

Adrien took a long, shaky breath. "I..."

"Come on, you can tell me anything," I said, touching his arm.

"I..." he swallowed, "killed someone."

I laughed nervously. "You mean your sister, right?"

"Yes, but also...someone else. Someone...very special...to you." He grabbed my hand. I felt him trembling. I searched his green eyes and saw pain so intense, it hurt me to look at them. He opened his mouth, struggling to form the words. "I... killed...Abby."

"What?" I yanked my hand away, like a kid who touched a hot stove. After it sunk in for a moment, I started laughing.

He looked at me like I was nuts.

Surely he was joking. This wasn't real. This *couldn't* be real.

"I killed her, September," he repeated, his voice cracking.

"What?" This wasn't funny. Who'd joke about something like that?

"Don't make me say it again," he whispered, his face gnarled in pain.

"You...? *You* killed her? It was you?"

He nodded.

It took me several seconds to digest his words. Or maybe it was minutes. Time was a blur at that point. We sat in silence, listening to a neighbor's cat make strange hollering noises.

And then it really hit me, like a skyscraper tumbling down, crushing me.

"No!" I said, stomping my foot. "No!"

"I killed her. I killed her." He was crying now. He crumbled into the steering wheel.

I threw my arms around my head, shielding myself from his words.

"I'm so sorry. So sorry," he said, sitting up, acting unsure whether to reach for me or pull farther away.

"It was you?" I echoed, too stunned to say anything else. I was confused. Really, really confused. It was too much for my tired brain to process.

"It was me," he said, resignation in his voice.

We sat saying nothing as a whisper soft rain began to fall. It was not a surprise. Moody storm clouds loomed above us all day. The rain quickly intensified. We listened to the drumming noises it made falling onto the car, falling onto rooftops, falling onto trash can lids. The sound was strangely soothing. We watched it collect on the windshield and wash it clean. Only a stubborn spider remained. It struggled for some time to keep its ground, fighting for its life. We watched it intently. The stream of water kept pulling it down. Tenacious, the spider would manage to climb back up. Finally, it lost its strength. It gave up. The water washed it away.

There was a second wave, an aftershock. It felt like someone had knocked all the air out of me. I struggled to breathe. Every muscle in my body tightened like an angry fist. Dinner seemed to be inching up my throat, little by little. And then I opened the car door and spewed everything on my parents' curb. A panic attack. I was having a panic attack.

I began weeping and rocking in my seat, making a sound so strange, so wild animal-like, I didn't realize it was me at first. Hesitantly, Adrien reached out to touch my shoulder, trying to comfort me. I pulled away.

How could this happen? Was this a sick joke? How could I meet and fall in love with the boy who killed Abby? I must be dreaming. This can't be real.

Adrien sat helplessly, waiting for me to calm down. "Horrible isn't a strong enough word to describe how I feel," he whispered, his face pain stricken.

Finally, after several minutes, I calmed down enough to say, "When did you—? How long did you—?"

"I figured it out that day I made you and Mary waffles," he said, reaching for me and flinching when I pulled away again.

"And you didn't say anything? You just let me fall in love with you?"

"I swear I didn't know that would happen. I didn't know we'd become so close. I wanted to tell you, believe me. But I was scared. I didn't want to hurt you—more than I already had."

"Then why now?"

"Because before, when I was going to kill myself, I knew the secret would be buried with me. But things have changed...I can't keep lying to you, September. You deserve to know the truth."

"How did it happen? And why did you just..." I squeezed my eyes shut, "leave us there? Leave Abby to die?"

The muscles in his jaw tightened. "I'd just found out my father had cancer. They sent him home, giving him four to six months to live. I hadn't seen or heard from him in years. He hasn't spoken to me much since the divorce. He never truly forgave me for what I did to my sister...

"You have to understand I was in turmoil. I couldn't eat, couldn't sleep. I finally gathered up the nerve to visit him. Whether he wanted to see me or not, I had to say goodbye. I thought about flying, but I needed time to think about what I was going to say to him. I chose to drive, a decision that would change the rest of my life...and the lives of many others. At the time my car was in the shop. Mike, my boss, lent me a van."

I clutched my mouth. *The ugly brown van.* In my mind I saw it flying across the freeway, crushing us.

"I was so exhausted. The depression, the anxiety, the lack of sleep. They all added up. I fell asleep at the wheel. I must have been out for only a few seconds. Before I knew it, I was hitting a yellow Volkswagen Beetle. I watched in horror as it flew off the freeway, turning over and over across the ground. I saw something green fly out of the window." Abby's scarf. "I knew—there was not a doubt in my mind—I'd killed the occupants. There was no way, I thought, they could survive that.

"I panicked, September. I don't know *what* happened. I'd like to think of myself as an honorable person. The kind of person who does the right thing. A good person. But then it all came back to me—the day I killed my sister. I watched in horror as the fire consumed my bedroom. I saw my sister's face. I saw her tiny body being taken away on the stretcher." He sobbed. "I saw her charred feet peeking out of the blanket. Those perfect little feet...I couldn't think straight. I just stepped on the gas and took off. Initially, it wasn't the consequences I'd have to face that made me flee. I just...lost all common sense. I was that seven-year-old kid again, hiding in the bushes, spinning the wheels of my toy truck.

"I never made it to Vegas. The pain was too intense. Depression paralyzed me. I thought about turning myself in at least a dozen times. I knew there was a very good chance I'd go to jail. Maybe even prison. But I couldn't bear to face the families I'd hurt. I did go to Abby's funeral—"

I laughed, because sometimes that's all you can do. "You were at the funeral?"

"I wanted to see what I'd done. Whose life I'd destroyed. I found an article about the accident online. I was relieved there was a survivor. Two deaths on my head are better than three, I suppose. Then I found Abby's obituary."

It clicked then. I saw him there. I saw Adrien at the funeral. He was the hot guy. "Did you see me? At the funeral?"

"No. I don't think I did. And I swear I had no idea Abby was your friend. Not until Mary said something that day I made waffles. It was all just a terrible coincidence. A sick, sick coincidence.

"Going to the funeral only made me feel worse, which I guess was the point. I was punishing myself. But after getting to know Abby at the funeral, I realized I'd killed an angel. Maybe I was hoping she was a dirtbag or something. But, man. I killed this amazing person. So I figured I'd take matters in my own hands...punish myself. Give myself the death sentence. This way no one else could get hurt. I wouldn't be able to destroy any more lives...

"I had it all planned out. I was going to leave the perfect

suicide note, placing no blame on the ones I'd leave behind. I was relieved, to be honest," he said, laughing through his tears. "I was almost happy for the first time in thirteen years. It just seemed like the perfect solution. But then I met you. At first I just thought of you as a pleasant distraction. A friend to kill time with. Someone to help me not think about what I'd planned to do. What I felt I *had* to do. But I screwed up. I started falling for you. And then I learned about your accident, about Abby being your friend. I knew right away, right as you described the accident.

"You probably remember, after you told me about the accident and I put two and two together, I left your apartment. Quite abruptly," he adds, laughing. "Never to return—or so I thought at the time. I went straight home, stunned. I thought about doing it right then and there. I had the gun in my hand. I had it pinned right under my chin. I was ready. I couldn't take any more pain. But then, in my mind, I saw your face. I saw you smiling at me. And I wanted to somehow make amends. I wasn't sure how I was going to do it. How it was even possible. But I figured if you knew who killed Abby it'd give you a sense of closure..." He shook his head in disgust. "I meant to tell you, but it was never the right time. I didn't want to ruin your first solo exhibit, your birthday. And all the while, I was falling deeper and deeper in love with you."

I opened my mouth, wanting to say something, anything, but I couldn't find the words. I was so confused. More confused than I'd ever been. Drowning in a bottomless lake of confusion.

"I'm so sorry, September. I could say it to you a million times and still, it wouldn't take the pain away. It wouldn't bring Abby back. It wouldn't change anything and that's why you and I would never work."

"I..." I said. Words jumbled inside my mind. Conflicting

feelings. But there was nothing to say. Nothing I *could* say. After all, Adrien had killed the one person who meant everything to me. "I don't—"

A knock on the passenger window startled us both. Chris's concerned face filled my view, his image warped through rain streaked glass. He spoke, his voice muffled by the patter of rain. "September, we need to talk."

I looked at Adrien, still in a daze. His tears had dried, but his knuckles grew chalk white, curled around the steering wheel. "It's okay, you can go," he whispered, his face smooth, void of emotion. "After everything you've told me…He seems like a really good guy." He laughed bitterly. "He'll make you a hundred times happier than I ever could." He gently nudged me. "It's alright, I swear. I'll be okay."

I looked at Adrien, then Chris, then Adrien again.

Torn.

Confused.

Exhausted.

"Adrien, I—"

"Just go!" he yelled, slamming his fist against the dash, making me jump in my seat.

Obediently, I pushed the door open and climbed out. He didn't wait for the door to close before he sped away, car tires screaming against wet pavement.

32

"September! You look like you've seen a ghost," Chris said, grabbing my arms, steadying me. His wet clothes clung to his body. Raindrops collected and fell from the hair that fell loose from his ponytail, from his chin.

"Chris," I said, collapsing into his damp arms. He held me close—closer than he ever had.

"You're shaking. You okay?" he said, resting his chin on my head. "What happened? Did he break up with you? Wasn't he supposed to be...dead by now?"

"Chris," I said. "Please, just get me out of here."

He helped me get into an old aqua-colored Mazda before sliding in behind the wheel. He turned the heat on full blast, but kept the car in park. I sat in a fetal position against the passenger door, my whole body trembling like the strings of a guitar.

"Come here," he said, pulling me into his lap, his arms calming my quivering body. I sobbed for a good fifteen or twenty minutes while he patiently waited, rocking me gently. His body was firm and warm and his cologne smelled amazing.

Finally, I laughed, feeling a little better now that endorphins flooded my body. I climbed back into my own seat, pushing snot away with the sleeve of my cardigan.

"Here," he said. "Let me grab you a tissue." He popped open the glove box and pulled a tissue out of a Snoopy box. I couldn't help but giggle.

"Snoopy?" I raised an eyebrow.

"This isn't my car. I don't have one, remember? I borrowed it for tonight. Are you okay now?" He dotted the tears away with a clean tissue.

I let out a long, quivery sigh. "Honestly? I don't know if I'll ever be okay."

"That bad?" he said, pocketing the tissue. "Look, I'm sorry I kissed you. I mean, I'd be lying if I said I didn't enjoy it, but I didn't know it would mess things up so bad."

I shook my head. "That's not it. It's something else."

"What?" he asked, stroking my damp hair. "What is it?"

I squeezed my eyes shut. "I know who killed Abby."

He dropped his hand mid-stroke. "What? Who?"

I opened my mouth, struggling to say the words. "Adrien. He killed Abby."

His brow furrowed. "Wait. *Adrien* killed Abby? Are we talking about the same Adrien—your boyfriend?" I nodded. "How do you know this?"

"He confessed just now. In his car."

"Are you kidding me? What kind of sick guy would—"

"He didn't know who I was when we started hanging out. He didn't realize it was me until later," I said, surprising myself that I was defending him.

"Wow," he said, shaking his head, appearing stunned. "That's a lot to swallow. What was his excuse for fleeing? After the accident?"

I inhaled deeply before telling Chris the entire story, beginning with Adrien's sister's death. Chris sat, mostly in silence, absorbing everything. He stopped me from time to time to ask questions. When I finally finished, he seemed almost as conflicted as I was.

"Why didn't you tell me any of this before?" he asked, touching my elbow, searching my face.

I shrugged. "I don't know. The story became increasingly complicated. I didn't even know a lot of it until a couple days ago."

"Are you going to tell Abby's parents? They deserve to know."

"I don't know. Maybe Adrien will. Even if he did, I'm sure they wouldn't press charges. They're too kind and compassionate to do anything like that. And Adrien's punished himself enough, believe me," I said, grabbing another tissue, playing with it, twisting it around and around my index finger.

"You really love him, don't you?" he said, clutching the steering wheel, looking straight ahead.

"Yes," I whispered, unconsciously drawing a heart with my finger on the fogged up window.

"Do you think you'll ever be able to forgive him?"

"Hmmm. I don't know. Everything's so fresh. I guess I have a lot to think about."

He closed his eyes for several seconds before putting the car into reverse, pulling away from the curb. By now the rain had stopped. The world around us was strangely quiet. Raindrops on the car, on the grass, glistened in the moonlight.

"Ready to go home?"

"I'm so sorry Chris. I didn't know. I didn't realize…" I bit my lip. I guess I did know Chris had feelings for me, but I didn't realize they were that strong. That he'd be willing to break up with his girlfriend and borrow someone's car and show up at my folks' house to save me. What was left of my mangled heart ached for him. I wanted to reach for him, comfort him. I couldn't lie to myself. I loved Chris, too. And he was finally here, finally mine for the taking—if I wanted him, if I chose to have him.

But Adrien had to come into my life and complicate everything.

Chris was quiet the entire drive home. He reached over and squeezed my hand when I sniffled once, but other than that he seemed to be punishing me for having feelings for someone else. Either that or he was in too much pain to talk. I couldn't imagine what he must be feeling now, after finally gathering up courage to break up with Megan, in part to be with me, only to be rejected.

Street lamps and traffic lights painted the wet pavement a rainbow of colors. The navy blue sky blackened. A cool breeze rushed in through the cracked-open windows, grazing our hair, filling our lungs with the scent of damp earth and baptized air. Several times I turned to him, wanting to read his face, wanting to know if he'll be okay, but it was concealed in the dark shadows.

"Are you going to be all right?" he asked when we parked in front of my apartment complex. "Do you want me to come in and hang out for a while?"

"I think I'm going to—somehow—be all right," I said, although I didn't know if it was true. Reluctantly, I unlocked my seatbelt. "Are *you* going to be okay? Are *we* okay? You're my best friend, Chris. I don't want to lose you."

He shook his head in frustration. "September, I don't want to be your friend. I want so much more than that. I want you. I'm in love with you. I have been since the first day we met. Every day, not getting to be with you…it hurt."

Each word wrapped a layer of barbed wire around my already wounded heart. I squeezed my eyes shut. "I don't know what to say. You know I love you, too, as my best friend, but…I also have feelings for you. I have for a while. But…"

He sighed. "But you love *him*."

"I don't know *how* I feel anymore," I said, coiling the tissue so tightly around my finger, it cut off circulation. "I don't know if I can love the person who killed Abby—not in that way."

Chris turned in his seat to face me, his expression desperate, his voice urgent. "Tell me I have a shot. That you and I stand a chance to be together."

I clutched my throat. "I…"

"Kiss me, September. Kiss me with all your soul and then tell me you don't want me," he said, his gray eyes burning holes through me.

"Chris, come on," I pleaded. "Be reasonable."

"Please. Just one kiss." His face contorted in pain.

"It wouldn't be fair to you *or* me. Not like this. Not when I'm so confused." I felt my body fighting against a powerful urge. I did want to kiss him. But Adrien's face touched my thoughts. Would I be able forgive him? Would I be betraying Abby if I did? What kind of girl would I be, choosing the guy who was responsible for her tragic death?

I bit my lip, gazing at Chris like a kid eyeing a giant lollipop at a candy store. I'd wanted him for myself for all these months. He could now be mine. For a moment I indulged in thoughts of a possible future together, a luxury I never had with Adrien. I thought about all the time we'd finally get to spend together, outside of work, without sneaking around behind Megan's back. Volunteering together at the animal shelter, taking some of the cats and dogs home. Going to farmers' markets and poetry readings. Snuggling on my couch, watching bad chick flicks (He admitted to me once he liked those). Maybe taking a few classes together at NYU. Here was my chance to be with the sweetest guy in the world. The person who I trusted the most. My comfort blanket. My best friend.

But I cared for him too much to make a rash decision. I had to be sure this was what I truly wanted. And I was in no shape to be making a choice right now.

Finally, I said, "Chris, I want to, trust me. That kiss at my parents' house, I'm not going to lie, it was great. And I know we'd be good together. There's no doubt in my mind. But I care about you far too much to let this get out of hand when I'm not sure if..." I frowned and gestured to my head. "I have to think." I kissed him on the cheek before pushing the car door open and climbing out.

"Wait—"

"I'll see you on Monday." I ran, afraid of what I might do if I looked back. I fumbled through my purse for my keys. As soon as I was inside, I ripped off my dress and ran straight to the bathroom to splash cold water on my face. I crumbled against the bathroom wall and waited for the inevitable tears. But they didn't come. I rolled into a ball and let my mind drift. I wanted to escape into an empty slumber, flee cold reality, but strangely I was too exhausted to sleep. I considered taking a sleeping pill, but the dirty bath mat became oddly comforting. I stroked its shaggy fur as I closed my eyes.

Adrien popped into my head, like a tired radio song that just doesn't quit. He could be mine. All mine. That's what I wanted, wasn't it? He was sticking around. He chose life in part to be with me. He was no longer a milk carton with an expiration date. If we still liked each other in five or ten years, we could maybe think about marriage. We could grow old together. God willing, of course. I loved Adrien more than I'd ever loved a boy. But how could I choose him over Chris when I'd known him for only two weeks? How could I choose anyone after only two weeks? Let alone the person who destroyed a precious part of my life? He killed Abby. He hit us and left us for dead. Nothing would change that.

But the two weeks we shared felt more like months or even years. Partly because we spent practically all day, every day together—and partly because it felt like I've known him forever. And if I didn't choose him, he'd become an eternal "What If?". Although he made some mistakes, he did eventually do the right thing, even though he knew he'd risk losing me and would possibly have to face legal consequences. It scared the hell out of him but he did tell the truth. He also proved he really loved me. He altered his path dramatically to be with me—and to prevent hurting the ones he loved. All of that must've taken a lot of courage, a lot of character.

Could I bear never seeing him again? Never hearing his adorable dying-donkey laugh again? I had to admit I'd miss his ridiculous green outfits. And those amazing baby grass green eyes that searched my face so attentively. Those hands that shot electricity through me whenever they touched me. That generous heart, the size of the moon. I'd miss the throw-out-the-clock days we spent together, the way he fit right in with my weird friends, his sloppy hair, his amazing smell, his perfect jaw. I wanted to read his funny stories and discuss music for hours and kiss those soft lips again.

But would we be able to get past the fact that he—even though by accident—killed my childhood friend? Would I hold that against him in moments of anger? Would I be able to separate him from the tragedy? Would we tell Abby's parents, or keep it buried in the past, a dark secret, like a spider, lurking in the corners? Could I really trust him? Would he really get help?

More importantly, could I trust myself to really love someone again? Could I trust *anyone*? Could I trust life again?

33

Mary found me in the morning, drooling on the red bath mat.

"Hello? Are you still in there? September, are you dead?" At first I melded her words with the weird dream I was having. She poked me hesitantly, like a kid poking a snake with a stick. "You're freaking me out. Wake up!" she said, yanking me out of a surprisingly heavy sleep.

"Huh?" I tried to open my eyes, but my lids were too heavy. I groaned. Every square inch of my body ached, particularly my neck. I felt as stiff as a corpse.

She folded her arms over her chest. "What are you doing sleeping in the bathroom in your underwear? Did you get wasted last night? Please don't tell me you threw up."

"No, no, no. Nothing like that." I struggled to peel myself off the floor. I cringed as I greeted the reflection in the mirror. Mascara circled my eyes. Lipstick smudged my cheek. The entire left side of my face had shaggy bath mat imprinted in it, making Play-Doh come to mind.

"You look like hell," Mary said, stating the obvious. "Are you okay? How did the thing go? Where's Hot Waffle Guy?"

My head was throbbing—I guess I had a crying hangover. "Please. Stop with the questions. I just want to fall into my bed and die," I said, stumbling into my bedroom.

She gasped, theatrically placing a hand over her O-shaped

mouth. "He broke up with you, didn't he? I knew there was something wrong with him. He was too good to be true."

"Something like that," I said, facedown in my pillow. I didn't have the strength to tell her the whole story.

She began babbling about who-knows-what. I tuned her out but found the familiarity of her voice soothing. I said nothing in reply, but occasionally a soft moan escaped my lips. I had to think...I had to think...I was out before she noticed I wasn't listening.

When I awoke later in the afternoon I knew I couldn't wait until Monday to see Chris. I had made up my mind. I knew what I had to do.

I sat up abruptly, making the throbbing pain in my head intensify. I swallowed an ibuprofen and made a mad dash for the shower. I scrubbed the bad night from my face and shampooed in record time. I barely did my hair, applied a minimal amount of makeup. I threw on some jeans and a t-shirt and grabbed an apple to eat in the taxi.

"Where to?" the cab driver said, bobbing his head to Bob Marley. The laid-back Reggae seemed almost comical compared to my urgent mood. I gave the driver Chris's address between bites of apple. This wasn't the first time I'd been to his apartment. He'd taken me there once during a work break because he had a "special needs" guest, a Rottweiler he had to check up on. In this case "special needs" meant a chewer. The first and only time I saw his place the couch was torn to bits. Chris, being the cheerful guy he was, had a good laugh about it for the rest of the night. I admired that in him, his ability to find humor in things.

After twenty painfully long minutes, I paid the driver and hopped out of the car. I climbed a few flights of unreliable looking stairs, passing graffiti on dingy white walls (that made me wonder if gang members lived there) until I reached apartment A34 and pressed the dirty, cracked doorbell.

"September," Chris said as he opened the door, his brows raised, his mouth gaping open. "What're you doing here?" he asked, throwing on a tie-dyed shirt. Seeing him in just his plaid boxers—shirtless—for the first time made me blush a little. He had a lingering summer tan, with nice abs and nice arms and nice, well, everything.

"I had to see you right away. We need to talk," I said, my heart hammering.

"Is everything okay?" He searched my face for clues.

"I hope everything *will* be okay," I said, walking over clothes and textbooks and shoes, making my way into his living room. He was kind of a slob. I wondered if Adrien was too or if he was the-change-your-sheets-every-week type. I also wondered if I'd ever get to see Adrien's apartment. The same destroyed couch was centered in the modest-sized room, but a blue blanket covered it now. I assumed Chris, being a student and living solely on a janitor's wage and student loans, wouldn't be able to replace the couch for a while. His apartment was a wreck. Every inch of his coffee table was cluttered with homework, paper-back novels, candles, candy wrappers, you name it. A half-eaten TV dinner was left out on a bookshelf, out of an animal's reach. The place smelled of chicken and instant mashed potatoes, pets and laundry soap. A dryer hummed from another room.

"Sit down," he said, a mixture of hope and dread written on his face. He knew why I'd come—to give him an answer. He cleared a spot for me on the couch.

As I sat, three dogs: a black lab and two poodle mixes, greeted me. One sniffed my legs while another licked frantically at the remaining apple juice on my fingers. A pompous-looking white cat glanced over at us before darting behind the entertainment center.

"What's going on? Is everything all right?" he asked, sitting up too straight, interlocking his fingers. "It's not every day you just show up at my apartment. I think this is a first."

"There's a first for everything," I said, swallowing twice. I studied his wonderful face, acne scars and all, the face I grew to love. His mop of golden hair was unruly, like he hadn't showered yet today. It made him look endearing. I studied a deep scar on his left leg I'd never seen before.

"I broke my leg skateboarding when I was fourteen," he explained.

"That sucks. Chris—"

His hands shot up. "Please don't say anything."

"What do you mean?"

"Let's just sit and chat. Pretend we're pals—like the good old days," he said, picking up the smaller poodle and stroking its puffy white cloud for a head. "I think we both know—after you choose, one way or the other—" he bit his lip, "things will never be the same again."

I stroked the black lab behind the ears. He peered at me intently with eager brown eyes. Occasionally he'd scoot in a little closer until he was stepping on my shoe.

"You really feel like talking about the weather? At a time like this?"

"Or sports," he said, managing to grin.

Chris hated sports. I just wanted to get this painful conversation over with. He was making it hard. I sighed. "We never talk sports."

"We could always start." He laughed. "How about those Jets?"

I squirmed in my seat. "I can't put this off any longer." I pleaded with him with my eyes. "Chris…you're my best friend."

"I don't like the sound of this," he said, probably guessing where this was going.

"The last thing I want is to hurt you—or to lose you. You mean too much to me. I don't deserve you, the way you've been there for me all these months since Abby."

He shooed my words away. "Please, you don't have to say it."

"But I do," my voice cracked, "I owe you the truth."

"I get it. You've chosen to be with Adrien."

I felt like I was Hitler as I watched his face twist in agony. I knew he was in love with me. I suspected it for a while, but after that passionate kiss and the way he was behaving now, I never realized how much. This was going to hurt both of us. A lot. I hated it. What rotten timing—meeting Chris and Adrien in the same chapter of my life. And then I had to be stupid and fall for them both.

But I made my choice. And the faster I ripped the band-aid off, the less it was going to hurt.

"I'm sorry," I whispered. "I'm so sorry."

"Can I just ask you one thing?" he asked, still stroking the dog asleep on his lap.

I leaned forward and touched his arm. "Anything."

"Would...would you have wanted me if I was free—before Adrien came around?" His face tightened in anticipation.

I bit my lip. Should I tell him the truth? Would that only hurt him more? Would I even be able to lie to him? Would he believe me if I did?

Finally, I said, "Yes. I had a thing for you from day one." And it was one-hundred-percent the truth. This seemed to injure him further. But he also seemed pleased.

"My cousin offered me a job at his restaurant. Can you see me waiting tables?" he said with a hollow chuckle, not meeting my eyes. His words sliced through me like a wire cheese cutter.

"What? You're quitting your job? Does this mean...?"

"You didn't honestly think we'd still work together, did you?" he said so bitterly, I was stunned. I'd never seen this side of him before.

"I—"

"September, I love you too much not to be with you. I don't want a little of you. I want all of you," he said, picking animal hairs from the couch, one by one, still avoiding my gaze.

I leaned back on the couch, feeling like someone just punched me in the gut. "So we can't even be friends?"

He shook his head. "Not when I go to bed every night thinking of you. Not when half of my dreams are about you."

I felt my cheeks burn. "But Chris. You can't mean—"

"I can't see you anymore. Not if I expect myself to ever get over you." He continued to pick at those damn animal hairs, refusing to look at me.

Look at me Chris! I wanted to scream. *Why won't you look at me?*

I sat, unable to speak for a moment, stunned. I slid my shaking hands under my thighs.

I'd lost my best friend—again. What was I going to do without my Chris? My Sunshine Boy? I wanted to cry, but I must've surpassed my yearly quota because once again, my eyes remained dry.

"Chris, I…" What was there left to say? He was right. It wouldn't be fair to expect him to swallow his feelings for me and pretend everything was peachy. I didn't want to hurt him anymore than I already had. "Just know that I'll be eternally grateful for the few months we had together." My throat tightened. "I'm going to miss you. So much. And I'll never, ever forget you."

"I'll miss you, too, but…Please. Just go," he said, still avoiding eye contact. I froze, unable to move. I knew when I'd get up to go, it would probably be the last time I'd ever seen him. I couldn't bear the thought.

"Chris, please. Let's not end it like this. At least give me a goodbye hug."

He shrugged. "Okay. That's a reasonable request."

We stood and embraced for a long time. I honestly don't know if it was for several seconds or minutes. It was the best—and worst—hug of my life. And the tears finally returned.

***

A very large part of me wanted to climb into bed and stay there for a week or two—or three. And the Twinkie cravings came back with a vengeance. Could this weekend have gone any worse? I lost Chris *and* discovered the boy I'd fallen for was responsible for Abby's death. Why did everything have to be so complicated? Would my life ever feel normal again?

In the taxi, I forced myself to push my hurt feelings aside. There was only one thing I had to do. Find Adrien. Not an easy feat when I never learned his address or phone number. Finding Adrien in New York would be like trying to find a dust mite on an elephant.

***

I looked for Adrien for four consecutive days. Some days in a cab, some days on foot. On one day, Mary and I borrowed her friend's car. She insisted we listen to her depressing goth music, but this time I didn't mind too much because it matched my mood perfectly.

"Where are we going today, miss?" a scruffy, heavyset older cab driver said, frowning. The car reeked of tobacco and body odor.

"That's the thing. I don't know," I said, snapping on my seat-belt, feeling panic mount inside of me. I was beginning to lose hope. What if I was too late? What if Adrien, in the heat of the moment, did something rash? Hurt himself? Or what if he assumed I didn't want to be with him and decided to move? After quitting his job there was nothing keeping him here.

"Give me something to work with. I've got to pay the bills," the driver said, glaring at my reflection in his rearview.

I replayed the two weeks we spent together in my head. Where would I find him? This could take days or weeks. Months even.

I spent hours today looking for him, feeling my hope dwindle little by little. First I tried Cooper Park. I hit a few bookstores because Adrien was really into those. And then Tim's Coffee popped into my head. I'd gone there every day, but it never hurt to try again.

"Try Tim's Coffee. It's on—"

"I know where it is," the cab driver snapped.

The ride to Tim's seemed to last an eternity. And of course today of all days, the traffic had to be as thick as congealed cream of mushroom soup.

My heart jerked as I climbed out of the taxi. There it was: Tim's Coffee. The place it all began. What were the chances Adrien would actually be there?

Slim to none.

Inside the café, I scanned the room frantically. I saw the usual crowd. Three teenage girls flipping through a gossip magazine, sharing a fruit smoothie. A balding business man opening his laptop. A middle-aged woman with a bad perm arguing with an older woman, probably her mother. In a panic, I scanned the room a second time. No Adrien. Of course.

Just as I turned to leave, I heard a quiet voice in my head. *Bagel with-everything-on-it.* Okay, admittedly, I was hungry. I'd only had a bowl of cereal today and it was nearly dinnertime. And it *had* been a while since I'd had one. I could grab one for the road and keep looking. The cashier, a vinyl thin boy around my age, took especially long ringing me up. He messed up twice. The time I rang Adrien up at Anderson Art and Frame came to mind. What a pathetic first impression I must've made. I wondered if he still remembered that. Just as the cashier was about to hand me my change, the middle-aged woman came up to the counter and began arguing with the boy about how he got the order all wrong and overcharged her. I groaned, maybe a little too loudly. I didn't have time for this. I needed to find Adrien as soon as possible. Now was not soon enough. As a young woman with a buzz cut handed me my order, I took off, no longer caring about my change.

Outside the sun was retiring, turning the sky a soft burnt orange. I sat on a bench and people watched as I ate my heavenly bagel, which was warm and oozing cream cheese. I saw a variety of interesting people, including a homeless woman swearing at an imaginary friend (or enemy?) and a man wearing a Cookie Monster suit. I saw someone who reminded me of Chris and it made me sad. Chris had quit right away. It was lonely cleaning restrooms without him. I wanted to cry every time I thought about how I would probably never see him again.

I popped the remaining seeds from the bag into my mouth and buttoned up my jacket—it was getting cold. I was emotionally and physically spent and decided to call it a day. I would start my search again early tomorrow morning. Deflated, I turned to head back for my apartment. That's when I saw the back of a man—tall and slender with messy chestnut hair—walking briskly ahead.

Was it him?

Yes, I was sure of it. The green jacket and shoes were a give-away.

"Adrien?" I ran after him, hoping I wouldn't lose him in the crowd. "Adrien!"

His long legs gave him the advantage. Panic shot through me like a rocket as I saw him disappear into the thick crowd. I zig-zagged through the cluster of people, no longer bothering to be polite. Elbowing and pushing became necessary as people stopped to watch a man in a plaid hat sitting at a TV tray doing card tricks.

I saw a flash of green.

"Adrien!"

He turned and recognized me immediately, his face giving away surprise and confusion.

"Adrien. Stop. Please," I said, closing the gap between us, a little out of breath.

"September," he said. He seemed to be in a daze. He placed his bags of groceries on the ground beside his feet.

We stood next to the steps of a brightly lit office building. I was glad because I could take in every beautiful inch of his glorious face. The face I missed dearly. The face I wasn't sure I'd ever get to see again.

His thick sap green scarf made me smile. Of course it was green. He looked especially handsome bundled up against the cold, his cheeks flushed, his nose red. It was brisk for an early fall evening. Winter seemed to grow impatient, not wanting to wait its turn. Although we were together only a few days ago it felt like months since I last gazed into those amazing baby grass green eyes. I wanted to hold him and kiss him and take in his Adrien scent. I ached to cling to him and never let go. We now had the chance to be together, but would he want me back? Would we get to spend our numbered days of mortality together, however many God or the universe would grant us?

"I can't believe I found you," I said. "I've been looking for you for days." He seemed surprised by this. "Do you live near here? Am I allowed to ask you that now?" I laughed.

He smiled a sweet smile. "Yeah. In that building right there." He pointed to some row houses down the street from Tim's Coffee. I laughed again, maybe a little too loudly.

"You're kidding me. All this time you were living right by Tim's? Right by *my* place?" He stood in silence, hands in pockets, his expression skeptical. "Adrien, we're neighbors."

"I guess we are." His lips curled upward, but the smile didn't reach his eyes.

"That's funny, wouldn't you say? Considering there's something like eight million people in this city? We're always crossing paths. I think the universe is trying to tell us something. Not that I need any convincing."

He kicked a weed growing through a crack in the sidewalk, crossed his arms over his chest. "I have to be honest. I never thought I'd see you again." The way he said it, almost mechanically, confused me. Wasn't he happy to see me?

I sucked in a long, shaky breath, feeling more nervous than the first day we met. For a moment the crowd thinned, giving us the privacy we needed.

"I love you, Adrien," I said, voice croaking. My heart was clobbering my ribs so hard it was challenging to get the words out. "And if you feel you need to hear it: I forgive you. I'm always going to miss Abby, but it *wasn't your fault*. I know you didn't mean to kill her and I know you'd bring her back, that you'd trade your own life for hers if you could. It was an *accident*. I forgive you, Adrien. I know Abby would want that."

His eyes flooded. He brushed a single fallen tear away with a shaky hand and finally grinned that goofy grin I love. "That means more to me than you'll ever know."

I waited for him to say something more. Would *he* still want *me*? Now that we had this burden, this secret to share? Would he feel guilty whenever I mentioned Abby's name? Was this going to work? Did he really love me—as much as I loved him?

"But I wish it were enough," he said, his face sad now.

"Can't it be enough?" I asked, feeling my heart plunge into my stomach. Just when I thought things couldn't get any worse. I took a step closer, grabbed the sleeve of his jacket. "Don't you…want me?"

He shook his head and laughed. "Of course I want you. More than anything. But it won't change the fact that I—"

"Then there's nothing more to discuss," I said, grabbing him by the neck, pulling him down and covering his mouth with mine, kissing him with all my might. He took a second to respond, but when he kissed me back, the intensity surprised me. All my remaining strength left me and I felt my knees give out and I began falling backwards. He caught me and wrapped his strong arms around me, steadying me, holding me as if he'd lose me if he let go. His lips trailed to my ear and he kissed it before saying, "Thank you."

"For what?" I asked.

"For everything."

Epilogue

"I don't know if I can do this," I said, my breath short, my heart palpitating as we walked down the front steps of Adrien's apartment building. Outside we squinted against the bright, cheerful sun. It was a perfect spring day. Seventy degree weather. I wore a brand new floral dress with a pair of Abby's Dr. Martens. An elderly couple walking an Irish wolfhound smiled at us as they passed by at a turtle's pace on the sidewalk.

"You'll be fine," Adrien said, taking my hand and squeezing it. "You can do this."

I gazed into his lovely face, hoping it would distract me from my fears. He looked better than ever—if that was even possible. Happiness agreed with him. The brooding guy I met months ago was replaced with someone determined to have hope. Hope was a choice, we were both learning. A daily decision. Rose taught us that. Adrien started therapy two weeks after I found him outside of Tim's Coffee. I saw a huge change in him the day he finally unearthed his secret—he finally collected the courage to talk to Abby's parents and apologize. As I predicted, they didn't press charges. In fact they forgave him right away. They were amazing that way. Of course they were emotional, but I think meeting Adrien and seeing how remorseful he was turned out to be a healing experience for everyone.

"You'll be fine," he repeated, amused by how tightly I was clutching his hand.

Today he wore a black t-shirt with green cargo pants. He was evolving—he added touches of black to his previously all-shades-of-green wardrobe. It gave him a sexy bad boy vibe that Mary approved of.

Adrien got his job back at Mike's Okay Cars, but he would not likely have to work there forever because a couple weeks ago his literary agent said she found someone who wanted to publish his book. It was a small indie company, but it was still a lifelong dream come true. I was sure to tease Adrien—several times. "See? Great things happen when you choose to stick around." And "Good thing you're still here, or else the world would've missed out on a masterpiece!"

Every time Adrien rolled his eyes but I knew he agreed with me. Now that he was healing the simplest things brought him joy: A pretty leaf on a sidewalk. A new song on college radio. Our bodies in a tangled lump on his couch, poking fun at B-grade horror movies that we both secretly liked.

As for me, I was still cleaning toilets, but now with a funny girl named Madison who happened to love photography as much as I did. We were doing an exhibit together in a small gallery next month.

"But what if—"

"I'm right here. You *can* do this. You're strong. You've proven that to yourself." He opened the driver's door of his car for me. A shiny new football helmet sat in the front seat. It made me smile.

"You remembered," I said, touched. "But you forgot the body armor."

"Body armor is harder to come by," he said, smiling, caressing my cheek. A sudden gentle breeze tickled my skin, carrying with it the sweet scent of lilacs and spring blossoms. He pulled me in for a long and tender kiss, dulling my anxiety. I hooked my thumbs into his back pockets and kissed him back. Even months later, his kisses had a powerful effect on me.

"I think I'm ready," I said as we pulled apart. He gingerly

placed the helmet on my head, secured the strap, then took me by my sweaty hand and helped me into the car. I took comfort in the familiar sandalwood scent and the warmth of the sunlight blanketing my face. Adrien climbed into the passenger seat and snapped on his seatbelt.

"What if I can't do it? What if I crash?" I asked, feeling a wave of nausea hit me. I hadn't driven since John took me car shopping so many months before.

His eyes locked into mine and he softly smiled. "Then we crash together. We've been through enough now to know that we can get through anything." His words gave me goose bumps. I knew, deep down, he was right. We didn't have to fear anymore. We'd both been through the worst and somehow made it out alive.

I thought of Abby and smiled. I knew she'd be proud of me and that in some way she was here with us. I thought of my new friends and the spaces in my heart they filled. I thought of life, what a precious gift it was and how it could be taken away at any moment. That was the beauty of it. I thought about love and how nothing, death included, could destroy it.

I sucked in a breath and turned the ignition.

September's Grieving for Abby Playlist

1) Pictures of You by The Cure
2) Touched by VAST
3) Tears in Heaven by Eric Clapton
4) Afterlife by Arcade Fire
5) I Will Follow You Into the Dark by Death Cab For Cutie
6) Lovesong by The Cure
7) I'll Be There by Escape Club
8) Missing by Everything But the Girl
9) Wish You Were Here by Pink Floyd
10) Angel by Sarah McLachlan
11) Goodnight, Travel Well by The Killers
12) Bridge Over Troubled Water by Simon and Garfunkel
13) People Who Died by Jim Carroll Band
14) I Grieve by Peter Gabriel
15) Here's to All the People I Have Lost by VAST
16) Always Something There to Remind Me by Naked Eyes
17) Map of the Problematique by Muse
18) The Hardest Part by Coldplay
19) Dark Paradise by Lana Del Ray
20) I Am Stretched On Your Grave by Sinead O'Connor
21) Hurt by Johnny Cash
22) Gone by The Striped Goat

Adrien's '80s Mix CD for September

1) But Not Tonight by Depeche Mode
2) With or Without You by U2
3) Unlovable by The Smiths
4) Hold Me Now by The Thompson Twins
5) Tower of Strength by The Mission UK
6) Crazy by Icehouse
7) I Know It's Over by The Smiths
8) Just Like Heaven by The Cure
9) Your Eyes by Peter Gabriel
10) I Melt With You by Modern English
11) Let's Dance by David Bowie
12) Drive by The Cars
13) There is a Light That Never Goes Out by The Smiths
14) Shake the Disease by Depeche Mode
15) The Killing Moon by Echo and the Bunnymen
16) Love is Stronger Than Death by The The
17) Heartbreak Beat by The Psychedelic Furs
18) Just What I Needed by The Cars
19) No One is to Blame by Howard Jones

September's '80s Mix CD for Adrien

1) Blue Monday by New Order
2) Cruel Summer by Bananarama
3) Don't You Want Me by The Human League
4) Time After Time by Cyndi Lauper
5) If You Leave by OMD
6) Never Surrender by Corey Hart
7) Running Up That Hill by Kate Bush
8) Tainted Love by Soft Cell
9) Broken Wings by Mr. Mister
10) Always the Sun by The Stranglers
11) Missing You by John Waite
12) Don't Dream it's Over by Crowded House
13) Eternal Flame by The Bangles
14) Bizarre Love Triangle by New Order
15) Fight by The Cure
16) Should I Stay or Should I Go by The Clash
17) Dancing With Tears in My Eyes by Ultravox
18) Take On Me by A-ha

If you enjoyed this book, please support the author. Tell your friends about it and leave a review on Goodreads, Amazon and Barnes & Noble.

About the Author

Juliette is a writer and painter. She loves travel and music with a passion, particularly '80s, alternative and indie. Like September, she lost her very best friend. Juliette lives with her family in Springville, Utah.